THE THIRD BROTHER

ANDY HAYES MYSTERIES

by Andrew Welsh-Huggins

Fourth Down and Out

Slow Burn

Capitol Punishment

The Hunt

The Third Brother

THE THIRD BROTHER

AN ANDY HAYES MYSTERY

ANDREW WELSH-HUGGINS

SWALLOW PRESS
OHIO UNIVERSITY PRESS
ATHENS

Swallow Press
An imprint of Ohio University Press, Athens, Ohio 45701
ohioswallow.com

Printed in the United States of America
Swallow Press / Ohio University Press books are printed on acid-free paper ⊚ ™

28 27 26 25 24 23 22 21 20 19 18   5 4 3 2 1

Library of Congress Cataloging-in-Publication Data
Names: Welsh-Huggins, Andrew, author.
Title: The third brother : an Andy Hayes mystery / Andrew Welsh-Huggins.
Description: Athens, Ohio : Swallow Press, Ohio University Press, [2018] |
  Series: Andy Hayes mysteries
Identifiers: LCCN 2017058847| ISBN 9780804011945 (hardback) | ISBN
  9780804040860 (pdf)
Subjects: LCSH: Private investigators--Fiction. | Columbus (Ohio)--Fiction. |
  GSAFD: Mystery fiction.
Classification: LCC PS3623.E4824 T48 2018 | DDC 813/.6--dc23
LC record available at https://lccn.loc.gov/2017058847

In memory of Landree Rennpage, 1984–2016

Fellow Kenyon College classics major,

devoted reader, aspiring writer

Postea vero, quam Tyrannio mihi libros disposuit,
mens addita videtur meis aedibus.

—Cicero, letter to Atticus at Rome, CXI (A IV)

"I have always dreamed," he mouthed fiercely, "of a band of men absolute in their resolve to discard all scruples in the choice of means, strong enough to give themselves frankly the name of destroyers, and free from the taint of that resigned pessimism which rots the world. No pity for anything on earth, including themselves, and death enlisted for good and all in the service of humanity."

—Joseph Conrad, *The Secret Agent*

Ah how shameless—the way these mortals blame
    the gods.
From us alone, they say, come all their miseries, yes,
but they themselves, with their own reckless ways,
compound their pains beyond their proper share."

—Homer, *The Odyssey,* Robert Fagles
translation

1

"GO HOME!"

"Go home!"

"Go home!"

I blinked in the late afternoon sun, processing what I was looking at across the parking lot. Two men shouting at a woman, one of them with something in his hand. The woman shouting back, struggling to retrieve what the man was grasping. Behind her several children, a couple of them wailing. Whatever was happening, it wasn't even the second cousin twice removed of a fair fight. I let go my shopping cart and started to run.

"Go home!"

"Go home!"

"Go home!"

She was black—I was guessing Somali—wearing a flowing yellow dress and orange head scarf. The older of the two guys was chanting while a younger and skinnier man tugged at the scarf like an old-fashioned vagrant trying to steal laundry off the line. Both of them white. She was no pushover; she was yelling at them as she tried with one hand to keep the garment from being pulled off while shielding her kids with the other. As I ran I looked out at Broad, hoping for a cop, but saw only a steady stream of cars speeding in each direction past a jumble of west-side fast-food restaurants, car lots, and payday loan joints.

"*Go home!*"

"*Go home!*"

"*Go home!*"

"Stop it," the woman said over the crying of her children. "Stop it!"

"Hey!" I said as I reached them a few moments later. I took a second to catch my breath. "What the hell do you think you're doing?"

"*Go home . . .*" The older guy said, the chant dying on his lips as he stared at me. He was a hard-living fifty or so, dumpy and balding with patchy grizzle coating his face and chin. He wore loose-fitting tan cargo shorts and a blue checkered button-down short-sleeve shirt with the bottom two buttons undone, exposing a flash of belly as white as butcher-shop lard. The kid with the scarf in his hand was scrawny, midtwenties maybe, in jeans shorts and a white ribbed wifebeater, with a shaved head and a thin face I might have paid more attention to had my eyes not been drawn to a prominent tattoo on his neck that seemed to involve rifles, barbed wire, and the sun. I couldn't tell if it represented a branch of the military or a prison break fantasy.

"The fuck are you?" Grizzle said. His eyes were glassy and he swayed as he spoke. "Some kind of raghead lover?"

Up close, I noticed for the first time the gun in a holster on his right side. Ohio's an open carry state, making it perfectly legal. I took a step back. Legal, but cause for concern with a guy in that condition? That was another matter altogether.

"I'm someone telling you to leave this lady alone."

"We'll leave her alone when she goes home. Where she belongs."

"She is home, you nitwit. That's probably why she's buying groceries."

2

"How do we know she don't have a bomb under that?" said the scrawny guy with the tattoo, tugging on the scarf as he pointed at her dress.

"Stop it!" she said.

"How do we know you don't have shit for brains?" I said. "Do everybody a favor and beat it."

"Free country," Tattoo said. "Except for *terrorists*."

"The only terrorists I see are you two clowns. Why don't you crawl back under the rock where you came from and we can all go about our business?"

"Make us," Tattoo said, grinning.

"Are you deaf on top of stupid?" I said, reaching out and tearing the end of the scarf from his hand. He looked at me in surprise, as if I were a magician at a kids' birthday party who'd just pulled a penny from his ear. I turned toward the woman, who rewrapped her scarf without meeting my eyes. I was turning back to face the cowboys when out of the blue Tattoo leaped onto my back. I reached around to try to pull him off, wobbling like a top at the end of its spin, and then gasped as he wrapped his right arm around my throat and cut off my air. *What the hell?* I thought. This was supposed to be a simple grocery run. I gasped as black specks floated before my eyes like flies hovering over dogshit. I staggered, spun around once more, summed up my available options, settled on one, and fell backwards, hard, into the car behind me. The kid made an "oof" sound like a guy who didn't realize the medicine ball he was catching was quite that heavy, and dropped off me like a leech doused in sea salt.

I stepped away from him, inhaling deeply. "I said, beat it."

"Let's hold it right there," Grizzle said, the gun out of the holster and in his right hand. *Lesh hol' it right there.*

"Easy now," I said, backing up.

He didn't reply. He nodded at Tattoo, who slowly righted himself, walked over to the woman, grabbed her scarf again, and this time pulled it clean off. He shrieked in triumph like a movie

Indian counting coup as the woman cried out and put both hands on her head.

I stepped in front of her, keeping my eye on the gun.

"Why don't we all calm down a little? No one wants to get hurt."

"Sure about that?" Tattoo said, charging up to me, scarf balled in his hands as he stuck his face in front of mine. I saw bloodshot eyes and smelled breath that would have wilted poison oak. "You shouldn'a gotten involved."

"And you should try picking on people your own size for a change."

"That's what I'm about to do."

"Have it your way—"

"Let's get out of here," Grizzle interrupted.

"What?" Tattoo said.

"I said, let's go." He held up a phone in his free hand.

"Gimme one minute with this douche. Just one fuckin' minute."

"Forget it," Grizzle said. He waved the phone at Tattoo. "He's saying JJ's, now."

Reluctantly, Tattoo took a step back, though his eyes never left mine.

"Don't try anything stupid, ya dumb shit," he said. "Raghead lover. Traitor."

"There's a cop," I said.

"What?"

"Behind you." He looked around. As he did I grabbed the scarf out of his hands for the second time that day.

He twirled back, eyes blazing, right arm cocked. But Grizzle whistled and held up his phone again. "*JJ's*," he said. Lowering his gun, he turned and limped toward a rusted brown pickup truck three rows over. Too far to see the plate.

"We ain't done here, douche," Tattoo said, following his partner.

"I'm free most Thursdays," I called after him. He flipped me the bird. A minute later they were gone in a squeal of tires and cloud of diesel and a long, defiant blast of their horn.

I took a breath and turned to the woman.

"You all right?"

She nodded unconvincingly, phone already pressed to her ear as she made a call.

I'd had worse shopping trips, I consoled myself, reaching for my own phone. I was conscious, anyway.

Then it hit me: I'd forgotten to use my coupons at checkout. *Shit.*

2

"*JJ'S?*"

"That's what he said."

"That a person?"

"Maybe. Or a bar. Or a pool hall in Spencer, Indiana, according to Google. I really don't know, and I'm not sure I care. I was too busy looking at his gun."

I was sitting in an Adirondack chair in my postage stamp of a backyard on Mohawk Street two days later. Sunday morning, the quiet kind that I don't get enough of. Until a minute ago I'd been on my second cup of coffee, reading *Dreamland* and starting to think about breakfast. Hopalong, dozing at my feet, stirred briefly as my phone went off. I saw from caller ID it was Burke Cunningham. I almost didn't answer, and not just because I liked listening to my new ringtone. A call from Cunningham on a Sunday morning was like the cluck of a dentist as she works on your teeth. The news can't be good. On the other hand, because he's one of the most sought-after defense attorneys in Columbus, Ohio, the news would probably involve a job, which I could use right at the moment. But it also meant an end to a quiet Sunday morning of the kind I don't get enough of. I answered anyway. Unlike my conscience, my bank balance always gets the better of me.

"What'd the cops say?"

"They said it was a good thing I didn't get my ass shot."

"They did not."

"Perhaps I'm paraphrasing."

"Any leads?"

"Not at the moment. They took the info. Put out a news release."

"I saw the coverage. You're a hero, again."

"Slow news day. A zoo baby would have bumped me off the lineup in a heartbeat."

"How about the woman? Is she all right?"

"Scared and angry. But physically OK."

"Any idea who they were?"

"No."

"Any guesses?"

"Let's see. Two redneck Americans looking to have a little fun at the expense of an immigrant who dresses funny to them. Other than that, no."

"And you're OK?"

"I'm out eighty dollars in groceries and my pride's a touch wounded. I never should have let the kid get the drop on me like that."

"What's with the groceries?"

"I lost track of my cart afterward. Is there, ah, anything I can do for you?" I glanced at my book and my coffee.

"Just the opposite. I might have an assignment."

"Now?"

"Something a bit more long term. If you're interested. Are you available tomorrow morning? Perhaps we could discuss it then."

"I'll have to check my calendar. Why, yes, it turns out I'm free. Anything you can tell me beforehand?"

"Probably easiest if we talk in person. Nine o'clock work? My office?"

"See you then."

I tried returning to my reading but made it only a page or two when I was interrupted by a sound at the back door. I turned and saw Joe, barefoot in red shorts and the Hogwarts T-shirt my parents bought him for his birthday.

"Morning."

He nodded, wiping sleep from his eyes. I held out my arms. He stumped forward, hesitated a moment, and climbed onto my lap. I hugged him. I tried not to squeeze too tight. I had at best three or four nanoseconds of his childhood left before he was too old for this kind of thing.

"How'd you sleep?"

"Fine. Can I play on the Xbox?"

"In a little while. Is Mike up?"

He yawned and shook his head. He looked down at Hopalong. "Can I take him for a walk?"

"Maybe later. Once we've had breakfast."

"He needs exercise. He's lazy."

"He's an old Labrador. There's a very slight difference."

"Can we go swimming today?"

"Not a bad idea. If it doesn't rain."

"What's it matter if it rains? We're wet either way. It's so hot. Why don't you have air conditioning?"

"It's a zoning code thing."

"Sure it is, Dad." He snuggled into me and I held my breath. He was a slight kid, just on the cusp of puberty, edges still soft here and there. Not like his half brother, already shooting up and bristling with muscles and testosterone and attitude. The window for lap sitting with Mike had been almost nonexistent, though most of that was on me. There'd been a scene with him the day before when I told him we couldn't stop at a food truck on the way to the Clippers game and were making sandwiches instead. Typical stuff between us.

"Do you think you'll ever get back together with Anne?"

"What?"

"You know, like get back with her. Like, romantically and stuff."

I looked at him. He returned the look, face full of innocence.

"Why are you asking me this?"

"Just curious. So, will you?"

"Probably not," I said, after a moment.

"How come? I thought you liked her."

"I did. But things just didn't work out."

"How come?"

A man, his son, his dog, and a Sunday morning inquisition about his failed love life. Could it get any better than this?

"Sometimes my job makes it hard for me to pay attention to people the way I should. Not a lot of ladies like that. It's hard to blame them."

"That's what I thought."

"Really?"

"Yeah. Plus she's got a new boyfriend."

"She does?"

He nodded, reaching down to thump Hopalong.

My stomach shrank a little. "How do you know that?"

"I met him. I was playing with Amelia the other day. He was at her house."

Against all odds, Joe and Anne's daughter had stayed friends even after Anne broke up with me, tired of too many dropped balls and missed dates. An English professor at Columbus State, she'd been the first girlfriend in years I hadn't treated like a door-mat with boobs. But I hadn't been there the times she needed me, either. Call it a draw, I guess.

"I'm glad to hear that."

"Amelia says he's not as funny as you."

"Probably a good thing."

We sat for a couple of minutes longer, listening to the sound of German Village waking up. Birds singing, cars juddering down the brick streets of the neighborhood south of downtown, the two Kevins having a just-shy-of-heated discussion across the alley about whose turn it was to clean the grill. A moment later Joe wiggled off my lap and planted himself atop Hopalong. The dog sighed in protest but didn't move from his Labradorean repose. I shifted in my chair and realized my right leg was asleep. I picked up my cup and took a drink of lukewarm coffee and retrieved my book and read a chapter without absorbing a single word. I put it down, got up stiffly, and went inside, trailed by Joe and the dog. It was time to start mixing pancake batter and frying bacon and figuring out the best places to swim for free on a Sunday in Columbus.

3

CUNNINGHAM'S LAW OFFICE WAS A TWO-story brick building on Front in the Brewery District. A maple tree shaded the front yard, so tall and thick-limbed it might have been there when Cunningham's grandfather was a bell-boy in the long-gone Neil House hotel. "Offices of Burke Cunningham III, Attorney-at-Law," said the weathered brass plaque set into the brick to the right of the door. At one minute to nine the next morning I rang the bell, looked up at the camera, and waited for his secretary to buzz me in. At the click of the lock I pushed open the door and walked inside, grateful for the crisp chill of the air conditioning on the already humid morning.

LaTasha sat at her computer at her desk in the small, wood-paneled lobby. It being summer, she was in her Egyptian period, meaning ankh earrings and a beaded gold necklace and a tan sleeveless vest adorned with hieroglyphic figures. Executive legal secretary, Queen Nefertiti style.

"Good morning. You're looking very Cradle of Civilization today."

"Good morning, Andy," she said, too brightly. There was something wrong with her face, as if she were trying to decide how she felt about the terminal illness of an unpleasant relative.

"Everything all right?"

"Everything's fine. Why do you ask?"

"No reason, other than you look like you just swallowed a mayfly."

"What a thing to say. Besides, it's June. Burke's ready for you," she said, gold bracelets clicking as she waved her right hand down the hall. "Go on in."

"Thanks, warden."

She laughed nervously. I walked around the corner to Cunningham's office and stepped inside.

"Jesus Christ," I said involuntarily.

"Oh, very funny," Freddy Cohen said.

"What are you doing here?"

He was leaning against the far wall, favoring his back. He didn't reply right away. First he glanced at Cunningham, sitting behind his mahogany desk, then at the ceiling, and then at me again.

"I need your help."

"My help?" I said.

A pause, during which galaxies spun and tectonic plates shifted. "I need help with a case," Cohen said. He shifted his position. He was standing between Cunningham's framed law degree and the "Whites Only" sign Cunningham hung up as part of his rotating display of Jim Crow memorabilia. "Lest we forget," he liked to say.

"What kind of case?"

"I'm getting to that."

"I can hardly wait."

"Don't take that attitude with me—"

Cunningham cleared his throat.

We both looked at him. His hands were folded atop his desk like a pastor at a mandatory counseling session. "Why don't you take a seat, Andy?"

I walked to the leather chair to the left of his desk and sat. I knew it hadn't been a request.

"Nice weather we're having," Cunningham said.

"Indeed," I said.

"Though perhaps a little warm."

"Very humid."

"You know what they say. It's not the heat. Good weekend?"

"Too short."

"They always are. Especially when you're saving damsels in distress. Which brings me to the matter at hand."

Before he could continue, LaTasha entered with a silver tray bearing large white porcelain coffee mugs, a tall carafe, and cut-glass containers of sugar and cream. If a plastic swizzle stick or a Styrofoam cup had ever despoiled the inside of Cunningham's office, I wasn't aware of it. We sat in silence while LaTasha poured our coffee; mine black, Cunningham's light, Cohen's with both cream and sugar. She left as gracefully as she'd entered. My eyes followed her out, admiring the thick, pleated cotton skirt completing her Nile ensemble. I hoped my figure held up as nicely when I was a mother of four someday.

"Go ahead, Freddy," Cunningham said.

Cohen picked up his mug, took a sip of coffee, and placed it back on the edge of Cunningham's desk beside a carved African fertility statue. He was still standing, which meant his back was bad again. Which was my fault, depending on how you felt about blaming messengers. Thin, gray hair receding, wire-rimmed glasses pushed down on his nose, he'd grown a trim salt-and-pepper beard, heavy on the sodium, since the last time I saw him. He wore a tailored, dark-gray suit, black shoes that uncharacteristically needed shining, and a frown suitable for an infant's funeral.

"Hassan Mohamed," he said. "Name mean anything to you?"

"No. Should it?"

"Try reading the news instead of making it for a change. Columbus man killed in Syria last month. Made CNN for five seconds between Cialis commercials."

The headline came back to me. Stories of radicalized young men sneaking overseas blurred in my mind anymore. But I remembered the local connection and the two days of news coverage it garnered.

"Now I recollect. Islamic State?"

"That's right. Everyone's favorite homicidal psychopaths."

"Was Mohamed Syrian?"

"Somali. Came to Columbus when he was four. Parents made it out of Mogadishu during the civil war and spent several years in a refugee camp in Kenya before emigrating."

That sounded about right. Columbus had the second-largest Somali population in the country, after the Twin Cities in Minnesota, thanks to its low cost of living, reams of warehouse jobs, and the snowball effect of one outpost of settled refugees attracting others. They'd clustered in large groups on the north and west sides and were now such a common sight they hardly turned a head any more. With some variations to the tale, it was the same reason Columbus once had half a dozen German-language newspapers. I thought of the woman in the parking lot. I'd learned her name since: Kaltun Hirsi.

"With you so far," I said.

"First for everything," Cohen said. "So, the feds are still putting the pieces together, but it sounds like a pretty familiar recruitment story. Hassan dropped out of high school, sold some drugs, ran with a gang for a while. Agler Road Crips, if you're counting. Guys like him are low-hanging fruit for Terror Inc. A week's diet of an extremist imam preaching on YouTube and he was in their pocket."

"Meaning?"

"Classic case of self-radicalization. First he cleaned up his act. One day he's running the streets, the next day—well, couple of days, figuratively speaking—he finds religion. Then he became superreligious. Changed his look: beard, robe, sandals, the whole nine yards. His parents were elated."

I took a drink of coffee and nodded.

"That didn't last long. Before they knew it he was tearing into them because they weren't Muslim enough. He demanded his mom and his sisters go full-on burka. When the imam at his mosque denounced a terrorist attack in France, Hassan called him an infidel on Facebook. He was asked not to return. He left the country not long after that."

"To Syria?"

"Turkey first, then he crossed over. He tweeted a picture of himself with his new brigade and a pledge to the caliphate. A week later he was killed in a firefight."

"It's awful. But what—"

"What does it have to do with you?"

"Is this about the other day? In the parking lot?"

"I'm getting to that. You can imagine how devastated his family was. It took them by complete surprise. These are basically hardworking immigrants trying to get by while they adapt to a new life. A new country. They had no idea what to do when his switch flipped and he veered fundamentalist. There's a lot of second-guessing going on."

"Who else in the family?"

"Older brother who works at a Walmart warehouse, and two sisters. One's a stay-at-home mom, the other's a teacher at a charter school for immigrant kids."

Cohen stopped, reacting to a back spasm. I reached for my cup, took another drink, but said nothing.

"There's a third brother. A kid named Abdi," Cohen continued. "Youngest in the family. If Hassan was the troublemaker, he's the golden boy. Decent grades, hell of a soccer player, starts at Ohio State in the fall. Wants to be a diplomat."

"Must have been hard for him, his brother going off like that."

"That's the impression everyone had."

"Had?"

"You heard me. That's the problem. He's gone. He disappeared three days after the family got the news about Hassan's death."

COHEN LEANED FORWARD, OPENED A MANILA folder on the edge of the desk, pulled out a picture, and handed it to me. I examined a photo of a rail-thin kid with a smile big enough for three, wearing a Columbus Crew soccer team cap while he gave the camera a hearty thumbs-up.

"Disappeared?" I said.

"Left school one afternoon, never came home. Week before graduation. Parents didn't think anything at first, figuring he was at a buddy's or maybe work."

"Which was where?"

"Bagged groceries at a Kroger. After a few hours his folks started to panic. They called his friends, but nobody knew anything. Eventually they called the police. Next day the FBI's at their door."

"Why?"

"To ask questions. Starting with, 'Tell us where he is before he does it.'"

"Does what?"

"Kill a bunch of people, apparently. He posted something on Facebook to that end after he went missing."

"What'd it say?"

Cohen pulled a sheet of paper out of the folder. "It rambles a bit. Well, a lot. But the main points are pretty scary." He scanned the document for a second, then started reading. "'America, stop interfering with other countries, especially the Muslim Ummah. We are not weak. We cannot be ignored.'"

"Ummah?"

"Community. Like the Muslim world. Then there's this: 'I will kill them in their own lands, behead them in their own homes, stab them to death as they walk the streets.'"

"How old's this kid?"

"Nineteen. And finally this one: 'I can't wait for another 9/11, San Bernardino, or Boston bombing!' "

Cohen handed me the paper. He was right, it rambled. But along the way, like poison ivy on a meandering trail, was plenty of ugly stuff. It wasn't the kind of thing you wanted to read on Facebook. It made me long for some of my relatives' screeds about their neighbors' dogs.

"Is this all?"

"A few other posts after that. Next couple of days. Images of the ISIS flag. Videos of suicide bombers, articles on martyrdom, attacks on the American government. The usual stuff."

"And the family says this is out of character?"

"Completely."

"But wasn't it out of character for his brother, too?"

"They say it's different. Hassan was an angry guy. He just shifted the focus of his anger. Abdi was happy-go-lucky, always in a good mood. And he didn't go through any of the stages of transformation. That's the key thing. His usual self one day, gone the next, Facebook posts the day after that."

"Did he go to Syria?"

"We don't think so. There's no evidence he left the country."

"Has he been charged?"

"Not yet. Right now the feds are just trying to find him."

"So how are you involved?"

"The family hired me, figuring something's coming down the line. I've represented a couple Somalis over the years for khat possession, so they know who I am."

"Khat?"

"The weed of East Africa. Nasty stuff, but nothing to go to prison for, in my opinion."

"So why am I here?"

He sighed. "The family asked me to bring you on."

"The family? Why?"

He sighed again and shifted his position. "Your little parking lot escapade."

"What about it?"

"Apparently they think you're some kind of hero. I tried to persuade them otherwise, but they were adamant. They think you can help."

"Help them how?"

"They want you to find Abdi."

IN THE SILENCE THAT followed, Cunningham got up from his desk, walked around it, and refilled my cup. He looked at Cohen, who shook his head.

"I tried to talk them out of it," Cohen said. "I told them everything you touched you made worse. You're like a three-legged bull in a china shop with narrow aisles. Should have heard Abukar try to translate that. What were you doing out there, anyway?"

"Who's Abukar?"

"Abukar Abdulkadir. He's a community liaison of some sort. He's the one who reached out on the family's behalf. Answer the question."

"Out where?"

"On the west side, where you helped that woman."

"I was grocery shopping."

"You live on the other side of town."

"I'd just wrapped up a job. I needed some things for the weekend. My boys were coming the next day."

"What kind of job?"

"I was following someone."

"In a grocery store?"

"At the casino."

"That makes more sense," Cohen said. "Who were you following?"

"Someone."

"Someone like who?"

"Freddy," Cunningham interrupted, taking his already deep baritone down a notch. "Perhaps we should stay focused on your situation."

"Of course, of course. It's just that the wanderings of Junior Lew Archer here always fascinate me."

"I'm sure they do, but—"

"First off," I said, "I see myself more the Continental Op type. Secondly, I was following a man who's having an affair with one of the blackjack dealers. I needed a picture of them together when she took a break. Satisfied?"

Cohen looked as if I'd punched him in the nose. The fact we both knew he'd been more or less asking for it didn't make me feel any less bad.

"Did you get it?" he snapped.

"Get what?"

"The picture?"

"Yes." It was one of my better efforts, in fact, the two of them holding hands over sodas at the bar like middle school kids at the roller rink.

"Good to hear," Cohen said.

"Freddy—"

"Don't," he said, putting up a hand.

Cunningham cleared his throat again, but this time he meant it. "You were saying the family wants Andy to look for the boy."

Cohen made a face as if he'd just sniffed sour milk. "To *find* him, were their exact words. They're determined it has to be

Andy. They said you kept helping the lady even after one of them jumped you. They said you were the only person to intervene."

"I was the first. There's a difference."

"They don't see it that way. They said"—he frowned and paused to cough, as if suddenly tasting bile—"they said you're a great man. That's why they want to hire you."

5

ABDI'S PARENTS LIVED IN CAPITAL PARK Village, a complex of putty-colored two-story apartment buildings off Agler Road on the north side. A pair of little girls in bright orange dresses playing in what passed for a front yard eyed me curiously as I found a space in the half-filled lot near the Mohameds' unit at four o'clock that afternoon. I glanced over at Cohen, who'd pulled in right ahead of me. He refused to make eye contact, staring instead at the pants and shirts and multi-colored scarves drying on the fence surrounding the apartments. Fortunately for both of us, our host arrived a minute later.

"*See tahay*? How are you? I am Abukar Abdulkadir," he said, introducing himself with a string of precisely clipped syllables. "You are the wonderful Andy Hayes. I recognize you from the TV. You're a very brave man."

"I did what anybody else would." We shook hands. He was thickset, with short-cropped hair starting to gray, a slightly rounded head, and an engaging smile, wearing a suit and tie that made me feel hot just looking at him.

"That's where you are assuredly wrong. Kaltun said you were the only person to help her. She's very grateful."

"How's she doing?"

"Much better, thanks be to God." Kaltun Hirsi had turned out to be a married mother of six—two other kids were at home with her husband at the time—studying to be a social worker. She'd been at the store picking up a few things for dinner when Tweedledum and Tweedledee approached and started taunting her.

"Have the police found those men?"

A cloud crossed Abdulkadir's face. "Not yet."

Cohen got out of his car and joined us, moving even more slowly than at Cunningham's office that morning. It was hard to tell whether he shook Abdulkadir's hand to greet him or to keep his balance.

"How are you doing today, Mr. Freddy?"

"I've been better. Let's get this over with."

The woman who met us at the door introduced herself as Farah, Abdi's older sister. The schoolteacher, I deduced. She was dressed in tan slacks, a white blouse, and purple sandals that matched her headscarf. She showed us inside. Her parents were seated on a couch in the living room. A soccer match played out on an enormous TV on the other side of the room. An aroma of simmering meat filled the air.

Abdi's father was thin, wearing a long-sleeve white shirt and gray slacks. Abdi's mother was a heavy woman, enveloped in a black scarf and dress. They both smiled and nodded but didn't speak. As Abdulkadir and I sat down, a girl, high school age, introduced as a cousin, appeared with cups of Somali tea. I had come to appreciate the sweet, cardamom-flavored drink the few times I'd had it. Cohen took his as if he'd been handed a witches' brew and sat down carefully on a folding chair beside me.

Abdulkadir said something in Somali to the parents. They nodded and replied. He turned to me.

"The family appreciates your help finding their son. Are there any questions you'd like to ask?"

I took a sip of tea and considered my approach. I made eye contact with Farah briefly before she lowered her gaze. "I'll start with the obvious one, I guess. Do they have any idea at all where he could be or where he went?"

They conferred for a moment. I waited for Abdulkadir to translate. But it was Farah who spoke next.

"None at all. He just vanished."

"No one saw anything?"

She shook her head.

"His friends?"

"They saw him at school that day. They don't know anything."

"Which school?"

"Maple Ridge. It was the second-to-last day of classes. It makes no sense."

I'd heard of the city school on the northeast side but didn't know much about it. "He worked at Kroger. Is that right?"

Farah nodded. "He had a shift that afternoon. He never showed up."

I took a moment to frame my next question. "The Facebook posts. Those were out of character?"

"Completely," Farah said. "Most of the time he put up pictures of himself or his friends. Or stuff about the Crew. He was soccer crazy. The Crew and Juventus FC. It was almost like it was someone else posting."

"Could his account have been hacked?"

"I have no idea." She paused. "Hassan posted similar things, right before he left. But for him, it made more sense. He was very angry. And of course—"

When she didn't finish, I said, "Hassan changed, if I'm not mistaken. But Abdi didn't."

"That's right. That's what makes this so difficult to understand."

"What was Hassan so angry about, if I may ask?"

"Everything. He had a hard time finding a job. He said he was always being picked on for being Muslim. He said America was never held accountable for the things it did to other countries. That American soldiers were killing Muslims."

"Was that true? That he was picked on?"

"Probably. We all are, to some degree. You get used to it, after a while. It's just something you expect to happen now and then. The stares and the whispers. Or like those two men and Kaltun, who you helped. People shouting 'Go home!' even if you were born here. We try to ignore it, or report it to the police if it feels dangerous. But Hassan was thin-skinned. He had a real problem with it."

"Hard to blame him."

"I suppose. But he didn't lose his job because he was a Muslim. He lost it because he came late every day." She spoke with bitterness, glancing at her parents.

"Abdi wasn't like that?"

"No, absolutely not. He loves America. And he loves Columbus." For just a moment the worry in her face disappeared and she permitted herself a smile. "If people said something cruel to him he'd laugh it off. He wouldn't hurt a fly. And he had no reason to disappear. His life was ahead of him. He'd already figured out who his roommate at Ohio State was. They were trading messages."

Farah stopped and spoke to her parents. They nodded in assent.

"Is it possible he's just holed up with a friend?"

"No. We've checked with everyone we know of."

"The school?"

"They say everything was normal."

"Freddy—Mr. Cohen—said the FBI was here. What did they say?"

"They were very rude," Farah said. Framed by the purple scarf, her pretty face hardened. "They accused Abdi of many things. They refused to believe anything we said. They threatened us, told us we could be held responsible. We could lose our refugee status."

"It's a common tactic," Cohen interjected. "Especially now, with everything going on in Washington. But in my opinion they don't have anything to go on, other than some completely uncharacteristic Facebook posts and a few tweets and of course the disappearance right after Hassan's death. On the surface, it's reasonable they'd ask questions. But there's nothing concrete. I've told them as much."

"How'd they respond?"

He waved dismissively. "They reminded me they have to bat a thousand percent every time and a terrorist has to succeed only once. They can't take any chances. Which means a kid who ran away is suddenly a dangerous extremist."

"He didn't run away!" Farah said.

"I didn't mean—"

"Hang on," I interrupted. I knew it was no use pointing out to Cohen, or Farah, for that matter, that the FBI had a damn good point. That, plus the fact Abdi's brother had been a bona fide radical didn't help matters. I had a bigger issue to bring up.

"I wonder if I'm the best person for the job."

"What do you mean?" Farah said. She was sitting on the edge of the couch, mug of tea in her hands, watching me closely. She had arresting eyes the color of melted caramel that seemed full of wisdom and something more painful, far beyond a woman of her years—which couldn't be much past midtwenties.

"It's a complicated case. I don't speak Somali, obviously."

"All his friends speak English," Farah said.

"I'm just not sure where I would start."

"I thought you said this was arranged?" Farah said, looking at Cohen.

"I warned you. He can be difficult."

"I'm not being difficult. I just—"

Abdi's father interrupted, saying something in Somali. He spoke for nearly a minute. Farah said something else, then Abdulkadir, then Abdi's mother. Abdi's father replied in turn. I sipped my tea while I waited.

Farah said, "There's the school, here. His teachers. Maybe they know something. Something they might tell you and not us."

"Isn't school over for the year?"

"That's why we need your help," Farah said, frustrated. "To work those things out."

"I'm still not sure—"

"You were sure about Kaltun Hirsi. In the parking lot."

"That was different."

"Different how?"

Good question. Helping the beleaguered woman was part of a pattern in my life of rushing in first and asking questions later. How many times had a coach threatened to bench me for tearing up the plan at the last second and play-calling on my own from the line of scrimmage? The fact that my choice was often the better one was of little consequence in a rule-bound sport bulging with sideline egos. I also hated bullies, since you often despise that which you yourself have been. It had worked out OK in Kaltun's case. But was I any more a hero than the person who'd called 911 as the pickup truck peeled out of the parking lot?

"I was just trying to help," I said.

"Like nobody else did," Farah said.

"I'm not sure that's true—"

"We think it is."

I took a sip of tea to buy some time. I thought about the family's situation. I considered what it had cost Cohen to agree to their request. Saying we had a history was like noting that summer storm clouds are black.

"I'll do what I can," I said at last, meeting Farah's caramel eyes, which were bright with indignation. "I can't make any promises."

"Thank you. I understand."

"Thank you very much, Mr. Andy Hayes," Abdulkadir said, clapping his hands as he stood.

"Yes, thank you, Andy," Cohen said, rising with difficulty. I moved out of instinct to offer a hand, but withdrew at the sight of his frown. "Thank you so much for everything."

6

CREDIBLE EVIDENCE INDICATES THAT
Hassan Mohamed died May 27 on the outskirts of
Aleppo. He appears to have left his home in Columbus,
Ohio, two months prior and made his way first to Turkey,
then into Syria. Preventing extremist recruiting of youth
is a top priority for the U.S. government.

I stared at my computer screen an hour later, sitting at my kitchen table. I clicked here and there for more, but there wasn't any. That was it. The sum total of the official government reaction to Hassan's death. Three sentences summarizing a young life consumed by the combustion of modern warfare and ideology masquerading as theology. Of the pain in his parents' eyes and the passion on his sister's face as she pleaded for help involving a second potential tragedy in the family, there was nothing.

I moved on to Abdi. Googling his name in combination with Maple Ridge High got me a few hits involving soccer games, including last year's state semifinals, when he'd scored three goals in an ultimately losing effort that still won him plaudits all around, including from the other team's coach. I searched for his

Facebook page and Twitter account, but they were long gone. Knowing I had no choice, I called the one person I knew who might be able to help find them. Bonnie Deckard picked up on the third ring. I heard yelling and a whistle in the background. I told her what I was looking for.

"If the accounts have been deleted, it could be pretty hard. There might be some posts left on friends' sites, if they're public. How soon do you need it?"

"Sooner the better, I guess, since he's missing." I told her about the threatening posts and the purported images of the Islamic State flag and suicide bomber videos.

"I can't do it until tomorrow. I'm at practice right now. We're just on a break." Bonnie played for the Arch City Rollers, the city's roller derby team, when she wasn't running her own website development company and bailing me out of technological problems beyond my capability, which was often.

"One thing?" she said.

"Sure."

"You still, um, owe me for the last job. It's not much, like a hundred bucks," she added apologetically. "But—"

"Right. I'm sorry about that. I'll stick it in the mail right now. Or I could drop it by."

"Maybe just do quick pay, with your bank? I'm pretty busy the next couple of days. And I sort of need the money."

"No problem. No problem at all. I'll do it right now."

"Thanks. And I'll take a look at your guy tomorrow. Just e-mail me the details."

"By the way, it's a national security case. Be careful about, you know . . ."

"Covering my tracks?"

"Something like that."

"Thanks for the warning."

FIFTEEN MINUTES LATER, SWEATING a bit from the uphill climb from my house, I walked inside Jury of Their

Pours at Mound and High. Despite my lobbying over the years, the courthouse watering hole had never deigned to stock Black Label. There's no accounting for taste. I settled for a draft Yuengling and a bowl of bar nuts instead. I drained the shoulders off the beer and munched some nuts. I needed to clear my head. Owing Bonnie money like that was embarrassing. It wasn't that I didn't have it, especially since Cohen had just written me a fat retainer check. It's just that I didn't have a whole lot to spare. And losing eighty bucks in groceries is not a small deal in the world I live in, bracketed by hefty child support payments and a cash-flow ledger that looks like a seismograph machine on a bad day in fracking country.

I looked around the bar as if hoping to find solace in the display of framed newspaper clippings of some of the great trials of the century. "Not Guilty" screamed the headline in the *Dispatch* the day after O.J. walked free. Below that front page, which hung on the opposite wall, sat a female defense attorney I'd seen here and there. She was chatting with an assistant male prosecutor I knew just well enough to say hi to. We nodded our hellos. They were doing a decent job of pretending to talk shop in an oh-so-professional-way, but their body language wasn't fooling anyone. I drank my beer and munched some nuts and enjoyed the floor show. A few minutes later the door opened and another customer walked in.

"Moose around?" the newcomer said, seating himself with one bar stool between us.

The bartender shook his head.

"Any idea where he is?"

"Went to see his mom, over in Martins Ferry."

"Is she OK?"

"I don't think so. Something about hospice."

"Sorry to hear that." He ordered a Coke. He was black, light-skinned, with blue eyes and a look of preoccupation. He pulled out his phone and made a couple of calls. One was to someone named Buck, the other to an acquaintance who apparently went by Big

Dog. He left voicemails both times. He didn't sound happy about it. He sighed and looked at his watch and took a gulp of his drink and glanced around. He settled on me with a look of surprise.

"Woody Hayes. I'll be damned."

I almost turned away. I still get called by my old nickname a lot and normally want nothing to do with it. But there was something about those blue eyes.

"I go by Andy now."

"Andy?"

"That's right."

"Why?"

"It's my name."

"Huh." He checked his phone as if hoping against hope that someone had returned his call in the fifteen seconds since he'd last checked it. He returned his attention to me.

"Michigan State, your sophomore year, third and thirteen, forty-two yard line, three minutes on the clock, up by twenty points. Snap's fumbled, you recover, drop back another five yards, roll left, scramble, juke this lineman who wasn't much wider than a double-wide beer cooler, look into the eyes of that guy's bigger cousin, and just as he nails you, you fire a perfect spiral and hit Drew Wade for the first down."

I stared at him.

"What?" he said.

"Other than the fact you'd probably make a hell of a good *Jeopardy* contestant, that's pathetic, if you don't mind me saying so. Who remembers that kind of shit? Especially a play that didn't matter."

"It mattered to you. And for the record, *I* remember that shit. Don't tell me you went by Andy then."

I gave him another stare. On the TV above the bottles of hard liquor the Indians were losing the first game of an afternoon doubleheader. At the end of the bar warm laughter indicated that final deliberations were underway for the two lawyers. Someplace in East Lansing, a baby was crying.

"OK," I said. I stuck out my hand. "Woody Hayes."

"That's more like it," he said, accepting with a firm grip. "Otto Mulligan."

"Buy you a drink?"

"No thanks. I stick to the soft stuff."

"Another one of those, then."

He shook his head. "Can't stay. I'm working. Supposed to be working."

"What do you do?"

"Bail bonds. Got a shop around the corner." He gestured out the door with his thumb. He took a card out of his wallet and handed it to me. It said:

Get Otto Here!
24-Hour Bail Bonds. Flexible Payment Plan.
Same Day Service.
Otto Mulligan, Licensed Bail Agent

"Are you new? I haven't seen you around."

"I'm old as dirt. Been out of town a few years. Came back because my dad was passing. Think I'm back for good now."

"Sorry about your dad."

"Thanks. You and half of Columbus, it turns out."

"Really? Who was he, if I may ask?"

"Patrick Mulligan."

"Judge Mulligan?"

"One and the same."

Half of Columbus made sense. Mulligan was a legendary common pleas judge and pillar of the local Democratic Party who'd served forty years on the bench. His death had warranted a front-page news article in the *Dispatch*. As Irish as they came. Unlike the man sitting on a bar stool beside me.

"So—"

"Ever heard of Joyce Brown?"

I shook my head.

"Jazz singer, out on the east side. Most beautiful voice you'd ever want to hear. Little whispery now, but she's still got it."

"And she—?"

"She's my mom. And yes, black is beautiful."

"Your mom—but not Judge Mulligan's wife."

"No indeed."

"Does Mrs. Mulligan know?"

"She does now," he said, bemusement in his eyes. "He wanted me in the hospital with him. Insisted on it."

I pondered this. After a moment I raised my glass.

"To complicated histories."

"*Sláinte,*" Mulligan replied.

I fingered his business card. "OK if I keep this?"

"Be my guest."

I handed him my card in turn.

"Private eye, huh? You any good?"

"I hold my own."

"Do any security?"

"Like what?"

"Like personal protection. The bodyguard routine."

"From time to time. But I don't carry."

"Don't, or won't?"

"Can't. There were limits to my plea deal, despite how generous it was."

"Right. The point shaving. How quickly we forget. So, doing anything right now?"

"Now?"

"Need a hand with something, and my usuals aren't picking up."

"Moose, Buck, and Big Dog?"

"They're sweet guys once you get to know them."

"Sweet as pie, I'm guessing. So what's the deal?"

"Minor little job. Guy on a bad check warrant missed his arraignment. It's a felony because he had the bright idea of writing one for a thousand bucks. Think I found him in a house off Weber Road."

"Weber east or west of 71?"

"East. But it's no big deal. He's a shrimpy guy. We'd be in and out in five."

"If it's no big deal why do you need help?"

"Two heads better than one, is my philosophy. What do you say? Two hundred bucks and I'll buy you a drink when we get back." He paused. "I might even spring for a burger and fries."

I thought about Bonnie and my bank account and the low-balance alerts that kept clogging up the screen of my phone like globs on bird crap on a windshield.

I said, "Two-fifty, since it's east of 71. And make it sweet potato fries."

He reached out and shook my hand again. "Dig it," he said.

7

THE ONE-STORY RENTAL HALFWAY DOWN
the block was the color of puke left in the sun for a week. The
blinds were drawn and duct tape covered a crack in the bottom
right corner of the front window. The chewed-up lawn looked
like a family of woodchucks had spent the night excavating it.
What appeared to be an actual sapling was growing out of the
front gutter, which sagged in the middle like a mocking smile.

"Good thing is, we don't have to worry about some prissy
home-and-garden editor interrupting us while we work," Mulligan said, eyeing the property from where we'd parked along
the street two houses up. He drove a battered Chevy Suburban
that looked like it was motored new off the lot around the time
Jimmy Carter was putting solar panels on the White House roof.
"You go around back, watch the rear door, just in case."

"In case of what?"

"Inclement weather. Come on."

He was out of the car before I could respond. I followed,
walking behind him down the gravel berm. At the house, a rusty
gate opening into the yard squeaked in protest. Mulligan signaled

for me to cut left. I tiptoed past several piles of dogshit I was hoping were not as fresh as they looked and crept around to the back. Concrete steps ran up to the rear entrance. There was a screen door without its screen. The backyard lawn ornaments consisted of crumpled-up Taco Bell and White Castle bags.

I positioned myself a few feet away from the stairs and waited. I heard a knocking on the front door, followed by an explosion of barking. So the shit was fresh. I tried not to think of my Louisville Slugger collecting dust in my van back in German Village. More knocking, more barking, then voices. At first the tenor of the conversation sounded reasonable enough, as if Mulligan were pitching an alternative natural gas supply. Then I heard a shout and still more barking and what sounded like a crash. A rapid thudding inside indicated someone running, and getting close. I bent my knees and adopted my best pro wrestling stance, minus the makeup and green spandex. A moment later the rear door burst open and a man hurtled out. A small man, no more than five five and maybe 120 pounds in the shower. Definitely shrimpy. But his eyes were glazed, and for a moment I thought he might be high, which would have complicated things. Instead, I saw he was terrified, as if he'd just seen a ghost while in the shower. He ran straight into me.

"Easy now," I said, grabbing him by the arms and turning him around. He didn't struggle. Maneuvering him was like putting a coat rack back in the corner where it belonged.

"Otto!" I yelled. "Back here." When Mulligan didn't reply I started marching my prisoner around to the front.

"Please," the man whined.

"Talk to Otto. I'm just the hired help."

"Please. *Save me.*"

"Save you? From what?"

"*From her.*"

"Her who?"

The answer came a second later. I heard a sound behind us, turned, and saw a two-headed monster rounding the corner and barreling towards us. I stared in disbelief. The bottom half of the monster was a woman the size and approximate shape of an extra-long chest freezer turned on end, snorting like a bull and yelling something that sounded like *Blobby Baby*. She was wearing too-tight black yoga pants and a black CD101 Radio T-shirt, her brown hair pulled back in a ponytail with a frilly white scrunchie. The top of the monster was Mulligan, clinging to her back and trying to restrain her as she charged in our direction. Tangled up in the woman's feet was a corgi, ears raised and fangs bared as it barked its little head off.

"Get him out of here, Woody!" Mulligan yelled.

I pushed the bail skip forward and started to run. But it was too late. The woman's forward momentum overtook me, even with Mulligan trying to hold her back, and we went down in a tangle of limbs and arms and barking canine. I pulled myself free, started to stand up, looked around for the little guy, and had just enough time to back up slightly before the woman's right fist connected with my left eye. I staggered, caught my balance, staggered again, and fell over. The corgi pounced and clamped its jaws onto my right sneaker, jerking my foot this way and that like a rat it had dug out of a hole. I rolled to my left, reached for something to pull myself up by, and found a fleshy, sockless ankle instead. I grabbed it with both hands and held on tight. For nearly twenty seconds I was back on my uncle's pig farm being dragged through the mud by a surly sow as the woman fought her way forward hollering *"Blobby Baby, Blobby Baby!"* and I bumped and scraped my way across the dug-up yard. I'm pretty sure I ran over an expired woodchuck. Finally, just when I thought there was no way sweet potato fries were ever going to cut it, the woman said, in a surprisingly high, girlish voice, "God damn you motherfuckers to hell." I stopped moving and she fell over with Mulligan splayed across her back like a rodeo rider at the county fair prelims. I took a breath, got to my knees, got all the way up, and rubbed my eye. I was seeing not just stars but entire constellations.

"Let's get out of here," Mulligan said. He ran up to the object of his pursuit and took him roughly by the left arm. The man was shaking like a leaf in a November breeze. He didn't resist. "Thank you," he whispered.

"Bobby baby," the woman wailed, lying prone in the yard as she squeezed mud and God knows what else between her fingers. "*Bobby baby.*"

"I'M TELLING YOU, YOU'RE a natural, Woody," Mulligan said an hour later, as I sat at the bar at Jury of Your Pours, an uneaten burger and a double helping of sweet potato fries before me. The lovebirds had departed, but the scent of their pheromones still lingered.

I adjusted the ice pack on my eye and took another drink of beer.

"You could have told me about her," I said, not for the first time.

"I didn't know."

"But I bet you guessed?"

"Life's too short to speculate, don't you think? Anyway, you did great."

"Tell it to Big Dog."

"Dig it," Mulligan said with a grin.

I DIDN'T LOOK MUCH WORSE THE NEXT
morning than a guy whose left eye and socket have been replaced
by an overripe eggplant. How I felt was another matter. I pulled
myself together with a second cup of coffee before setting off for
a romp in the park with Hopalong. After breakfast, a shower, and
more breakfast, I got in my Honda Odyssey and headed to the
northeast side of town.

Maple Ridge High was a 1970s special: flat roof, brick exterior
the color of fish sticks, a bank of recessed glass doors at an entrance guarded by poured concrete pillars that brought to mind
abandoned Olympic villages. I had to wait to be buzzed in. Once
I was inside, a custodian reluctantly pointed me down a gleaming
hall toward the office. I could feel the resentment in his eyes like
little death rays in my back as I tracked molecular-sized grains of
dust onto the newly waxed floor.

I explained to the woman sitting at a desk why I was there.
She didn't reply, but instead stared hard at me, which was a puzzle
until I remembered my eye.

"I'm not sure Ms. Paulus has time today," she said at last.
"We're trying to wrap up the school year."

"Ms. Paulus?"

"The principal?"

"Right. It won't take but a minute, promise. Or I can wait." I leaned forward, folded my hands on the counter and smiled.

She didn't return the smile. She had a full, brown face and a streak of red in her straightened black hair that nicely matched her lipstick. Her dark eyes were the sort you could fall into if you had a thing for school secretaries who brooked very little crap. She glanced at an open office door behind her and to her right. A poster of a female swimmer doing the butterfly filled the upper half of the door.

"I'll have to see." She studied her desk phone for a moment. I couldn't tell if she was hoping it would ring or deciding whether to call 9-1-1. At last she stood with a frown and click-clacked on red summer heels back to the principal's office. I looked around the room and caught the custodian glaring at me through the office windows. Like the secretary, he didn't appear to feel I was conducive to the school's educational mission. I waved. He stalked off. A moment later the secretary click-clacked back to her desk, followed by a woman with a pen in her hand and impatience on her face.

"I'm Helene Paulus. How can I help you?"

I got the same puzzled look at my eye. I smiled and handed her my card and told her my name and reason for my presence. She took the card and studied it like a copy machine invoice she hadn't been expecting. When she was done she turned the card over and seemed disappointed the back was blank. I get that a lot. It always makes me think I should buy a set printed with a cartoon of a hound wearing a Sherlock Holmes hat and sucking on a churchwarden pipe, to show I'm a real investigator and all.

She said, "But I thought . . ." She paused. She lowered her voice a notch. "I thought Abdi was overseas."

"Not as far as anyone knows. We think he's here."

"We?"

"The family. And the government, too, for that matter."

"And you're a private investigator?"

"Yes, ma'am," I said, which I could tell she didn't like since she couldn't have been that much older than me. I pulled out my license and presented it.

"Just a couple of questions. In hopes of finding the boy."

"We can talk in my office," she said doubtfully, and gestured for me to come around the counter and follow her back. I smiled at the secretary as I passed her desk. She shot me some of the custodian's death rays. As we entered the principal's office I looked at the poster on the door. "Dream Bigger," it said, beneath a photo of the swimmer taken from an underwater angle.

"I don't mean to be rude," Paulus said, as she sat behind her desk. "Your eye—"

"Cue ball," I said, sitting down across from her. "Took a bad hop. About Abdi . . ."

She frowned. "The FBI was already here. I'm not sure what more I can tell you. Or should." She had short, white hair in a boyish cut and the tan of someone who's outdoors a lot. Given the profusion of house plants in the office I was guessing gardening over triathlons, though she had a nice enough figure. She was dressed professionally, even with school out, in a sleeveless patterned blouse and white slacks. No wedding ring. Her tone was cool and guarded, as if I were an errant teacher begging to be rehired despite a file full of student grievances.

"Whatever you're able to answer," I said, trying to decide where to start. My eyes strayed across her desk. Beside a pile of manila folders sat a copy of *Dreamland*. She followed my gaze.

"It's a book about the opiate epidemic," she said, taking her time pronouncing 'opiate.' "There's several chapters about Ohio."

"Yes. I'm reading it myself."

"You are?"

"That's right."

"Is it for a class, or, or something?"

"Actually, I'm just reading it. You know, for pleasure, so to speak. It's good, don't you think? But quite disturbing." I waited a moment, but she didn't respond.

I said, "Don't worry. I have a friend who helps me sound out the really big words."

"I'm sorry. I just didn't think—"

I waited, watching her blush. I felt bad, but it was worth seeing. It made my embarrassment at owing Bonnie money literally pale in comparison. Plus, the color didn't do any harm to her features.

"I meant—"

"Don't worry about it. Sounds like a topic we're both interested in. I imagine it's a big concern in a school. Maybe we could talk about it sometime over tea and crumpets. But right now I'm here about Abdi Mohamed. I guess I'm wondering if anyone here has any idea where he might have gone. And if these accusations are a surprise in any way."

"Yes," she said, recovering. "Yes, I mean they are a surprise. A huge surprise. You think you know the students, and then something like this. It's hard not to wonder now, with his brother and all. But Abdi was a good kid. We didn't suspect anything like this. None of his teachers did."

"And no idea where he is?"

"Of course not. We would have told the authorities."

"His family says he was on the way to work. After school got out?"

"That's right. He always had a job of some kind. Very hardworking. Not like—"

"Not like Hassan?"

"Yes," she admitted. "They were very different young men, despite the fact they were brothers. Hassan was a real troublemaker, to tell you the truth. We have a gang problem here, and he was headed in that direction. That's what made his turnaround so surprising." She paused. "And frankly, a little hard to swallow."

"What do you mean?"

"He just traded one set of problems for another, in my opinion. Instead of just, I don't know, doing the right thing in the first place."

"In my experience, doing the right thing is a high bar for a lot of people."

"Is that so?"

"Present company excepted, of course." The expression on her face told me I hadn't won any favors with the remark. I smiled, hoping to tone it down a little. The smile wasn't returned. I forged ahead anyway. "So was there anything about Abdi that might have signaled a change?"

"Like what?"

"I'm not sure. A difference in his mood, maybe. Something suggesting he was subject to, I don't know, some kind of outside influence. Going down his brother's path."

"Not at all. His grades were fine. He wasn't an 'A' student or anything like that, but he was no slouch. There were no signs of a senior slump." She sighed. "Not like a lot of the kids in his class. He was upset after his brother left town, of course. I talked to him briefly a few times. Barbara would know more of the details, but I can't really say I noticed a big change."

"Barbara?"

"Barbara Mendoza. One of our counselors. She worked closely with Abdi. She helped him apply to Ohio State, and look for scholarships. She has—"

"Yes?"

"She has a different opinion, I guess. I believe she told the FBI it wasn't out of the realm of possibility that Abdi could have, well, turned."

"Sounds like you disagree."

"I wouldn't say that. She knew him much better. I'm not in a position to second-guess her. She's a veteran counselor."

"Is she around?"

"She's off for the summer."

"Is it possible to speak with her?"

"I'm not sure. I suppose I could ask. She was very upset when this happened. Still is. I think she—"

I waited while she gathered her thoughts. She said, "It's almost as if she took it personally. After all the time she spent with him."

"She feels betrayed?"

"Something like that."

"I think she'd be good to talk to. If you could reach out to her, maybe, let her know my interest. That I'm trying to help. Maybe explain I'm an OK guy. That I read books from time to time."

"There's no need to be rude, Mr."—she put her index finger on my card and raised a pair of readers onto her eyes—"Mr. Hayes."

"My apologies. I was aiming for impertinent. And call me Andy."

Her face reddened again, but not from embarrassment this time. "Maybe you're accustomed to this kind of thing, Mr. Hayes. In your line of work." Her tone implying septic tank cleaning might be a step up in the world. "But this has been utterly traumatic for us. Especially now, after Hassan, and happening right at the end of the school year."

"I can imagine."

"I doubt it."

"I'm sorry you feel that way. So. The counselor?"

"I'll see what I can do."

"Thank you."

When I didn't go on, she said, "Was there anything else?"

"Could you ask her now? The sooner I can get some answers, the better."

"Now?"

"No time like the present."

"And if I say no?"

"That's your prerogative. I'll probably find her anyway. But I was hoping we could, you know, collaborate."

"Is that so?"

I realized I was folding my arms against my chest like a kid challenging detention. I unfolded them and put my hands in my lap instead. "It is, as a matter of fact."

She looked at me for a long moment before standing up from her desk and marching into the outer office. I heard her conferring with the no-nonsense secretary. I looked around

Paulus's office. Where one might expect framed diplomas hung a couple of George Bellows prints I recognized from the art museum. A nice touch. Interspersed with the plants on the office bookshelves were plaques and photographs and several representations of people on rearing horses, from plastic statuettes to yellow-and-white pennants. It came to me after a second: I was sitting in the home of the Maple Ridge Riders. Some framed photos of grown-up looking kids I took to be hers sat next to the mascot displays—no husband in the pictures, I noticed. I'm observant that way.

"I left a voicemail," Paulus said, reentering the office. "I explained it was important. I can let you know when she gets back to me."

"Thank you. One other thing."

A sigh. "Yes?"

"Did Abdi have a lot of friends?"

"What do you mean?"

"Just that. Was he popular?"

"Very, as a matter of fact. It was part of his charm. A joker, but not obnoxious. He had an easygoing way about him that naturally attracted people."

Like Islamic State recruiters? I thought. "Any particular students I should talk to?"

"There might be a couple." She sighed again. "I could get you some names."

"And numbers?"

"I'm not sure I can do that."

"I'm thinking you can do anything you want. You're the principal, right? We're not talking missed homework here, Helene. It's life or death."

"It's Ms. Paulus, and thank you for that insight. It hadn't occurred to me. Is there anything else you want from us, as long as you've barged in here like this? Or is that just how private detectives operate?"

"I'm a private investigator," I corrected her. "And under normal circumstances I would have waited for you under a streetlamp while the mist curled around my iron jaw and the dark night fell like a blanket over a grave. I figured I'd mix it up a bit."

"I think we're done here," she said, rising again. This time she waited for me to do the same. I walked into the main office and bided my time examining the other inspirational posters on the walls while she gave the secretary instructions in a curt voice to pull the files of a couple students. The secretary handed me the names on a piece of Maple Ridge stationery, glaring as if I was the one who'd personally talked Abdi into joining a terrorist front.

"Thank you," I said, folding the paper in thirds and tucking it into my pocket. "You'll get back to me about the counselor?"

"I said I would," Ms. Paulus said.

As I headed for the front door I saw the custodian at the far end of the hall, eyes locked on my wax floor–defiling shoes. I tried another wave. This time, as if a tremor had gripped his arm, he waved once in return.

I DROVE DOWN MCCUTCHEON TO STELZER
Road, glanced in my rearview mirror, and headed back toward
the highway. I figured I'd give Ms. Paulus-not-Helene a few hours,
no more, to persuade the counselor to talk to me before tracking
her down myself. It probably wouldn't earn me any extra credit
points with the principal, whose Christmas card list I was assuredly off of after our encounter. Not that I blamed her for her
reaction to my visit, or my insistent manner. The fact was, I *could*
imagine how rattled the school community was. The thought of
a homegrown extremist in my town was rattling me, too.

Right before the entrance to 270 I glanced in my mirror again
and changed my mind and decided to take the scenic route home
instead. I took Stelzer back to McCutcheon and turned right,
heading west. A quarter mile down I put on my signal, braked,
and turned into a newish-looking subdivision. I slowed to the
residential street's posted limit of twenty-five miles per hour and
for the next several minutes drove up and down the lanes of the
small suburban neighborhood, taking in the scenery and trying to
guess the median age of the houses. Best guess was late nineties,

early aughts. Calling them cookie cutter would be implying too much diversity. At last, I ended up back on the street where I'd entered this little slice of real estate heaven. I pulled up to the intersection with McCutcheon. Instead of putting on my turn signal, I placed the van in park, activated my flashers, turned off the engine, and pulled out the keys. I pocketed them as I got out of the van. I walked back to the black Ford Explorer stopped behind me and gestured to the driver to roll down the window. I did that sideways stirring motion, as if using a spatula to scrape out batter from a mixing bowl. One of those anachronisms that everyone still understands, like saying tinfoil or calling a band's latest release an album. After all, practically no cars have hand-cranked windows anymore. Kind of funny, if you think about it—

"There a problem?" the Explorer's driver said. If he had eyes, you couldn't tell through his mirrored aviators.

"Not really. Just that you need a buffer."

"I'm sorry?"

"Like a decoy. A car in between." I took a step back and used my hands to illustrate. "It gives you cover but not so much you lose visual contact."

"I don't know what you're talking about. Could you just—"

"OK. How about this? Why don't you cut the crap and explain why you're following me?"

I HAVE TO GIVE the other guy credit. Or gal, as it turned out. Unlike the driver frowning at me from the front seat of the Explorer—who might as well have turned a siren on from the moment he followed me away from the school—I hadn't spotted the second car at all, a fact I determined as it pulled up a moment later right on cue. Doors on both cars opened simultaneously and four people in dark suits surrounded me. I felt like the first customer on a slow day at a Brooks Brothers outlet.

I looked at the woman, whom I knew. I said, "I didn't bring my bathing suit, in case this is the part where you waterboard me. But I am wearing Scooby-Doo underpants, if that counts for anything."

"Don't be an ass," Cindy Morris said. "Sorry: more of an ass. What the hell happened to your eye?" She took off her own sunglasses. Her expression indicated she'd had one of those days just since breakfast. Her short, dark hair had come down with a mild case of snow flurries since the last time she'd flashed her FBI badge at me.

I gave her the cue-ball line, which earned me a look several degrees below Kelvin. "You have a funny way of asking me out to coffee," I soldiered on. "Did you lose my number?"

"Maybe we could take this someplace less public," said the driver of the Explorer I'd busted, standing next to Morris. Flushed from his lair, he stood tall and broad-shouldered. I was guessing two parts basketball, one part free weights, with a twist of jujitsu on the side. His stance suggested people usually took his etiquette suggestions.

"Good idea. How about Capitol Square, in front of the *Dispatch* office, downtown? There's a decent bagel place next door. I'm buying."

Morris looked up the street. A minivan had pulled to a stop behind the line of parked cars. The female driver eyed the vehicles and the five of us standing in the road. Morris nodded at another of the men in black, who happened to be black, and he stepped back and signaled for the woman to drive around.

"There's a Wendy's up the street," Morris said.

"A local restaurant. Trendy of you," I said. The fast-food chain was headquartered just up the highway in suburban Dublin. "I'd heard the bureau was very farm-to-table these days. Unfortunately, I'm comfortable right where I am. This traffic stop feels like my second home, without the patio. And I apologize for my slip of the tongue: it's the CIA that waterboards, not you guys. You just psychoanalyze people to death. To repeat: why are you following me?"

"It really might be easier—"

"Actually, I think I can guess why. How about I tell you what I've been up to and save us both some time?"

"Listen, Hayes—"

"I started with a good breakfast, since that's the most important meal of the day, as I'm sure they taught you at Quantico, where you probably grilled rabbits over bonfires. After that, I drove to Maple Ridge High School to meet with Helene Paulus, the principal, whose social security number I didn't manage to snag but I'm thinking you already have that, plus all her pin numbers. We had a nice chat about the country's opiate epidemic and cooperation and the fact that if Abdi Mohamed wasn't a Boy Scout, he was the next closest thing and therefore a highly unlikely recruiting target for Islamic extremists. Unless they've started infiltrating Kroger checkout lines. From here I'm headed to the house of worship Abdi attended for some palavering with the elders there, although I'd wager my last Sacajawea dollar they won't tell me much. After that, I fly to Istanbul to meet a guy named Ahmed parked in a black Mercedes under the third streetlamp down from the Hagia Sophia mosque. Hope to be back in time for Sunday dinner with my folks." I stopped and pressed both forefingers against my temples in a thinking pose. "Oh, I also need to pick up kibble for the dog. OK. I think that about sums it up."

Special agent Morris was not amused. The look on her face made my conversation with Helene Paulus seem downright convivial in comparison. Without breaking eye contact, she took out her cell phone, glanced for a fraction of a second at the screen, power-typed a message, and replaced it in her coat pocket. She trained her baby blues on me like a predator weighing which limb to tear off first.

"Listen carefully, *Woody*. We're not screwing around here. You're interfering with a national security investigation."

I bristled at her use of my nickname. For a Feebee Morris was all right. But she wasn't on the short list like my new best friend, Otto Mulligan. "I don't go by Woody anymore. It might be more effective to throw in my middle name instead, the way my mom does. As for interfering? I'm not even at hindering—"

"By rights I could have you arrested. Questioning government witnesses on a terrorism case."

"And I could have you slapped with a bar association complaint. Let's see—harassing an officer of the court during the lawful conduct of his duties. How's that for starters?"

She snorted. "Officer of the court? Give me a break."

"I'm working for Freddy Cohen. Cohen is representing the family of Abdi Mohamed. Ipso facto, that makes me an extension of Cohen."

"You're working for Cohen?"

"Don't tell me you didn't know that. Or did your surveillance drone run out of petrol already?"

"You and Cohen. That's amazing, I have to say, even for you. After what you—"

"Careful, Agent Morris."

My tone caught the attention of the tall agent, who shifted his feet in a manner that suggested a flying tackle was a misplaced adjective away.

"I'd be sensitive about it too, I were you," Morris said. "But the fact you're working for Cohen doesn't change anything. You're still tramping around where you don't belong. Per usual, I might add."

"Now see, that's where you're wrong."

"Oh?"

"The way I see it, you're carrying out your duties as a law enforcement agent tasked with investigating federal crimes. I'm helping Freddy find a man presumed innocent under the U.S. Constitution. We're really two peas in a pod, don't you think?"

"I think I'd like to know what Helene Paulus told you."

I thought about the names of the students in my pocket, and about the school counselor's close relationship with Abdi. Her feeling, according to Paulus, that the suspicions against the boy were warranted. Surely Morris knew all that already. I said, "She told me Abdi's hiding under her desk along with two of Osama bin Laden's drivers and an Islamic State player to be named later. In other words, go ask her yourself."

"I'm serious."

"So am I. But like I said, I'm under attorney-client privilege."

"You think this is a game? There are lives at stake here, Woody. We're lucky Abdi's brother died overseas. The alternative is these people coming back home carrying grudges and trained to do something about it."

"These people?" I said, cocking an eyebrow.

"Terrorists," Morris snapped. "Real or wannabe. You know what I mean. Don't try to misconstrue my words."

"Let me guess. Some of your best friends are Muslims?"

Between the murderous look that flared in Morris's eyes and the intake of breath from the tall, dark, and muscle-bound agent beside her, there was a good chance I might have ended up in the backseat of a bureau-issued car in the next few seconds had Morris's phone not gone off just then. Eyes never leaving mine, she planted the cell against her right ear and listened to someone on the other line for a full thirty seconds without speaking. "All right," she said at last, cutting the connection without saying goodbye.

Maintaining her vacuum-locked gaze, she said, "As much as I'd love to continue this conversation, something's come up I need to attend to. You're free to go."

"Oh goody. So what's up? Two peas in a pod, remember?"

"Don't flatter yourself. We're not even in the same garden."

TEN MINUTES LATER I WAS SITTING IN THE parking lot of Masjid Omar, the mosque that Abdi's family attended off Sunbury Road. I was reviewing the encounter with the agents when I was interrupted by the sound of Tom Petty's "Free Fallin'" coming from the passenger seat. Caller ID blocked. I answered the phone anyway.

"You're lucky to be alive."

"Excuse me?"

"You heard me. Those guys don't fool around."

"Who is this?"

"Name's McQuillen. Thought you could use some help." His voice low and conspiratorial, like someone passing along a horseracing tip.

"What kind of help?"

"Finding those guys."

Confused, I thought of the three agents acting as Cindy Morris's backup band just now. "What guys?"

"The ones in the parking lot who rolled you. I might know who they are. Depending on what you can tell me."

"And how would you know that?"

"I study guys like them."

I get this kind of call a lot, which doesn't make them any less annoying. Most of the time I waste precious minutes explaining why I don't look for lost cats or collect video evidence of ectoplasmic trails. Usually. I looked out my van window. Abukar Abdulkadir pulled in three spaces away. I waved. He nodded, a look of distraction on his face.

"Back up. Tell me again who you are. And why you're calling."

"Told you. Name's McQuillen. I analyze those people."

"What people?"

"Right wingers. Hate groups. Citizen militias. Three percenters. The lot."

"McQuillen your first name or last?"

"Ronald J. McQuillen. Ronald, not Ron."

"And you analyze these people? Like, as a hobby?"

"I'm a consultant."

"For who?"

"For people who know less about these groups than me, which is pretty much everyone."

"Does that include the police?"

"Sometimes."

"Anybody else?"

"ACLU. Southern Poverty Law Center. Anti-Defamation League. NAACP. Others." His voice got even lower, as if he'd stepped back into the shadows after spying someone from the state racing board. "I know what I'm doing. I might be able to help you."

"OK, Ronald J. McQuillen. I'm in the middle of something right now. Any chance I could call you back?"

"I'll text you my address. Come by and we'll talk. Just not before ten. I'm usually not up. And not after two or three in the afternoon. I'm working."

"Where do you live?"

"Watch yourself, all right? These people are a lot more dangerous than you think."

"But—"

It was too late. He'd hung up. Which also happens to me a lot.

THE MOSQUE WAS A cement-block building painted a drab green, with a basketball court on one side and a small playground of slides and climbing structures on the other. A tall chain-link fence ran around the perimeter, concluding with a rolling gate at the entrance, which had been open when I pulled in. Inside, I followed Abdulkadir's lead and slipped off my shoes, grateful that I was wearing matching socks for a change. I placed my shoes in a cubbyhole built into a set of floor-to-ceiling white shelves, where they joined a few other pairs.

A young man introduced as Sammy, the mosque youth coordinator, gave me a tour. It didn't last long. The carpeted prayer room looked to have capacity for a couple of hundred worshippers. You could tell the community had worked hard to create a functional sanctuary, installing wood wainscoting around the room and painting the cinderblock walls a slightly less drab olive than the outer walls, but it didn't take a lot of imagination to see it as its former incarnation: a central warehouse storage area filled with whatever equipment had once been housed here. A kitchen opened up to the right and classrooms ran down a hall next to it. On the other side of the prayer hall was a recreation area with some workout equipment. An electronic sign by the entrance noted the upcoming prayer times.

The tour finished, we walked back to the front of the mosque and sat around a table in a conference room whose walls were lined with explanatory posters about Islam and travelogue images of a pristine and no doubt long-ago Mogadishu. Abdulkadir served me coffee in a paper cup from a drip machine sitting atop a dented file cabinet in the corner. Settled, I was introduced to the imam, a man whose gray hair partially covered by a prayer cap put him in his late sixties or seventies. He nodded, glance lingering on my black eye.

"Thank you for meeting with me," I said, after Abdulkadir made the introductions. His suit and tie set him apart from Sammy and the imam, who both wore robes. Abdulkadir smiled as I spoke, though it seemed like he was making an effort to stay positive. I explained who I was and why I was there, knowing full well I was giving them information they already had. "Do you have any idea where Abdi could be?" I said, ending my short speech.

Sammy glanced at the imam before responding. "Aren't you going to ask if we think he was radicalized?"

"I guess not. Should I?"

"That's what the FBI wants to know."

"And for good reason, don't you think? But I was hired to find him, not figure out his theology. If you think that will help me, then tell me by all means. Otherwise, it doesn't matter one way or the other. Does it?"

Abdulkadir roused himself and stared at me like a man who's brought himself up short just inches from the edge of a cliff. "Of course it does, Andy Hayes," he said. "It matters most of all."

11

THE IMAM INTERRUPTED, SPEAKING TO Sammy for a minute or two. When he was finished, Sammy said, "What will you do if you find him? He faces arrest, correct?"

"Probably."

"So regardless of what happens, his future is uncertain."

"Well, he's got a good attorney." I hesitated. "A very good attorney. If I find him—when I find him—Freddy, Mr. Cohen, will handle everything. He'll make sure Abdi gets a fair shake, right from the beginning. He knows his stuff."

Sammy said, "And if Abdi is innocent?"

"If there's a good explanation for why he disappeared, and for what he's been posting on social media, he might not face charges. That's a stretch, in my opinion. But the explanation could go a long way toward resolving the case in his favor."

"What do you mean?"

"Well, let's say there's nothing to the threats. That he just got carried away. Maybe he disappeared because he was upset after Hassan died. Maybe he was worried about guilt by association. Maybe he posted those things and then panicked. He wouldn't be the first nineteen-year-old to do something he regretted later. That would all need sorting out. But none of that can happen until we find him."

Sammy nodded thoughtfully. Before he could speak again, I said, "Did his brother come here? Hassan?"

"Rarely. Perhaps during Ramadan a few times."

"How about after he changed? Got religion?"

"He came more often, yes. But he was disruptive, shouting things during services. We asked him to leave and to stay away."

"Things like what?"

Sammy smiled sadly. "He accused Imam Ali of kowtowing to American imperialists. If that's what you call being grateful for the refuge he was offered here by the government, then I guess we're all guilty."

"Could Hassan have influenced Abdi, in your opinion?"

"It seems the most logical explanation. What do you know about the boy?"

I recalled what Helene Paulus told me. "Decent grades. Very good soccer player. Lots of friends, or at least well-liked. Popular. Was going to college to be a diplomat."

"He's also a loyal person," Sammy said. "Dedicated to his family. He's closer in age to Hassan than his older brother. He spent time with him when other people in the family dismissed him as a lost cause. And he's a hard worker. Of course, he has to be."

"Meaning what?"

"The family has little money. Even with his scholarship he had expenses to think about at Ohio State. I know there was a question about whether he could afford it. Isn't that right?" The last question directed to Abdulkadir.

"It is possible," he said. "I know it's something he didn't like to talk about."

"Could his disappearance be related?" I said. "Ashamed he couldn't pay for this great opportunity?"

"I do not think so," Abdulkadir said quickly. "We have no indication of that."

The imam said something in Somali. Sammy and Abdulkadir both nodded.

"He says the boy was too smart to follow his brother," Sammy said. "He thinks something happened to him against his will."

"Hassan hung out with boys in a gang," I said. "Could they have been involved? With Abdi's disappearance, I mean?" Like almost every city these days, Columbus had a vicious gang problem, with black-on-black shootings a weekly if not daily occurrence. Often it seemed like one person was just in the wrong place and in the wrong crosshairs at the time.

"It's a possibility," Sammy said, translating my theory to the imam. The elder nodded, frowning.

"If that is what happened, perhaps it's for the best," Abdulkadir said.

Now it was my turn to stare at him. "What are you talking about?"

"I do not mean it like that, Andy Hayes," he said, sitting up straighter. "Of course I want Abdi found safely. But it would be a comfort, a small one, to know that he had not turned down the wrong path."

"Very small comfort if he's been murdered."

"Our community is accused of so many bad things these days," Abdulkadir said. "For some outsiders, the path of extremism is less forgivable than breaking the law by committing street crime. That is what I meant. I have noticed—"

"Noticed what?"

"That Americans will turn a blind eye to many things that shock us. Like the guns. Everywhere, guns, guns, guns. For us, who lived through war, it is hard to understand. Constant death on the streets. That is accepted. But if someone expresses opinions the way Hassan Mohamed did. Or the way Abdi is accused of? It is considered a far worse offense. It is a funny thing in this country. You have people who go to church every week who don't seem to mind the gun violence. Those same people criticize our religion, which is a faith of peace. That is all I was trying to say.

That depending on what happened to Abdi his story could have very different meaning. Even though for us, the loss is the same. But either way, I want what everyone wants. For Abdi Mohamed to be located and returned to his family."

12

I LEFT THE MOSQUE ALONE A FEW MINUTES later, pondering Abdulkadir's concerns. It was a harsh way to look at the situation, to say the least. To conclude that dying by Columbus gang violence was a more genial fate than becoming a self-radicalized extremist. Yet according to Abdulkadir's thinking, the former would lead "merely" to city-wide headshaking, the latter to condemnation with far worse ramifications. It was a cold calculus, and it saddened me for what it said about the state of our society right now.

I sat in my van and checked my messages: among them was a text from Ronald J. McQuillen with his address. I thought about his parting words. *These people are a lot more dangerous than you think.* Still considering that, I called for Helene Paulus to see if she'd had any luck getting ahold of Barbara Mendoza, Abdi's school counselor. After the way we'd left things that morning, I was doubtful I'd get past the secretary. A bit to my surprise, Paulus took the call. But the news wasn't good.

"She doesn't want to speak to you. She said the whole thing has been too traumatic. The FBI interviewed her at length, and that was hard enough. She's not sure what else she could tell you."

"She's standing by her suspicions? That Abdi went down the same path as Hassan?"

"Apparently. As I said, she's devastated."

"I think it would help if I spoke to her myself. Could I get her number?"

"I'm afraid not. She specifically asked me not to pass on any of her information."

"Really?"

"She's upset, Mr. Hayes. She's been through a lot. I have to honor that."

"You understand I'm trying to help, right? The FBI wants to put Abdi behind bars. For a long, long time. If he's innocent, I'm somebody who might be able to stop that from happening."

"I understand you perfectly well, believe me. I looked you up."

"That's nice. Wikipedia or LinkedIn?"

"You have a checkered reputation. I don't know whether to trust you."

"Trust, but verify, is my motto. I didn't look you up, but I appreciate anyone with George Bellows paintings on their office wall. *Summer Night, Riverside Drive* is one of my favorites—the interplay of shadow and light. You know he's from Columbus, I assume?"

"Fascinating. You read books and appreciate art too?"

"Now who's being rude?"

"My humblest apologies. I've just never met a private investigator before. To tell you the truth, I wasn't sure they existed."

"I hear that all the time. Us and boy wizards. So now that we've got that out of the way, perhaps you could give me the counselor's number?"

"Barbara was adamant. She wants to be left alone."

"I don't have to say where I got it."

"I would never do that to her."

"How about doing it for Abdi?" She was unmoved, and sounded offended as she said goodbye, like someone who'd been asked for money after first receiving happy birthday wishes.

It didn't matter. Even on my phone, it took me less than ten minutes to find out on my own where Barbara Mendoza lived. It was the kind of computer database search I could perform without spending money on Bonnie Deckard's services, which tended to involve Internet probes of places beyond my capabilities and not always 100 percent legal. I pointed my van in the direction of her house. I didn't think a cold call would cut it in this situation.

THIRTY MINUTES LATER I was parking beside Mendoza's house in Pickerington on the far east side. Her neighborhood was another cookie-cutter collection of pastel split-levels planted atop what had been a soybean field a decade or two ago. The house was the light blue of a washed-out early summer morning, with a lawn that looked as if it should have been mowed three or four days earlier. Weeds poked through patchy mulch on either side of the front door. One of the house numbers, a 2, was off-kilter by a half inch or so. The property wasn't ill-kempt, but it had a distracted air, like the house of someone on a long vacation, or as though Mendoza—or her husband, or someone—was having a hard time keeping up with everything.

The door opened a crack after my second knock. A small, dark-haired woman looked up at me suspiciously. I explained who I was and what I wanted. A factory farm lobbyist might have gotten a warmer look from a vegan keeping gluten-free.

"I told Helene I didn't want to talk to you. Did she—?"

"She didn't tell me where you lived. She refused to, actually. So none of this is on her, just to be clear."

"How did you—"

"I'm sorry to intrude. It's just that I thought you might have some information about Abdi. Something that could help me find him. Or find out what happened to him. Helene—Ms. Paulus—said you worked closely with him."

Lines of worry warped her forehead. She glanced behind her, back into the house.

"I can't help you," she said, turning back to face me. "I told the FBI everything. There's nothing more to say."

"Do you have any idea where he could be?"

"I . . . I have no idea."

"Did he ever mention anyone who might, you know, be influencing him? Or talk about any plans? Was he angry about anything?"

"I'm sorry. I can't talk to you. Please understand." Tears filled her dark eyes. She started to close the door.

"Ms. Paulus said you believe the allegations. Is that true?"

She didn't speak for a moment, casting her eyes downward. When she looked up again I saw she was now trembling, as if I'd shouted an obscenity at her. I took a step back. I was walking the edge of harassment and I knew it. It was one thing to joust over information with Helene Paulus and another to show up uninvited at Mendoza's house. I didn't know how much a counselor in the city schools made. But I was guessing that no matter how generous her salary, it didn't cover the ordeal of seeing a beloved student surface in the middle of a terrorism investigation, and then answering questions from every Tom, Harry, and private dick that came along. There was also something else bugging her, a sense I got that someone was in the house, listening in on our conversation. Someone she didn't want me to know about. Wildly, I wondered: Abdi? Could she be hiding the boy inside? But that seemed improbable at best. And if I'd thought of the possibility I knew damn well it had made Agent Morris's punch list, and that would have been that.

So instead of pressing further I thanked her and handed over my card and asked her to call if she thought of anything important. From the look on her face and the click of the deadbolt sliding into place after she shut the door, like the snap of a bone, I was guessing the card was in the trash before I made it back inside my van. It was OK. It wouldn't be lonely once it hit the landfill. There were a lot more there just like it.

Are you coming or not??

I puzzled at the text from the unfamiliar number as I got back into my van and checked my phone. Coming where? Then I remembered. Ronald J. McQuillen. The hate group consultant, whatever that meant.

Why not? I thought after a moment. It could be novel talking to someone interested in helping me.

I IMAGINED MCQUILLEN LIVING in a home way out in the country bristling with antennas and high-tech surveillance equipment and protected by dogs that eviscerate first and sniff later. It turned out that he lived in an altogether normal-looking two-story stone-and-stucco house on Eddington Road in Upper Arlington, the tony old suburb on the northwest side of the city. I strolled up the walk and lifted my hand to push the doorbell. But the door swung open first.

"'76 Sentries," said the man standing before me.

"I'm sorry?"

"Your parking lot guys," he said. "I'm guessing 1776 Sentries. Private militia, offshoot of an offshoot of an Aryan Nation group that was active in the eighties in eastern Ohio, out between New-ark and Cambridge. It's also possible they were 1861 Copperheads. Been seeing signs of activity from them as well. Sometimes hard to differentiate. One of the Sentries married a Copperhead sister's niece, which adds to the confusion. Copperheads were Demo-crats in the Civil War, opposed—"

"Opposed to the war and supporting immediate peace with the Confederates. Not to be confused with scalawags, like I did on my sophomore year midterm. OK, just to stick with the niceties here, you are, ah, Ronald McQuillen?"

He seemed to consider the question. He wore red Converse high-tops, black socks, faded jeans shorts, and a gray T-shirt em-blazoned with the words "This is your brain on bacon" and an illustration of the self-same organ doing a happy dance. His right hand held a half-full two-liter bottle of Mountain Dew. Prob-ably midforties, medium height and stocky, shaggy brown hair retreating on top, with gold-rimmed glasses and the beard of a folksinger whose last album did OK but not enough to take him off the road for more than a month or two.

"Ronald J., yes," he said, finally. "Sorry. Been a long day al-ready." He stuck out his hand. I expected cold fish and got hail-fellow-well-met instead. He stood to the side while I came in. "Garden's back here," he said, gesturing for me to follow.

"Garden?"

Though it was bright outside and getting hot, the house was dark and cool, with curtains drawn and blinds down. We walked to the rear and stepped down into an office with the lights turned off. In front of me was a desk dominated by a keyboard and three wide computer monitors, each alive with graphs, charts, videos, documents and message balloons, as if I had stumbled across a trading desk in the New York Stock Ex-change. Beside that impressive setup, another monitor was split into four closed-circuit TV views of angles around the house, including the front walk, where McQuillen had no doubt spied me before I had a chance to ring the bell. I glanced at a wide-screen TV hanging above his work station and saw soldiers running through plumes of dust somewhere. The embedded station icon said BBC World News.

"Sorry," McQuillen said. "I work better in the dark."

He picked up a remote from the desk and pointed it at a wall panel pulsing with red and green lights. Above us, recessed lights running along the back and side walls like runway markers slowly brightened. McQuillen grabbed a chair on wheels on the other side of the office and slid it my way. I sat down, looking around. The contrast of the electronics-heavy room with the rest of the drab house was striking, like finding a chemistry lab aboard a clipper ship making a tea run to Cathay.

"Garden?" I said.

"Garden of Eden. The nickname I gave it."

"Because?"

"In memory of my father, I guess. Ironic, given that I'm an atheist, but what are you going to do?" When I didn't respond he shrugged and continued. "I thought I could at least try to figure out where the evil originated. As a way of trying to contain it. And what better place to study evil than *in* the garden. Where it all began. You know?" He took a pull from his Mountain Dew. Seeing the look on my face, he added, "Garden of Eden, like in the Bible?"

"I've only been east of there. You said your father?"

He nodded. "He would have loved all this technology. It was still mostly paper in his day."

"His day? I'm not sure I'm following—"

"You are an investigator, correct?"

"So the license tells me."

"And you didn't check me out? Or are you more a bodyguard type? I always thought—but never mind. Or"—he paused, a worried look crossing his face. "Sorry, I don't mean to pry. But is it a memory thing? All those concussions? From your junior year, mostly, right? The one at Wisconsin especially. It's called chronic traumatic encephalopathy, if I'm not mistaken. Getting clocked like that probably doesn't help, either." He pointed at my eye. "The parking lot guys do that?"

I felt like a man who's walked into the wrong cocktail party on the wrong continent, and in dungarees to boot. I thought of Otto Mulligan's memory of my meaningless, two-decades-old play. What was it with people in this town and college football?

I said, "I don't have CTE, though I know quite a few people who think I do—or maybe wish I did. You're right about junior year, but it was the Penn State game where I really got my bell rung. My eye's none of your business. But in any case, I'm still not sure I know what you're talking about. Your father died?"

"John McQuillen. I figured you knew all that." He gestured to the far wall before turning around and attacking his keyboard. I got up and walked over to examine a framed newspaper article.

"Prosecutor Killed in Car Bomb Attack," read the head-line. The clip was thirty years old. I skimmed the first couple paragraphs:

> A veteran federal prosecutor died Tuesday in south-ern Ohio after an explosion tore apart his car in what investigators are calling an assassination with a car bomb. Jonathan McQuillen, an assistant U.S. Attorney based out of Columbus, was investigating right-wing hate groups and was on his way to interview a witness when the at-tack happened, according to several sources.

"Your father. Got it. I'm sorry."

"No worries. Just figured you'd know."

I should have, I reflected. I recalled the case now, though just barely. I said, "So, forgive me for asking this, but what happened? Was someone arrested?"

"Arrested, no. Not enough parts left." Picking up on my puzzled stare, he continued: "The guy who did it accidentally blew himself up in his garage two days later. Maybe planning an-other attack. So there's some comfort there."

"Who was it?"

"Guy named David Derwent, may he rest in hell. So, your guys."

"My guys?"

"The ones in the parking lot."

"What about them?"

"One of them had a tattoo. The younger guy. It's a '76 Sentries design."

"How do you know that? I mean, about the tattoo."

"It's in the police report."

"You have that? The investigation's still open."

He rolled his eyes. "Let's just say I obtained it, OK? But that's beside the point. What matters is who these guys are, and what they're up to."

"You're farther along than the cops, if what you're telling me is true. I'll give you that."

"That's only because I do this full time and don't have to stand and squeeze my butt cheeks together every time somebody with more stripes walks into the room. One of the things that drove my dad crazy. So, anything else about these clowns? I have to say your description was pretty good."

"Thanks," I said drily. "That's about it, I guess. Well, that and JJ's."

"JJ's?"

I told him about the older guy's command, based on what looked like a text he'd gotten in the middle of the assault.

"That wasn't in the report," McQuillen said, frowning.

"Maybe I forgot to mention it. It seemed sort of random at the time. Does it mean anything to you?"

"Not really."

I told him about the Google search I'd done to no avail.

"Could be a business or a person," McQuillen said. "It's not ringing a bell. You never know with these guys. I'll run it through the database." He minimized his Internet browser, and I caught a glimpse of his desktop background: a young boy and a tall, thin man. Father and son?

"This guy Derwent," I said. "He was a white supremacist?"

"A high holy one. He was also one of the original Sovereign Citizens in Ohio."

"Sovereign Citizen?"

"It's an antigovernment group. One my father was investigating. They don't recognize any law enforcement authority except sheriffs. Won't get driver's licenses. File a lot of liens against people—especially judges—and specialize in not paying taxes and teaching others how not to either."

"He was one of them?"

"Not just one of them. He was their king."

MORE SOLDIERS BOUNDED INTO VIEW ON
the TV. I caught something on the crawl about heightened security alerts in Belgium. I wondered under what conditions I would
ever drink Mountain Dew.

"King?"

"Closest analogy I've come up with."

"King in what way?"

"It's a bit of a long story."

"I've got time."

"But I don't. Got an e-mail address?"

I gave it to him. He turned and his fingers danced across the
keyboard, the clacking like dozens of beetles scrabbling over a
sheet of hard plastic.

"Just sent you all you need to know about David Derwent and
Sovereign Citizens and the 1776 Sentries and more. You could also
check Wikipedia, except I wrote that entry, and this is more up
to date. Yours is a little stale, by the way. Didn't you catch a serial
killer last year?"

"By the skin of my teeth, if that counts."

"It does in my book. I can update it, if you want."

"That's OK. I need a little mystery in my life. So you think those guys in the parking lot were from this Sentries group?"

"Fifty-fifty," he said. "Fits the profile, and the tattoo might cinch it. Except sometimes they filch each other's insignia to throw people off. Some of these guys are actually smart in addition to being batshit crazy."

"If it is them, what's their thing?"

"Thing?"

"What do they believe in?"

He leaned back in his chair and took another pull of Mountain Dew. "Well, short version is anti-immigrant, anti-government, anti–Federal Reserve—probably against their own grandmothers if pressed. Opposed to pretty much anything that smacks of authority. Also, they're truthers, birthers, deathers, 3 percenters, and every other conspiracy theory du jour."

I held up my fingers and ticked them off as I spoke. "9/11 was a government conspiracy; Obama was born in Kenya; Osama bin Laden is still alive. With you so far. But 3 percenters?"

"That's a good one. They believe only 3 percent of colonists fought in the Revolutionary War. It's their way of justifying so-called patriotism against heavy odds."

"Sounds a little scary."

"A little? Some of these guys bake cakes on Hitler's birthday, for God's sake. Then there's the Third Brother thing with Derwent, which is a whole other set of kookiness."

"Third Brother?"

"It's all in the e-mail. But essentially, according to the theory, Adam and Eve had a third son, Seth, to replace Abel. He was supposed to be this particularly righteous guy. Derwent claimed he was a descendant of Seth. A pure, lily-white descendant, naturally."

"A descendant of the third brother?"

"That's right."

"So, another reason you call this place the Garden?"

"You're catching on. Maybe you don't have CTE after all."

"That dynamic duo in the parking lot. Are they followers of Derwent?"

"Hard to say. The older guy could have been around in those days. But the movement sort of imploded after Derwent died. He had two sons, neither of them up to the job—not for any lack of trying, I might add."

"Are they still around?"

"One's in the supermax, the other's on death row. The only thing they're leading these days is the chow line."

"They were his only kids?"

"Supposedly."

"What's that mean?"

"The word was that Derwent's wife couldn't have any more. No surprise, rumors cropped up over the years about him casting his seed elsewhere. I've never found anybody else, though. Closest I ever got is a story that some girl died in childbirth and she and the baby were buried in the woods someplace. But it could be all part of the mythology."

I thought about the young guy with the tattoo. I asked McQuillen what the chances were that he was a lost bastard son of Derwent.

"He'd have to be in his thirties to match. Your description made it sound like he was younger than that."

"You're probably right. So what am I supposed to do with all this stuff, anyway?"

"Stuff?"

"Everything you've told me."

"Whatever you want, I guess. Tell the police. Study up for the next time you run into them. Hunt them down yourself—though I'd be really careful if you go that route. I just figured you'd want to know. The more we can expose these people, the better."

I thought of Abdi Mohamed. "I'll be honest with you. It's not real high on my priority list. But I appreciate the heads-up."

"Whatever. I'm just letting you know your options."

"Thanks. So, how long have you been doing this?"

"Doing what?"

I spread my arms and looked around the room.

"As something I get paid for? Since a few years after college. As my life's work? Since the bombing, I suppose. No secret there. I loved my dad. I was only ten when it happened. It ruined our lives, in so many ways. My mom died a few years later, basically of a broken heart."

"Are you, I don't know, making any progress?"

"Fits and starts. These groups come in waves. A lot of it has to do with the economy. Militia types bloom in recessions, like mushrooms after a rain. But they're around even when unemployment dips again. Like I said, the main thing is to be careful."

"Don't worry—"

He turned in his chair to face me. Something in his face had changed. In the blink of an eye he'd gone from bedraggled folk-singer to a Renaissance depiction of an Old Testament prophet.

"I'm serious," he said. "Don't underestimate them. They've killed just as many people as all these homegrown Islamic terrorists that people are bent out of shape over. Derwent's a perfect example. After he blew himself up, they found a notebook he'd kept, with all these prognostications about his plans."

"Like what?"

"All this lofty bullshit. 'We will build a fire of pure white flame that reaches to heaven.' Crap like that. The problem is these people seem kind of clownish sometimes. And their beliefs!" He shook his head. "Some of them think the last legitimate government was the U.S. postal service in the late 1700s. And they've got a whole theory about the government using citizens as collateral against the country's foreign debts. Bonkers, I'm telling you. But that's the mistake everyone makes. They're dismissive. They write them off as nutcases. They focus on people wearing turbans. Then the next thing you know: *Pow.*" He smacked his right fist into his left palm. "Oklahoma City."

15

I FELT ODDLY RELIEVED WHEN I PULLED away a few minutes later, as if the Garden was someplace you'd have a hard time escaping if you weren't careful. McQuillen's expertise impressed me, despite the over-the-top image he presented. The vengeance-seeking son in full hacker mode fighting the good fight with NASA-caliber computing capability and an endless supply of Mountain Dew. The whole Seth / third brother thing was intriguing and chilling. And of course the irony, if McQuillen was to be believed, that guys like the ones who attacked Kaltun Hirsi were just as dangerous as the radical Islamic fundamentalists they claimed to see behind every scarf, prayer cap, or robe.

All this stayed on my mind as I drove up the street, pulled into the Upper Arlington library parking lot off Tremont, and checked my messages.

How's it going?? Freddy Cohen had texted, with customary abruptness.

Nothing yet but I did find the Lindbergh baby

He didn't respond. I called and left a voicemail for the detective handling the parking lot assault case. I gave him McQuillen's name and told him about the 1776 Sentries. After I hung up I checked the time. It was still early enough to try tracking down Abdi's friends, whose names I'd pried from the chilly hands of Helene Paulus at Maple Ridge High. I examined my notes. The first kid was another Somali boy, Abshiro Ali, who was in Abdi's graduating class. I called and texted him, but didn't get an answer either way. I texted Abukar Abdulkadir to see if he could help track the boy down. With no elaboration, he texted back to say he'd see what he could do.

I had better luck with a boy named Mike Parsell, a soccer teammate who answered on the third ring. He was at home, and didn't mind if I came by.

"I wish I knew where he was," he said, his lanky frame sprawled on the couch in his living room in a house off McCutcheon, a mile or so from the high school. His parents were at work.

"He didn't tell you he was going anywhere?"

He shook his head. "We were supposed to hang out this summer."

"Were you surprised? That he disappeared without saying anything?"

"Yeah."

"Why?"

"It wasn't like him."

I asked him about extremism and recruiting and any residual anger from Abdi's brother's overseas death that might have made him go around the bend.

"Hassan was a prick," Parsell said. "It's hard to believe they came from the same family."

"So I've heard. You knew him?"

"Enough to know he was a jerk. He had this huge chip on his shoulder. Everyone was against him and he never did anything wrong."

"Was that before or after he converted?'

"I didn't know him after. He'd graduated. But I saw him once at the coffee shop. Seemed like he was still an asshole, just one wearing a robe this time."

"Coffee shop?"

"Place near the school. A lot of us hang out there. Do homework."

"So Abdi wasn't like that? Like his brother?"

"No way. Friendliest guy you'd ever meet. Even my parents liked him." He lowered his voice a notch. "They're a little prejudiced, even though they say they're not." He was slouched on the couch, his hands idly holding a video game controller, though the screen across the room was dark. You could tell he was itching to play.

"Your principal—Helene Paulus? She said there's a gang problem at the school."

"Yeah, I guess."

"Any chance Abdi could have, you know, gone that way?"

"Nah."

"You sure?"

"Yeah." He sat up. "The thing is, he tried to talk guys out of that stuff. You'd see him, joking around with them."

"He wasn't scared?"

"Not really. Not that I knew. I mean, I was. Those guys were rough."

"I bet."

"This one kid, DaQuan or LaQuan or something? He was a real badass, but Abdi was always messing with him, teasing him, telling him he should just play soccer instead."

"Did he?"

"I don't know. I think he dropped out."

"Abdi talked to him at school?"

"Sometimes. Maybe at the coffee shop or something. Wherever."

I pulled out my notebook. I wrote, *DaQuan or LaQuan*. Then I wrote, *Grasping at straws*. But as I did, the obvious occurred to me. "Did Abdi have a girlfriend?"

It took him a second to respond. "I'm not sure."

"Not sure how?"

"Just that," he said quickly. He relaxed back into the couch and feigned boredom. "It didn't seem like any of the Somalis did. Dating wasn't part of their culture or something."

"But what about Abdi? Did he have a girlfriend or not?"

"Well—"

"Well what?"

He lowered his voice again and looked out the window. "There's this one girl. Sister of a kid on the team. I don't think you could call it dating. But they liked each other."

"Who was it?"

"I'm not sure . . ."

"Not sure what?"

"Thing is, I don't want to get in any trouble."

"I'm just asking for a name. If anybody's in trouble it's Abdi. And if there's anything or anyone who can help him, I'd like to know."

He wrestled with his thoughts for a moment. Finally, he said, "Faith Monroe. Paul Monroe's little sister."

"You know where she lives? Who her parents are?"

"Couple streets over. But—"

"But what?"

"I don't think her parents knew they were, well, whatever it was. And her dad's a pastor. And he *is* prejudiced."

16

A GIRL WHO LOOKED TO BE IN HER LATE teens answered the door at the home of Felicia and David Monroe a few minutes later, wearing flip-flops, shorts, and a Maple Ridge Riders T-shirt. I was guessing it was the daughter, Faith, but didn't ask her point blank. My suspicions were confirmed when I told her who I was and—without bringing up what Matt Parsell had divulged—my efforts to find Abdi Mohamed. "Mom," she yelled, a stricken look on her face. She turned and disappeared down a hall.

"May I help you?"

Felicia Monroe had the same strong brow and high cheekbones as her daughter, the same dark brown complexion and a similar, suspicious glare. The look only got worse when I repeated my spiel and handed her my card.

"I have no idea where he is. I just hope the police find him in time."

"In time for what?"

"In time to stop him from doing something bad."

"You think that's what he's up to?"

She stared at me. "Don't you?"

"I'm not sure. First I need to figure out where he is."

"Maybe look a little harder. But it's nothing to do with us. Now if you'll excuse me—"

"I'm told your son—Paul?—was on the soccer team with Abdi. Is he here?"

"He's at work. He won't be home for a while."

"Your, ah, daughter? Did she know Abdi?"

"Not really. Listen, this isn't a good time."

"I understand. I just figured someone might know something that could help me find him."

"And like I said, I hope you do. Everybody knows about his comments on Facebook. What he threatened. And of course his brother . . ."

"But those comments were after Abdi disappeared, right? How about before?"

"How should I know? What difference does it make?"

"People said he was a good kid."

"You mean, like his brother?"

"Everyone I've talked to says Hassan was different. A trouble-maker, extremist or not. They say Abdi was the opposite. That he'd never do something like this." I relayed the story Mike Parsell had told about DaQuan or LaQuan. "That's why I was hoping to talk to some of his friends. Like Paul or Faith. See if they know where he might have gone."

"They don't know," she said firmly. "Either of them."

I was starting to understand Mike Parsell's reluctance to tell me about Abdi and Faith. What I couldn't tell was whether, as Parsell speculated, Faith's parents didn't know about their relationship. Or conversely, that they did and were in deep denial.

"Was he ever over here? Abdi, I mean?"

She hesitated, the lie she wanted to tell stuck on the tip of her tongue like something bitter she needed to spit out but couldn't quite bring herself to.

"Once or twice. We had pregame potlucks. They were a good bunch of kids. Mostly."

"It sounds like it. I don't mean to pry, but was there any possibility that Faith and Abdi were, you know, involved? Dating?"

Her brown eyes flared with anger. "Who told you that?"

"Is it true?"

"No," she said, unconvincingly.

"Could I speak to her?"

"Absolutely not."

"What about your husband?"

"What about him?"

"Perhaps I could talk to him."

"That would be his choice. But he's not here either."

"I understand he's a pastor?"

"That's right."

"What church?"

"Mount Shiloh Baptist."

"Could I get a number for him?"

"Sure. Look it up online."

She folded her arms across her chest in a pose that meant the same thing in almost any language: get the hell off my doorstep. Reluctantly, lacking any counterargument, I did.

17

I DECIDED FOR NOW AGAINST WHAT I WAS guessing would be a fruitless trip to Mount Shiloh Baptist. Instead, I settled in at a nearby Tim Horton's with a cup of coffee, connected to the wireless, and checked my messages. McQuillen's e-mail was waiting for me in my inbox. His address was gardener1@eden.com. I clicked on the PDF attachment and sat back to read the document titled "76SentriesAbstract." It was a fascinating story, whatever its relevance was to the parking lot escapade.

According to McQuillen, David Derwent was a back-to-the-lander originally from Cleveland. A spoiled only child, he'd been an authentic hippie in the seventies, on the far left of the political spectrum, when he failed out of Ohio State—which took some real doing in those days—and decided to chuck it all to live in a tent in the Ohio woods. He got by doing a series of odd jobs in local towns, thumbing his nose at anything close to a real occupation, which he deemed the province of the patriarchal establishment.

Over the years Derwent had run-ins with local sheriff's deputies sent to evict him from various farmers' and timber companies' properties east and southeast of Columbus. Things got ugly a couple of times. So ugly that on one occasion Derwent ended up in the county jail on charges of assaulting a peace officer. Sitting behind bars for a month, he found himself at the mercy of a bunch of black gang members from Columbus being housed by the feds ahead of a racketeering trial. When those guys weren't picking on Derwent, he took it from the good ol' boy white jail deputies, who might not have liked black gangbangers much but liked long-haired semicerebral nature lovers who cold-cocked one of their own even less. Derwent ultimately pleaded to a reduced disorderly conduct charge, paid a fine, and got sent packing with time served. But if that was the end of his time in jail, it was the beginning of a deep and abiding hatred for cops, judges, jailers, prosecutors, people with brown skin, and pretty much everyone in between.

It was around that time, the abstract went on, that Derwent started cooking up his whole Third Brother origin story. Eventually he met a drug addict named Gloria as pissed off at the cops as him, with an equally thin grasp of biblical history, got her sober, married her, and had the two sons. His main source of income in those days may or may not have involved gold bars lifted during a never-solved Brink's truck robbery on the east side of Columbus. Over the years, he inculcated his boys with the same fire for civil disobedience in the name of Seth, and together they spread the word in little towns up and down the eastern half of the state, where some of their ideological descendants might very well include the two numb-nuts who ruined my perfectly good afternoon of stalking the wild adulterer. As McQuillen had already explained, Derwent *père* died in the garage explosion two days after the car bombing, and his sons were enjoying extended stays in secure public housing. The report concluded with the speculation of out-of-wedlock heirs, including the unknown girl who died in labor in the woods with her baby.

It made for good reading, even if I was getting a little far afield from the more important task at hand: finding Abdi Mohamed. I was reminded of this fact when my Tom Petty ringtone sounded again. I didn't recognize the number. The brusque tone was more familiar.

"You went to see Barbara Mendoza. After I specifically asked you not to."

Helene Paulus. And she wasn't using her indoors voice.

"Hang on. You said you would ask her, and she declined, through you. Fair enough. I decided to follow up on my own, as I suggested I might. I'm not working for either of you."

"I told you how upset she was—"

"And I believed you. And I saw it firsthand once I got there. Which is why I left after a minute or two."

"But why go against my wishes?"

I tried to keep the frustration out of my voice. "My job isn't to placate one of your employees, *Ms.* Paulus. It's to find Abdi Mohamed. Find him and help him, if he's in danger, or find out where he is in hopes of stopping him if he means harm to others."

"But still—"

"But still nothing. I'm not apologizing for doing my job. And here's the thing. I left when she asked me to. I can promise you the feds didn't offer her the same courtesy. And won't in the future, when they presumably circle back to her again. And again."

"Maybe if you'd told me you were going to do that, I could have—"

"Could have warned her?"

"No! I don't know what, but . . . It's just that she's so upset again."

"I'm sorry about that. I really am. But I'm not in the habit of telling someone I talk to what I plan to do next."

"That's obvious."

"What's that supposed to mean?"

"You have a history of doing what you please, no matter how it affects people. Don't you?"

I thought of what Cohen said. *Like a three-legged bull in a china shop with narrow aisles.* "Maybe. But most of the time they've invited me into their lives. And most of the time they're better off afterward than when I started."

"Better? Like that reporter you got killed?"

That stopped me for a second. I took a breath to compose myself. I said, "Is that what this is about? If you knew anything about that case, you'd see—"

"See what? That you fell down on the job?"

The death of investigative journalist Lee Hershey, murdered in the Ohio Statehouse when I was supposed to be protecting him, was a low point in my professional life, to be sure. My whole life, when it came down to it. I wasn't proud of the circumstances that led to that awful event. But it was useless to explain to Helene Paulus—or anyone else, as I'd learned over the years—that it wasn't entirely my fault.

"At least I don't spend my life hanging inspirational posters on my office door," I said. "Some of us actually go out and get shit done, even if it isn't always pretty. What's that old saying? Those who can, do, those who can't—"

"How dare you. Here I am trying to help, and the best you can do is insult me and my profession?"

"Help would involve giving me something I can use. Like the cooperation of Barbara Mendoza. Not calling me up with holier-than-thou speeches."

"You won't have to worry about that in the future. I can assure you."

"About what?"

"About me calling you," she said as she disconnected.

18

I SET THE PHONE FACE DOWN ON THE table, stood up, and walked up and down the restaurant. I sat back down, rubbed my face with my hands, and groaned the way I do when I'm hung over or paying Hopalong's vet bill. I stared at McQuillen's PDF. That conversation had been low, even by my standards. Paulus was right—insulting educators? I lowered my head in shame. I thought of my mother, a high school math teacher for nearly thirty years. What was I thinking?

I didn't have time to answer that question. My phone rang again. It was Crystal, ex-wife no. 2. Joe's mom. I sighed. I glanced outside to see if storm clouds were gathering.

"I'm sorry to ask this," she said. "I know it's last minute. And it's not your night. But any chance you could pick up Joe, bring him home? We're in a bit of a bind. One of the cars is in the garage."

"Can't Bob do it?"

"His practice is on the other end of town. You know that. It'll be another couple hours before he can get there. Listen, never mind. Forget I asked—"

"It's fine." Pushing this kind of favor onto my ex's husband, who I didn't like that much anyway, was the last thing I wanted to do. This was my son we were talking about. "Where is he?"

"You're sure?"

"I said yes."

"OK. I really appreciate it. Anyway, he's at Anne's. He and Amelia were doing something."

"Anne's?"

"That's right. Is that a problem? I thought you two were still friends."

"Sure. Best buddies. And it's not a problem. I'll be right there."

"Great. Thanks again."

Problem, I thought, hanging up.

TWENTY MINUTES LATER I knocked on the door of Anne's half-a-duplex on Crestview in Clintonville north of campus. It was a nice neighborhood filled with trees, the houses a collection of brightly colored cottages and side-by-side rentals and Dutch colonials, porches full of plants and flowers and wind chimes. Once upon a time I'd imagined living there. In this very apartment, in fact. Right around the time I'd cut a deal with Anne's landlord, who happened to be Bonnie Deckard's father, to trim the rent Anne would pay in exchange for a job I did for him. The deal didn't include me, initially, but I'd harbored fantasies—

"Help you?"

A man I didn't recognize was standing in the doorway.

"I'm here for Joe. Is, ah, Anne around?"

"Oh," he said, puzzled. "Sure. Hang on." He retreated into the house and called Anne's name. After a minute or so she appeared.

"What are you doing here?"

"Didn't Crystal tell you? She asked me to get Joe. She said he was over here. Playing with Amelia?"

"No. I mean, yes, he's here. But no, she didn't say anything. Last I knew she or Bob was going to pick him up."

"Well, sorry about that. How does it feel?"

"How does what feel?"

"You've been Crystal-ed. First time, I take it?"

"That's not a very nice thing to say."

"It wasn't a very nice thing of her to do. Not to put you on the spot or anything, but any chance you mentioned to her that, ah"—I hesitated, stumbling for words—"that your boyfriend was here today?"

"I don't think that's any of your business. I . . . Let me get Joe." She turned and headed back inside. A moment later she stopped in the front hall. "Come in," she said impatiently. To my relief, she didn't ask about my eye. Probably because she'd seen worse when we were dating.

I went in. The living room was filled with the same comfortable clutter of books and newspapers and magazines that I remembered from days gone by. Anne read the way other people did things like eating or breathing. I picked up a book on top of a pile on the coffee table and examined the cover.

"That's a good one." The boyfriend, standing awkwardly at the far end of the room. "Have you read it?"

"Yes." I took a breath—there was no point in forestalling it. "I'm, ah, Andy." I switched the book to my left hand and took a couple steps in his direction. "Andy Hayes."

"Ben Layton," he said eagerly. He walked over and shook my hand. Once again I expected cold fish—strongly desired it, this time—and once again was disappointed. Not longshoreman, but hardly shy and retiring either. He was thin, thinner than me, anyway, with a runner's physique I suspected was part of the attraction for Anne, who when she wasn't reading was always training for one race or another. Sandy hair starting to thin, glasses, a sharp nose and friendly eyes. A guy who looked like he could save you a lot of money on your taxes and talk Kurosawa movies with you in the next breath. I already disliked him.

"Sorry to barge in like this. Signals got crossed, I guess."

"Not a problem. It's nice to meet you. Anne's told me a lot about you."

"She has?"

"Well—the things you've done. I mean, I've read stuff, too." He trailed off. I imagined him and Helene Paulus trading notes.

"Don't believe everything you read."

"Of course not," he said, nervously. "I only meant—"

"Do you live nearby?"

"Couple streets over. We, I mean, Anne and I, we go to the same, we're in a running group together. Meets at Park of Roses every Saturday."

"Sounds fun."

An awkward silence descended. We glanced around the room, staring at anything but the other person, like guys trying to fit in at a baby shower knowing full well the big game is on.

"I—"

"Yes?" I said, too quickly.

"I don't know if Anne mentioned, but I invited her and Amelia downtown for Red, White & Boom. My office is right near Broad and High. We're going to hang out there beforehand, then walk down and see the show. Everybody's welcome back up afterward to wait out the traffic."

"Sounds fun," I said, and mostly meant it.

"The thing is, Joe's welcome to join us. You too, if you're interested."

"Thanks. That's a kind offer."

The annoying thing? It really was. The city's annual fireworks display, one of the largest in the Midwest, is an unrivaled twenty-minute spectacle on the banks of the Scioto River. The downside is you share the view with four hundred thousand other people standing elbow to elbow on the streets. After the brief window of ooh-ing and ah-ing ends, it typically takes two or more hours sitting in your car while you try to get home. One year we'd ridden bikes from my German Village house and had been back and eating ice cream in less than half an hour. I'd been meaning to suggest that the boys and I consider that again. But I realized now I'd left it too late—the holiday was just a few days away. And I was going to guess that sitting in an air-conditioned conference room beat riding bikes on crowded city streets by a Roman candle or three.

"It would be great if you could make it. I mean it," Layton said.

"Thanks. It's—"

"Andy!"

Anne's daughter ran into the room. To my surprise she wrapped her arms around my waist as if I were a favorite uncle dropping by for a couple of days instead of the ex-boyfriend on the outs. Joe entered behind her but hung back a bit, his nose in a book.

"I miss you," Amelia said.

"I, ah, miss you too," I said, avoiding Layton's eyes.

Anne entered the room. "Are you reading that too?"

"I'm sorry?" I said, relieved as Amelia disengaged herself and flopped onto the couch.

"*Ready Player One,*" Anne said, pointing to the book I'd picked up from her coffee table.

I explained I'd seen it as I came inside a couple minutes earlier.

"It's set in Columbus, you know. I'm going to teach it next year." Anne specialized in science fiction novels and films. Her first book, on women sci-fi writers, was coming out in a couple of months.

"Ben recommended it," she said warmly, glancing at her boyfriend.

"What a coincidence. So did I."

"You did? To whom?"

"To you."

"No you didn't."

"Sure I did. I offered to buy you a copy, at the Book Loft. Signed copy, on sale."

"You must be mistaken, Andy. I don't remember that at all."

"I remember it like it was yesterday. You said, 'I'd love to, but I'm reading five other things and trying to finish my syllabus.' I asked if you were sure. I said I'd heard it was pretty good and kind of a natural, since it was set here."

I glanced at Layton. He wore the expression of a man who would have flung himself headfirst into a quicksand pit that very second if the option magically availed itself. And not even take his glasses off first.

"Andy," Anne said. "I really don't—"

"Joe, are you ready?" I said to my son.

"Do I have to go?"

"Yes. Your mom needs you home."

"Why?"

"You'll have to ask her."

"Why didn't my dad come? Why are you here?"

I could almost taste the sand as I gritted my teeth. Joe had been just young enough when Crystal and I split and she hooked up with her current husband that Bob was also "Dad" to Joe. Look who has two daddies. Though I knew it was the best outcome for Joe, the habit never ceased to bother me, especially since my older son, Mike, called his stepfather "Steve."

"Your mom asked and I was happy to do her a favor."

We said our goodbyes and walked outside. Joe climbed into the van. I was headed around to the driver's side when I heard my name called. Anne walked down her porch steps, holding *Ready Player One*.

"Why did you say you recommended this to me? To get under Ben's skin? There's no reason to be petty, just because I'm with someone else."

"I'm not being petty. I said it because it's the truth. It's not my problem if you don't remember."

"I wouldn't forget something like that."

I looked at her. She was angry, which meant the long scar on her cheek stood out against her pale skin; the Chile-shaped wound a souvenir from her murderous late husband, inflicted just before stabbing himself to death. I was sorry she was upset. But I was too.

"He seems like a nice guy. He's obviously got good taste in women. And good taste in books, too. But for the record, so did I. Which is why I recommended you read that."

"Andy—"

"He was also kind enough to invite me to Red, White & Boom. I'll check with Crystal about Joe going. I'm sure it won't be a problem."

"How about for you?"

"How about for me what?"

"You, coming with us to see the fireworks?"

"Have to check my calendar," I said, getting in the van. I shut the door and drove slowly up the street. As I signaled to turn at the next corner, I looked in my rearview mirror. Anne was still on the sidewalk, watching us go.

19

EARLY THE NEXT MORNING I JOGGED UP
Mohawk to Sycamore, watching my footing on the brick streets
as I ran, cut over to Third, and headed north. As I passed the Book
Loft I looked at my reflection in the windows, reviewing the scene
at Anne's the day before. I gave it two thumbs down. It was just
six but it was summer and light out. The sidewalks were crowded
with dog walkers and other joggers. At Town I went left and ran
across Columbus Commons, skirting a few other early morning
types wandering on the lawn and gravel paths that ran up to the
edge of several city blocks of luxury apartments. Bounding up
the stairs to High Street I passed a couple power walkers and a
trio hunting Pokemon Go characters. Maybe I should enlist them
in finding Abdi.

At High I turned right and ran through downtown. Across
the street the limestone exterior and Greek revival columns of
the Statehouse glowed softly in the humid air as the shadows
lightened. I tried not to think about the reporter who died there.
I crossed Broad, and then turned left at Long, jogged a little farther, and came to a stop in front of the downtown Y. There was

a morning aerobics class I was trying out. It was a co-ed mix of type A lawyers and bankers who might have shared three ounces of body fat between them. I ran home much more slowly.

After twenty minutes of sit-ups, push-ups, and pull-ups, I showered, grabbed a banana and the leash, and set out for Schiller Park with Hopalong. As usual, we hung out with the other dog walkers who gathered on the lawn just down from the Shakespeare in the Park stage. It would have been a good place to meet women if I were fifteen years younger and understood Snapchat. Most of the time I talked with the two Kevins while Hopalong nosed back and forth with their pugs. After the dogs lost interest in each other I bid the Kevins a good day and walked back up the street to my house at 837 Mohawk.

I was finishing breakfast, trying to figure out my next move, when my phone rang. It was Freddy Cohen.

"We've got a problem."

Tell me about it, I thought. But what I said was, "Abdi's in Syria?"

"It might be better if he was. Because otherwise, it looks like he firebombed the church down the street from his family's mosque."

"What?"

"You heard me. I need you to get out there. Figure out what's going on."

"No problem. Which church?"

"It's called Mount Shiloh Baptist."

I GOT AS FAR as a strip mall a quarter mile from the scene. I knew I was in the right place when I saw reporters from three separate TV stations doing stand-ups at the far end of the parking lot. Even from that far away I could smell the acrid stink of smoke in the air. I got out and strolled casually toward the media throng. One of the reporters, the best-looking by far, wrapped up her shot, did a double take and marched straight toward me.

"What the hell are you doing here?"

"You know me and conflagrations," I said, retreating. "I just can't stay away from them."

"You are so full of shit. Spit it out."

Under normal circumstances Suzanne Gregory was hard to say no to. I should understand this better than anyone: not only was she the muckraking-est TV journalist in town, with a shelf full of Emmys to prove it, she was also my ex-fiancée. She was cursed with cover-girl good looks that routinely lulled hapless bureaucrats and politicians into complacency as she used her relentless reporting to nail them for screwing taxpayers. There was even an expression for it: getting Suzy-Q-ed. She was back on the job after maternity leave, although you wouldn't have guessed she'd just had a baby, I thought, eyeing the way she fit into her sleeveless heathered gray dress. I powered up my defensive shields and gave her the movie trailer version of my involvement with Abdi Mohamed.

"You're looking for Hassan Mohamed's brother on behalf of Freddy Cohen?" she said when I was done. "I truly think I've heard everything now. Didn't you—?"

"I caught his wife having an affair with someone in their synagogue, yes," I said, doing my best to avoid looking directly into her stomach-flipping blue eyes. "There's more than one person in town who thinks she was completely justified, by the way. Next question."

"Fine. What can you tell me about Abdi?"

For the next couple of minutes we jousted a bit the way old lovers do, which is to say with affection and more than a bit of rancor, until we'd exhausted our mutual goodwill.

"How's Isabella?" I said as she turned to walk back to her post.

"Crabby, beautiful, and perpetually hungry—"

"Just like her mom," we both said at the same time.

I limped back to my van, staggered by the wry smile that that cute exchange had won me.

I called Cohen. He explained that Abukar was hearing rumors about witnesses identifying Abdi as the culprit. In turn, I filled him in with what Suzanne told me, starting with the report of a fire called in about ten o'clock the night before.

"Always with the media," he interrupted. "She going to put you on the noon news?"

"No," I protested. "We were just talking."

"You always say that, and the next thing I know I'm staring at your mug on a screen."

"Are you coming out here?" I said, ignoring him. "Or going to see the family?"

I decided for now to leave out the minor detail that Abdi may have attacked the church pastored by his girlfriend's father. I needed to wrap my head around that concept further before telling Cohen something that might make his noggin up and explode.

"Neither. My back's not good this morning."

"I'm sorry. Is there anything I can—"

"Yeah, right. Call Abukar. See if he's heard anything else."

He hung up before I could reply. I punched in Abdulkadir's number, got him in two rings, and explained my whereabouts.

"I'll be right there."

Sure enough, he pulled up a couple of minutes later. Though it was barely nine o'clock, he was dressed in his usual suit. I wondered idly if he was ever out of it. I started to open the van door, but he signaled me to stay inside. He climbed into the passenger seat and stared out the window in the direction of the church. "This is everything we dreaded," he said. "Two brothers like this. The repercussions we could face."

I thought about my conversation with Faith Monroe's mother. Her denial of the suggestion that her Christian daughter was dating the brother of a martyred Muslim extremist.

"Why would Abdi do that?" I said, carefully. "Attack a church?"

"I can't answer that. It's not the boy we know. That the community knows. But—"

"Yes?"

"There was a lot of tension with Mount Shiloh. Boys were always throwing rocks at the mosque. Taunting our children.

That's why we had to put the fence up, you know. Believe me, it was not something we wanted."

"Boys from the church?"

"Some of our children play basketball at the mosque, in the evenings. If the boys from Mount Shiloh see our youth they come over and start things. The two groups don't get along."

"Which groups?"

"The African Americans and the Somalis. And of course everyone hates Muslims now."

"Not everyone."

"Perhaps not you, Andy Hayes. But everyone else."

I let that one go for now. "It really could have been anyone. A coincidence." But even as I said it, I wondered if it were true. If I really believed that.

"From what I am hearing, the witnesses seemed sure it was him."

"Like, recognized him?"

He nodded.

"That doesn't make sense."

"No, it does not."

It didn't make sense for a lot of reasons. Why would you disappear, only to reappear and attack a church in practically your own neighborhood? Especially *this* church? It seemed like someone intent on doing harm would take the opposite approach. If you're already under suspicion, why do something to increase the scrutiny? Ramp up the search for you? Or was this the attack that Abdi's Facebook post hinted at? Had we escaped with nothing worse than a firebombed church and, to judge by the reports I was seeing pop up on my phone, no injuries? And how did his relationship with Faith Monroe—or perhaps more to the point, with her father—fit into all this?

We talked a few minutes more about the history of tension over the mosque, before movement on the street distracted me. I looked up and saw three black Ford Explorers roll past the strip mall, speeding toward the church.

"Looks like you're not the only one drawing conclusions about Abdi," I said.

"What do you mean?"

"Those are feds." I explained about my encounter after meeting Helene Paulus.

Panic filled Abdulkadir's face, as if he'd just realized he'd lost track of a friend's child in his care.

"I should go," he said, and opened the van door.

"Everything all right?"

"I will talk to you soon, Andy Hayes," he said, getting out and slamming the door shut. He walked to his car without turning around. A moment later he was gone.

20

I TOOK ON A NEW ASSIGNMENT LATER
that morning. The FBI wanted to question Abdi's parents again,
and this time they wanted them at headquarters in the Arena District north of downtown. Cohen insisted on being there, but his
back was so bad he couldn't drive. He told me to pick him up at
his house. He made it clear that under no circumstances was I to
come inside, or even step foot on the property.

Instead, I sat in my van on the street on Bullitt Park Place
in Bexley, the well-heeled suburb parked like a comfy couch between two gritty spurs of Columbus's east side. I tried not to
gawk as Cohen hobbled out the front door. He descended the
stairs slowly, one hand on the railing, the other on the knob of
his cane. He approached my Odyssey like a man twenty years his
senior. I thought I saw someone standing inside watching him
leave, but I couldn't make out who it was. Ruth? Unlikely, since
the last I'd heard they were separated, perhaps divorcing. Thanks
to me, according to the one and only shouting match Cohen and
I had had after it all came out. At the time, Cohen was still in
denial that his wife's lover might have been just the teensiest bit

responsible too, even though the relationship hadn't survived the glare of discovery.

I decided against getting out and opening the passenger door. I knew the Driving Miss Daisy thing would be hard enough for Cohen without me underlining his infirmity.

"What's wrong with your eye?" he demanded when he was in and buckled.

"Poked myself with my toothbrush. You OK?"

"Just drive."

To fill the silence, I went over what we knew so far. According to Abdulkadir, Mount Shiloh Baptist, along with neighbors in a small nearby subdivision, had filed complaints with the city when the Somali community purchased an old paper products warehouse, intending to convert it into a mosque. The complaints predicted problems from increased traffic along the road and challenged the commercial zoning code waiver that would allow the mosque. The words "Islam" and "Muslim" were never mentioned, though the subtext was clear. Meetings between the imam and Faith Monroe's father smoothed things over, and for a time everything went fine. But boys will be boys, particularly boys from religious congregations equally ignorant of the other. Tensions flared into rock-throwing and fistfights more than once. Taking a breath, I concluded by telling Cohen about the apparent romance between Faith and Abdi. He looked at me, incredulous.

"Abdi was dating the daughter of this church's minister?"

"Dating might be a little strong. Allegedly involved with? That's according to one of his friends. The girl's mom did a bad job denying it."

"And you didn't think to tell me?"

"It didn't seem that significant until today. It was just one more piece of the puzzle."

"You're a real piece of work, Hayes," Cohen said. He shook his head and looked out the window as we passed Franklin Park Conservatory going east on Broad, the greenhouses just visible through the foliage of the park's trees. "Every time I think you've hit rock bottom, another trap door opens up."

"That's not fair. I just didn't think it was relevant enough to call you up out of the blue. Obviously, the fire changed all that."

"You think?"

We didn't speak again until we reached the FBI building, a bland, stand-alone brick edifice that might have doubled for the IT annex of a midlevel insurance company. Farah Mohamed and her parents were already there. Cohen opened his door after I parked and killed the engine.

"Stay here," he said.

"Why?"

"I threatened to pull Judge Rafferty off the fourth hole at Muirfield just to get in on this interview. There's no way in hell they're letting you in too."

"Can I at least help you to the door? It looks like you can barely—"

"In your dreams. I'll text you when we're finished."

And that was that. I watched while Cohen inched his way toward the Mohameds, pegging the asphalt with his cane like a novice mine hunter. I considered what I knew of the circumstances that led to his back injury, related to the affair—but yet a different mess, too. I looked and caught Farah staring at me, confusion written on her face. I shrugged. She scowled and reached out an arm to Cohen. After a moment's hesitation he took it. They all went inside.

I LOOKED AT MY watch: nearly noon. One thing was for sure. I wasn't going to just sit there like an ersatz chauffeur, no matter Cohen's order to stay put. Instead, I locked up and walked down the street to Betty's. The usual sign was on the door of the bar: "Open when I get here, closed when I leave." I went inside. I guess she was there. I ordered a Bud and a hamburger and sat at the bar and thought about Freddy Cohen and Abdi Mohamed and Anne and my ex-fiancée and whether I'd paid the water bill this month.

I was on my second beer and starting to wonder if I was going to lose the entire day to chaperone duties when my phone went off. The number was blocked.

"What is it with you?" the voice on the other end said. "You're not busy enough ruining marriages? Now you're getting beat up by white supremacists?"

My mood darkened. It couldn't be good that Henry Fielding, a Columbus homicide detective, was calling like this.

I said, "I wouldn't say beat up, exactly. And for the record, it's not me having the affairs. I just expose them."

"A real social worker, you are. So back to your Ku Klux Klan guys."

"That might be giving them too much credit. They seemed a lot lower market than that."

"Not according to Ronald McQuillen. He made them sound like trouble."

"You talked to him?"

"That's what we do over here, in case you ever need some tips. It's called legwork. Yes, I talked to him. I recognized the name from your message. I met his father, briefly, when I was first on the force. Good man."

"It sounds like it. And of course it's always a delight to hear from you. But mind if I ask why I'm talking to you and not the detective assigned to the case? Nobody got killed here, as far as I can tell."

"No one yet, anyway. It's always a game of chance with you, isn't it?"

Fielding was a tall, skinny cop with a shiny, Mr. Clean pate whose appearance had earned him the nickname Voldemort among fellow cops and perps alike. I guess I was the Harry Potter he'd always wanted to obliterate. He'd had it in for me from the day we met and he found out where I lived. His great-grandparents had dwelled in German Village back when the language was actually spoken there. They'd been forced to change their name from Feld to Fielding when anti-German sentiment swept the city during

World War I, a loss of cultural identity which apparently Fielding—like Cohen with his wife's affair—blamed me for personally. He couldn't get over the fact I lived in his ancestral 'hood, one of the priciest zip codes in Ohio, while he was forced to shack up in a suburban nightmare of nice lawns and good schools. My explanation for my address, that my landlord cut me a deal in thanks for rescuing his heroin-addicted daughter from a pimp a few years back, fell on deaf ears. Which were rather prominent in Voldemort's case, though I tried not to point this out.

"I repeat. There's no homicide involved," I said. "So why are you calling?"

"Departmental policy."

"Regarding what?"

"Straight from my commander. Woody Hayes's name shows up on a case file, I get called. Lucky me."

"I go by Andy now."

"So you keep telling me, Woody. Anyway, the reason I'm calling is we got a possible hit on your Nazis."

"Go on."

"It looks like you weren't the only one scoping out the casino that day."

21

FIELDING WENT OVER WHAT THEY KNEW.
They'd taken a number of reports in recent months of casino patrons robbed by people too lazy to play the tables themselves but
more than happy to relieve winners of their own proceeds after
following them home.

"There's security camera footage of a couple of guys hanging
around inside the casino that fit the description you gave. Some-
what annoyingly, you were right on the mark with what you told
the patrol guy. If I send you a screen shot can you check it out?"

"Sure. Did they get a plate number?" I knew the casino garage
and surface parking lots also seethed with cameras.

"They got a plate. Not that it helps us any."

"Why not?"

"The tattoo the kid had, the one that jumped you?"

"What about it?"

"That's what's on the plate, if you can call it that. It's a fake,
not real. I'm told it's a Sovereign Citizen thing, to refuse to license
your vehicle. Gotta give them credit for balls, driving around like
that. But it's nothing we can trace."

"So if they were stalking people in the casino, how'd they end up at the grocery store? Was it just a coincidence they harassed Kaltun Hirsi?"

"Who knows? You keep telling me these guys weren't rocket scientists, right? And the grocery store was a five-minute drive. Maybe Nazis need milk and eggs too. Give me a couple minutes on the picture."

There was no mistaking it when the photo arrived. The two guys who'd harassed Kaltun Hirsi and cost me eighty dollars in lost groceries had definitely been hanging around the casino an hour earlier. I might have walked right past them as I trailed my philandering mark. I called Fielding back and confirmed the information.

"We're running this stuff past our intelligence unit," he said. "We'll see what they dig up. And we'll put out the word. Maybe somebody in eastern Ohio has run into these clowns, since that's home sweet home."

"Maybe," I said, doubtfully.

"What's up with your terrorist, while I've got you? Burning churches now?"

"How'd you know I was working on that?"

"Please. Woody Hayes carrying water for Freddy Cohen on a homegrown extremism case? It's the talk of the town. I take it you haven't seen the kid, or you would have told somebody."

I confirmed his analysis.

Fielding said, "You happen to run into anybody along the way who mentioned gang affiliations?"

"Affiliations for who?"

"For Abdi."

I drained my beer and shook my head as the server swung by. It wouldn't win me any favors with Cohen to show up with three drinks under my belt. I said, "Are you kidding? He's a soccer player with good grades going to Ohio State."

"Nothing about the Agler Road Crips?"

I recalled my conversations with Helene Paulus and Mike Parsell, Abdi's soccer teammate. I mentioned DaQuan or LaQuan. I said, "He was friendly with a lot of kids. Sort of fearless. But in a gang himself? No way."

"You're sure?"

"Sure. So what are you hearing?"

"I'm hearing the feds are itching to take this church attack away from us. As a result, I'd appreciate it if you come across anything and felt like dropping a dime."

"In return for what?"

"In return for maybe that helps us keep this on the state side, which is a helluva better deal for the kid than the U.S. Attorney's Office coming down on him."

I couldn't argue with his logic, despite his supercilious tone.

"I'll definitely keep that in mind," I said. "But listen—"

"Gotta run. Enjoy my ancestors' rightful property."

I tried not to fume over his parting shot and focused instead on the conversation. Abdi part of a gang? It fit with nothing I knew. I'd have to circle back with Abdulkadir and—I blanched a little at the thought—Helene Paulus. I'd also have to let Cohen know about Fielding's offer of cooperation. I had to give the evil wizard credit on that front: he was right about the benefits to Abdi if we kept the case out of the federal courthouse.

My phone buzzed with a text. I looked at the message. Mike, my older son.

If Joe's going to Red, White & Boom can I go too?

I sighed. I should have seen that coming. I recalled Ben Layton's firm handshake and the sincerity behind his invitation. *It would be great if you could make it. I mean it.*

I texted: I'll talk to your mom. I guess it's OK.

He didn't text back. Why bother? He'd gotten the answer he'd hoped for.

I was about to call Kym to see what she thought when Cohen texted me to say they were finished with the interview. I paid my tab and walked back up Nationwide. I met them as they came out the door.

"How'd it go?"

Cohen frowned and shook his head. I glanced at Farah but she looked down, hiding shiny eyes. Abdi's parents walked to their car wordlessly, like mourners in a midwinter funeral procession.

"So?" I said when Cohen and I were back in the van, alone.

"So it's not good."

"Why?"

"They've got security camera footage."

"Of Abdi?"

"Of Abdi or his clone."

"You saw it?"

"Saw a still. That's all they'd show us. But it sure looked like him, at least from behind. He's got a black head scarf on, so you can't see his face. Just like those Islamic State guys. He was wearing the same clothes he had on the day he disappeared."

I drove out of the parking lot and turned left on Nationwide. I related Fielding's call and the implication that Abdi was in a gang. I mentioned the offer to try to keep the charges out of federal court if we cooperated. Cohen chuffed with skepticism.

"I take it you disagree?"

He glanced at me dismissively. "Don't be a bigger idiot than you already are. Fielding's blowing smoke up your ass. This kid's public enemy no. 1."

"Believe it or not, I get that."

"I don't think you do. No way it's staying stateside. The feds catch you sniffing around now, they'll throw you in jail and maybe me too."

"What are you saying?"

"That it's probably time to go back to staking out motel rooms and dating C-list starlets, or whatever it is you do."

"Give up, in other words."

"Fuck you. You had your chance. But we've gone from simmering to high boil in a day."

"Which is why it's more important than ever to find Abdi."

"I said—"

"Give me a day. Two days. Three max. I'll watch myself. I promise."

He shook his head like a father sick of excuses from his wayward son. He said, "You screw this up, I may not be able to help you."

"Able to or willing to?" I waved off the retort I saw forming on his lips. "Don't worry. I'll finish this, one way or the other."

He thought about it for a long minute. I examined the FBI building. I wondered if they had microphones on the parking lot. I thought about some choice observations about Agent Morris I could offer, to test the theory.

"All right," Cohen said at last. "But Jesus, be careful. We're running out of time."

"That's obvious—"

He turned to me. "I mean it, Andy. The clock is ticking."

The use of my name like that caught me up. "I told you, I get it—"

"There's something I haven't told you yet. Something else they had." He gestured toward the FBI office. "There was a post on some kind of file-sharing service this morning. Something the extremists all use. It's untraceable."

"What kind of post?"

"It was a picture of Abdi, and a screen shot from the news about the fire. And a warning."

"A warning?"

"It said: 'This is only the beginning.'"

I DROPPED COHEN AT HIS HOUSE, LINGERING long enough to be sure he made it safely inside. I didn't see anyone at the door. I took my time driving home, thinking about how far I'd come with Abdi, the things I'd learned, the things I needed to pursue now, with the stakes so much higher. Cohen was right. I'd been lucky the day I caught Cindy Morris and her minions tailing me. She wouldn't give me a second chance, despite the fact I'd helped her out in the past. They weren't going to screw around with an alleged extremist firebombing churches on the side. Not in this day and age. Not anytime, to be truthful.

As a result, when Bonnie Deckard called later that afternoon with an update on Abdi's social media postings, I told her straight up she needed to be even more careful. That I'd understand if she bailed. I had to give her credit. She dismissed the suggestion of danger out of hand. Maybe that's why she excelled at Roller Derby.

"It's pretty easy to see the transition you were talking about," she said, laying out what she'd found so far. "Right before his brother was reported dead it's all stuff about soccer. He even posted something that day, about a Crew game he was pumped to go to. Presumably he hadn't heard yet. But once Abdi disappeared it's all that Islamic State stuff, the black flags, talk about a caliphate, calling for the destruction of the West. The things you hear about on the news."

"So he started posting after Hassan died?"

"After his disappearance," she corrected.

"But how about in between?"

"I didn't find a whole lot. A couple articles about his brother, and one newspaper story about the prejudice that Somalis in Columbus face and the way Hassan's death might make it worse. It probably reflected his reality at the moment. But that article was a long way from the stuff that came afterward."

"It seems strange he went from nothing to all that, if you know what I mean. The Crew to the Caliphate."

"Maybe. Or maybe he was too upset to post anything really radical until he'd made up his mind to do whatever he's going to do. I'm just telling you what I found out there. I could be missing things, too. I'm sure the government's taken down most of it."

I wondered aloud, as I had the day I met Abdi's parents, about the possibility he'd been hacked. She conceded it could have happened. But that only assumed he hadn't self-radicalized, she pointed out. And of course, there was Hassan's precedent.

"Well, I'll pass all this along to Freddy Cohen. Thanks for everything. And send me your invoice—I'll process it faster this time, I promise."

After pondering my next move, I decided to take the riskiest one of all. I drove to Mount Shiloh Baptist Church to see if I could find Pastor David Monroe. I promised myself I'd turn around at the first sign of black Ford Explorers.

SEVERAL CARS WERE IN the parking lot when I got there, but none of them looked like they were registered to three-letter government agencies. The church was a one-story red brick structure with a central entrance flanked by long wings on either side and a large, square, story-and-a-half building on the back. Yellow crime-scene tape wrapped around the covered walkway leading to what was left of the charred entrance. I followed hand-lettered instructions on squares of cardboard directing me to the back. A gray folding chair propped a metal emergency exit door open. I went inside.

I found myself in a gym at the rear of the church, a space housing a full-size basketball court along with an array of weights and workout balls and yoga mats. I tried to remember where I'd seen a similar setup recently and realized it had been at the mosque just up the street, minus the indoor court. Inside, people were putting out folding chairs as makeshift pews. That meant the damage had extended farther inside than just the entrance. Several black faces turned in my direction as I stationed myself near the midcourt line and looked around. Whether I would have looked more out of place had I simply pranced in naked was up for debate. After an awkward couple of seconds a heavyset woman in sweat pants and a purple "Sanders Family Reunion 2012" T-shirt walked up to me.

"Something I can help you with?"

"I was looking for Pastor Monroe."

"Was he expecting you?"

"I—"

"He's a little busy, is all. Trying to get reorganized. Are you a detective?"

"An investigator, yes," I said, hoping she wouldn't press beyond that. "It won't take long."

She sighed and walked across the gym, her tread heavy and slow. She disappeared through a door into the church. A minute later she returned, trailing a man dressed in work boots, jeans, and a red golf shirt stained with sweat.

"I'm Pastor Monroe. How can I help you?"

I handed him a card and explained who I was and why I was there. Anger brightened his eyes.

"I think my wife explained we have nothing to say to you."

"That's true. But that was before all this happened."

"Which is now a matter for the police. So if you'll excuse me—"

"So you've told the police that Faith and Abdi were dating?"

He cast a panicked look around the gym and lowered his voice to a whisper. "That's not true. Where did you hear that?"

"It's not important. But I'm curious: did you also tell the police you put your foot down? Forbade them to be together? And that that might make a decent motive for Abdi attacking your church?"

He glared at me, perspiration darkening the pencil mustache that seemed to float in place on his upper lip.

"Let's go to my office."

WE WALKED A GAUNTLET PAST SEVERAL stone-faced parishioners. We left the gym, went down a hall, turned, and entered a small room with a panoramic view of the parking lot. Bibles, books on religion, and family photos crowded a bookshelf behind the pastor's desk. The walls were covered with more photos, along with framed diplomas and the quintessential Columbus office accessory: a framed poster-sized picture of Ohio Stadium on game day.

Monroe moved behind his desk but stayed standing, arms folded tightly across his chest. Almost identical to the pose his wife had struck in her doorway the afternoon I stopped by.

"You have a lot of nerve coming here. As if we haven't gone through enough."

"I wanted to do this in person. I also didn't want to talk about this at your house. In front of your wife and daughter. To show you that respect."

He brushed the peace offering aside. "Just tell me what you want. Money? You're in the wrong place. We were struggling to make ends meet before this happened." He gestured to his left, toward the front of the building where the homemade bomb had hit.

"Don't be ridiculous. I don't want your money. I'm trying to find Abdi Mohamed. Until yesterday, his family and the lawyer they hired were convinced he was in trouble. That he didn't leave to follow in his brother's footsteps."

"What do they think happened to him? He just disappeared? Please."

"They don't know. A lot's changed because of the fire, obviously. It might be the explanation we're looking for. If he's really the one who did this, it's inexcusable and he needs to pay for his crime. But that's different than showing sympathy for a terrorist organization. Even you can see that."

"That's supposed to make me feel OK? We built this church from scratch. People invested their life savings."

"And if you help me find him, he'll be punished. You can be sure of that. But first I have to figure out where he is. And that takes us back to Faith."

"It was nothing," Monroe said. He produced a white handkerchief from a rear pants pocket and wiped his brow. "She was confused about her feelings."

"That's not what I heard. I heard they were involved. And I'm guessing from your denials you haven't told the police any of this."

"There's nothing to tell. It's hardly a motive for trying to burn down my church. The tension between the mosque and Mount Shiloh was well-known. Some of those young men there are openly aggressive to our youth. That's more than enough reason."

"I've heard the opposite was true. That kids here threw stones at the mosque."

"That's not—"

I waved away his objection. "Let me put it to you this way. Either you tell the police about Faith and Abdi, or I will."

"No!"

"Why not?"

"Because," he said with emphasis, "there's nothing to tell."

"I have a different theory."

"A different theory about what?"

"I think you don't want the fact your daughter was dating a Muslim to make it into any kind of official record. Sure, some kids know. You know how they gossip. But a police report? That's different. That's fodder for the news. And how's it going to look that the pastor of a church let this happen under his own roof? The brother of a terrorist, dating a good Christian girl?"

"Stop it."

"Help me, then."

"Help you how?"

"Help me find Abdi."

MUSIC DRIFTED DOWN THE hall. Someone was playing a piano. I recognized the tune from one of my uncle and aunt's country church hymns, though theirs was a decidedly more staid version. The heavyset woman in purple appeared at the door.

"Pastor Monroe? Someone from the insurance company—"

"Just another minute, Sister Andrea."

She smiled at Monroe, shot me a dead-eye, and slowly walked away.

When she was gone, Monroe said, "All right. They were dating. Secretly. Until we found out. Satisfied? I'd like to credit myself enough that it wasn't just a question of Abdi's religion that gave me pause. Faith is so young. She's barely sixteen, and not all that mature. Show me another father who wouldn't have done the same, looking out for his only daughter. Do you have children?"

"Two boys. The oldest is the one the people with the daughters need to worry about. Listen, nobody's trying to make this about religion any more than it already is. And I can't force you to call the police. I can only suggest it will help in the long run. But like I said, if you have any idea where he might be, I need to know."

"And I've told you, I don't."

"Your daughter?"

He shook his head. "We've asked her. We made her show us her e-mails and share her Facebook password. There were some innocent messages back and forth. But nothing for several weeks. Definitely not since he disappeared. I'm telling you the truth. We have no idea where Abdi Mohamed is. Unlike him."

"What do you mean?"

"He knows where we are," he said, his shoulders sagging. "He knew right where to come, didn't he?"

I WENT HOME, WALKED HOPALONG AROUND
the block, came back inside, and started making notes. I needed
time to think about the case. To figure out my next step. I also
didn't have any other options that night. Anybody to do anything
with. I was like the guy who decides to stop drinking because he
ran out of beer. I thought fleetingly of Anne, and then pictured
Ben Layton, and walked into the living room to hunt up the remote. A minute later my phone buzzed. It was the parson calling,
inviting me to see *Hamlet* around the corner in Schiller Park.

"It's practically your autobiography," he said. "Not to mention it's two blocks from your house and I'm bringing the wine."
The productions were staged each summer on a permanent stage
not far from where dog walkers gathered each morning and
evening.

"I suppose I could drag myself across the parapets for that.
What kind of wine?"

Roy Roberts made an improbable best friend, to say the least.
I'm one rung up the ladder from atheism, whereas he's an Episcopal priest. I'm Black Label, he's craft beer. I'm Browns, he's Bengals.

He and Lucy have been married thirty-plus years. Me? Moving on. But the fact he was once Major Roberts as an army chaplain in Iraq means he takes a greater than usual interest in my work. Meanwhile, I appreciate his rough-and-tumble ministry at his church in Franklinton, the poor neighborhood just west of downtown. It was the usual bromance, with occasional undercover work thrown in.

I walked to the park just before seven, passing under several of the tall oak trees on the park's outskirts before reaching the theater's sloped viewing lawn. Roy and Lucy were already there unfolding their lawn chairs. As we settled in I explained about my so-far failed search for Abdi.

"The fire at the church may have been the last straw," I said. "It lends credence to what the FBI thinks the kid's up to."

"It's hard to avoid drawing conclusions," Roy said in agreement, filling my glass.

"I just don't want to believe it."

"I don't blame you. But does that feeling make it any less probable?"

"It just doesn't make any sense, is the problem."

"Religion has a funny way of gumming up people's minds," Roy said. "People confuse belief with ideology, and then we're off to the races. It's a problem all faiths have. I see it every day even in my little church."

I acknowledged his point. "The issue is that the stakes are so much higher in Abdi's case."

"As are the prejudices, it sounds like. And both are dangerous."

"I'm starting to see that, believe me."

We raised our glasses and toasted moody princes. After a couple more minutes of conversation I excused myself to use the restroom. I was walking back out of the park's dark-brick recreation center when I looked up and to my surprise saw Helene Paulus strolling toward me. She stopped, uncertain.

"Small world," I offered.

"I guess so." Her colorful outfit—a long, red floral summer dress with a blue jeans vest—didn't match her cold expression.

"I live around the corner. I'm here with some friends."

"How nice. I'd tell you where I live, but I'm assuming you already know."

"Why would I know that?"

"Isn't that what private eyes do? Snoop?"

"You're thinking of Cold War spies. Mostly I sit around and drink rye whiskey and let the afternoon sun cut shadowed patterns on my desk through the blinds. Speaking of rye, you're welcome to join us." I gestured back toward Roy and Lucy. "My friend brought wine. He's an Episcopal priest, but don't hold that against him. The wine's actually drinkable. A nice Lake Erie Riesling."

She kept at it. "You snooped on Barbara."

"I thought we went over this already."

"Given the unusual coincidence of me seeing you here, this week of all weeks, I thought it worth mentioning."

"'Unusual coincidence' is redundant. It's like saying an astonishing surprise. More to the point, lots of like-minded people in Columbus come to Shakespeare in the Park."

"Like-minded?"

"Books and art appreciation, remember?"

"I've been trying to forget. Do you enjoy doing that, by the way?"

"Doing what?"

"Needling people. I think I know what a coincidence is."

"As a matter of fact, I don't enjoy it. It's one of my worst habits, right after politely asking for information that could help rescue a lost kid."

"Politely?"

"Forget it. I'm sorry if my methods offended your sensibilities." I paused, trying to figure out a way to salvage the conversation. "You heard about the fire, I presume?"

She nodded.

"If I may just say, one more reason it would be helpful to speak to the counselor."

"Just the opposite, in my opinion. She's even more upset now."

I was about to ask her about Faith Monroe and Abdi when a young man walked up.

"How's it going?" he said. "I'm Gabe." He stuck out his hand. I shook it, taking measure of a firm, friendly grip. What was it with guys and their handshakes anymore?

"My son," Helene said, frowning.

"Nice to meet you. Are you looking forward to the play?"

He laughed. "Sort of."

"Sort of? It's *Hamlet*."

"It's my fifth time seeing it. My girlfriend plays Ophelia. But it's still good," he added quickly. "And she's really good."

We chatted for a couple minutes while his mother stood silently beside us. He was a sophomore at Ohio State, majoring in history. His girlfriend went to Otterbein. He was a good-looking kid, black hair flopping over his eyes that he pushed back now and then with an easy brush of his fingers.

"If you'll excuse us," Helene interrupted. "We packed a picnic, and we haven't eaten yet."

"Drop by for some wine if you want."

"Sounds good," Gabe said, his expression not exactly mirroring his mother's.

I turned to let them pass. Gabe walked ahead of Helene, who hesitated a moment.

"It just doesn't add up," she said.

"What doesn't?"

"Abdi. Attacking a church. It's not the student we knew."

"Who?"

"Those of us at school."

"Including Barbara Mendoza?"

Her face darkened and she turned away, following her son without responding.

"She's cute," Lucy said when I returned to my chair. "Someone you know? Or were you just exerting your usual animal magnetism?"

"My poles reversed recently, so my magnetism's been on the fritz. She's the principal at Abdi Mohamed's school. I'm not in her particular good graces at the moment."

"Really? From the way she was looking at you I wouldn't have guessed."

"Sarcasm has never suited you."

"I'm serious. Could you really not tell?"

"Since I was trying to avoid the little daggers coming out of her eyes, I guess not."

"Your loss, then. Also, 'particular good graces' is redundant, just so you know."

"Thanks for the tip."

Roy poured more wine and Lucy produced a pecan pie. As I took a bite and washed it down with a swallow of Riesling, I thought about my encounter with Helene and her son. What struck me, I realized, was not her continued anger at my methods, including contacting Barbara Mendoza. It was how bewildered she remained by the accusations against Abdi, even after the fire. Finally, something—after books and art appreciation—we had in common?

25

I WAS STILL THINKING ABOUT ABDI WHEN
I woke up the next morning and headed out for a jog along the
bike path running south of downtown to the Scioto Audubon
metro park. *It's not the student we knew.* But what did that mean
anymore, such surprise at unexpected wrongdoing? We'd grown
accustomed to disparities in people's lives as tragedies flashed
across our screens with depressing regularity. The husband who
guns down his wife and kids before killing himself. *He always said
hi.* A student opening fire in a high school cafeteria. *He was quiet,
never bothered anyone.* The serial arsonist. *I just talked March Mad-
ness with him the other day.* Was it possible to know anyone anymore in an age of mass violence, when calamity was a trigger
pull of a legally owned weapon away? Of course, it always turned
out that trouble stalked most good guys who did bad things. A
little digging turned up what casual encounters missed. A pleas-
ant façade can only take you so far when the devil has you by the
short hairs. But was this true in Abdi's case? Could everyone—his
family, his friends, Helene Paulus, even Barbara Mendoza—have
missed something so fundamental in his character? Failed to see

that the amenable class clown and aspiring diplomat was headed down the same path as his black sheep brother?

On my way back up the trail I approached the Town Street Bridge and saw that the expanse was lined with food vendors. Yet another downtown festival was under way. Before circling around the Statehouse and heading back down to German Village I checked out the variety of food trucks lining the bridge. I decided I might have some deep-fried eats in my future, even if they were kale balls.

I was out of the shower and eating breakfast when the phone rang. It wasn't blocked, but I didn't recognize the number. A telemarketer was all I needed right now. I answered anyway.

"Is this Andy Hayes?" A woman's voice.

"That's right."

"You're a detective?"

"Investigator. Was there something—"

"You the guy got beat up helping that Arab lady in the parking lot?"

"Beat up might be a little strong. And she's Somali, not Arab. And if you're calling to harass me about it, you might want to read the Constitution and then take a ticket—"

"Calm down, soldier. I'm not calling to harass you. I need your help."

"With what?"

"Finding those two."

"Which two?"

"The two that beat you up."

I didn't correct her this time. "I wouldn't mind finding them myself. But first I need to know who they are."

"I'll tell you who they are. It's my brother and his boy. They're missing. And I need them found."

HER NAME WAS PATTY Bowden. She'd pulled my number off the website Bonnie set up for me. "Columbus Investigative Services." Not quite the ring of "Pinkertons," but I was getting there. She told me she lived east of Columbus, not all that far from Zanesville.

"So your brother's missing?"

"My brother and his boy. Mike Bowden's my brother. His son Todd is my nephew."

I described the tattoo I'd seen on the skinny guy.

"It's them, all right. I figured as much when I saw it on the news."

"Why's that?"

"Kind of thing Mike would do. Can't stay out of trouble. And his boy's no better."

"They live near you?"

"Closer to Newark."

"Any idea what they were doing in Columbus?"

"Up to no good, I guess. They'd been going there a lot recently."

I thought back to Henry Fielding's call while I sat at Betty's Bar. I said, "The police think they were scoping winners out at the casino. Maybe looking to rob them."

"I don't know about that. Not out of the realm of possibility, you know what I mean."

I glanced at my kitchen clock. "So what can I do for you, Mrs. Bowden?"

"Mrs. Bowden was my mother. Call me Patty. I want to hire you."

"For what?"

"To find them."

"Have you talked to the police?"

"No, and I ain't going to."

"Why not?"

"I've got my reasons. Any chance you could come over here? Let me explain a little. I can pay, don't worry."

"I'm a little, ah, busy at the moment." I didn't mention the urgency of the job at hand: finding Abdi Mohamed before further disaster struck. "When were you thinking?"

"How about right now?"

"Now?"

"You heard me."

"I'm not sure that's going to work. Any chance you could come here?"

"I don't get around so good. Won't take you that long to get over here. Like I said, I'll pay."

I balled my left fist in frustration. It went against my nature to turn down a paying client. But I didn't have time for this kind of random field trip, despite my curiosity at who those two guys might be. And why they were missing.

"Tell you what. Give me the directions. I'll see if I can make it this afternoon, depending on what's going on."

"Is that a yes or a no?"

"Yes," I said, after a moment.

I wrote down her address and told her I'd be in touch. I tried to decide if that were more a white lie or a straight-out prevarication. I didn't have the opportunity to think much more about it. My phone rang again, with another unfamiliar number. My lucky day, I guess. I answered and found myself listening to the voice of the last person in the world I expected to hear from just then.

"It's Barbara Mendoza. Please. I need your help."

26

I SAT UP STRAIGHT AND PRESSED THE PHONE tight against my ear.

"Help with what?"

"My . . . my daughter. She's missing."

"Missing?"

A whisper. "Someone has taken her."

"Taken? You need to call the police."

"*No.* I can't."

"Why not?"

"I just can't. Please. I don't know who else to go to."

"How long has she been gone?"

"Since yesterday evening."

"And you know for sure she's been kidnapped."

A long pause. "Yes."

"You really should—"

"*I can't. Please.*"

I stared across the dining room at one of my framed James Thurber cartoons, one of the few pieces of art in the house. My mind ground out possible responses. None of them were good.

"OK. I'll be right over. We'll figure it out when I get there."

"No. I don't know—"

"Don't know what?"

"If someone is watching me."

"Watching you?"

"My house. I can only assume. The other day, when you came by . . . They knew about that."

"They?"

"Whoever took Angela."

"Are you home now?"

"I'm at the airport."

"The airport? Are you leaving town?"

"I knew they had payphones here. It was the only place I could think of that did. I'm worried they may be tracking my calls somehow."

I tried to remember the last time I saw a payphone. Barbara Stanwyck in *Double Indemnity* came to mind, but it may have been more recently than that.

"OK. I can be there in twenty minutes." So much for my field trip to eastern Ohio.

"No. If they followed me, if they see you—"

My mind raced through several more possibilities. I said, "What if I had someone else meet you? Pick you up at the curb outside."

"Who?"

"A friend."

"Is he . . . someone I can trust?"

"It's a she I'm thinking of. And yes."

I told her to call me back in ten minutes, and if I didn't answer to try again in five. I hung up and punched in the number I had in mind. She answered on the third ring.

"QB," Theresa Sullivan said on the other line. "I got a good one for you. You know why Toledo doesn't have a professional football team?"

"Listen, I don't have time—"

"Yes or no?"

"*No*. I give up."

"If it did, then Cleveland would want one, too."

"Very funny. Now listen—"

"Thought you'd like that. You played for Cleveland, right?"

"Very briefly, yes, between snowstorms. Now would you please pay attention?"

I told her why I was calling. And what I had in mind.

"You can't ever just call to see how I'm doing?" she said when I finished.

"If I did that, would you tell me?"

"Probably not. Call me back when it's set up."

I hung up and waited for Barbara Mendoza's call.

THERESA SULLIVAN WAS PROBABLY the closest thing I had to a friend who happened to be a girl and not the other way around, as they say. I'll let you draw your own conclusions from the fact the only woman who fits this bill is an ex-prostitute whose heart is definitely not made of gold. When I first met her she was a foul-mouthed wraith who could count the number of weeks she'd been sober and free from a pimp's controlling fists on less than one hand. These days she ran an outreach center for trafficking victims sponsored by Roy's church. When you came right down to it, we didn't have much in common other than a bunch of demons we kept in locked closets of the mind, difficulty committing long term to the opposite sex, and an abiding hatred of bullies. As with me and Roy, friendships have been forged on less, I suppose.

If someone had seen me at Barbara Mendoza's house, there was a chance they knew where I lived. So my place in German Village was out for the purposes of meeting her. The church was an option, except I didn't want Roy pulled into anyone's cross-hairs. I ran through a list of other locations before settling on one that just might work.

Fitzy's twenty-four-hour diner sits on Schrock Road on the north side, just a hop, skip, and clandestine jump from the airport if you come up the Interstate 270 outer loop as I instructed Theresa to. I was sitting in a corner booth under a poster of Marilyn Monroe when Theresa and the counselor walked in right on time forty minutes later. I looked not at them but outside, where Theresa had parked her Honda Civic beside a Suzuki bike a man had ridden up on a few minutes earlier. He didn't look like a kidnapper, but I kept my eye on him just in case. Theresa and the counselor slid in opposite me, sitting side by side.

We waited while the waitress brought us waters and coffee and dropped off menus. I told her we might need a couple of minutes. When she was on the other side of the restaurant, I nodded at the counselor. She looked up at me, shell-shocked.

"I don't know what to do," she said.

"We can help, I promise. But the first thing is, I have to repeat what I said before. If your daughter's been kidnapped, we need to call the police. The FBI. I know people—"

"*No.*" She glanced around the diner, panic on her face.

"Why not?"

"We can't. They'll . . . they'll harm her."

"They said that?"

She nodded, misery filling her eyes.

"Barbara. I'm sorry. But if a crime's been committed—"

"You don't understand. The harm I'm talking about. What Angela will face, if they find out."

"If who finds out?"

"The police. The government."

"Find out what?"

A long pause. "That she's not really my daughter. And that she's here illegally."

27

SHE STARTED TO CRY. THERESA YANKED napkins from the dispenser on the table and handed them to her. All my instincts screamed to shake the details out of the counselor. If the girl was in danger and there was something we could do to help, we needed to do it now, and fast. Instead, I let Barbara compose herself. After a minute the waitress returned. I ordered us all omelets and home fries and bacon and more coffee when she had the chance. She had the chance. They always do at Fitzy's.

Barbara apologized, blew her nose, and started speaking.

"I've raised her like my own. But she . . . she's my niece. And she isn't documented. And—"

We waited.

"And I've lied about it on forms and papers." She started to cry again.

As gently as I could, I said, "Where is she from?"

"Mexico," she said, recovering a little. "Like me. But I came a long time ago, for college. I'm the oldest in the family. I'd been here more than ten years when my youngest sister came up. Angela was just a year old. Then my sister had to go back home and she left her with me. I promised I'd take care of her. It was only supposed to be for a little while. Maybe a few months. But months stretched into years. I thought eventually her mother would come back and we'd work things out. But then something bad happened, and I had to make a decision."

"Bad like what?"

"My sister was killed six years ago in Tijuana. Shot on the street. No one was ever arrested. And Angela's father—they never married—he disappeared. He's in prison or perhaps dead too. So Angela has no one."

"You adopted her?"

"I should have. It would have made everything easier. But I was worried even that process might jeopardize her. You don't understand the atmosphere we face now."

"What do you mean?"

"How right-wing everything is. The things people say. 'They might be children now but they'll take American jobs eventually!' 'Build the wall!'—you still hear that, all the time. One day, right after I found out my sister died, a lady at the park yelled at us when Angela was playing with another child. Said we shouldn't be allowed here. Even though I've been here almost twenty-five years! I became so scared I decided to pass her off as my daughter. Got her a fake social security number. Lied on school forms." She started to cry again. "This country, it was my dream to live here. A place of hope. But now—"

Theresa said, "Does Angela know?"

Barbara shook her head.

"I have to tell her. I was about to. But then—"

"Someone found out," I said.

"That's right."

"How?"

"I have no idea. An e-mail just popped up one day this spring. The subject line said *Angela*."

"What's the e-mail address?"

"A bunch of numbers and letters."

"And you think that's the same person who took her?"

"It has to be. They've warned me."

"Warned how?"

"Threats—"

I waited.

"Threats to expose the truth if I don't keep telling the police how certain I am that Abdi Mohamed was a secret extremist."

OUR FOOD ARRIVED. AS the waitress distributed the plates I contemplated what Barbara was telling me. Someone was blackmailing her to keep up a front that Abdi was a terrorist. They were using supposedly secret information—that her daughter was actually her niece, and here illegally—as a sword to hold over her head. Now the girl had been kidnapped and I was supposed to do something about it without alerting the authorities.

"How'd they take Angela?" I said when we were alone again.

"She'd gone for a run. She's doing cross-country in the fall, so she's already in training. Normally I don't worry—you've seen our neighborhood. It's very safe."

"And how do you know she's been kidnapped? As opposed to, I don't know, just being a teenager and not checking in?" It was an issue Kym faced constantly with Mike, something she was always on me to do something about.

"Someone texted me this."

She retrieved her phone from her purse and showed us a photo. My heart sped up a bit as I looked at a terrified girl with a gag in her mouth.

"No chance this is a prank? Maybe some friends—"

"No. Never."

"Have they made any demands?"

"They said they'll return her unharmed as long as I don't screw around anymore. That's their phrase. They mean with people like you."

"Did they say when? When they'll return her?"

"No."

"And that's it? No other demands?"

"They said it's symbolic. A reminder I shouldn't violate our deal again. But next time it could be worse."

"What's that mean? Violate your deal?"

"When you knocked on the door the other day. They accused me of calling you."

"Do they know who I am?"

"I don't know. But they had the date and the time."

Which meant someone besides the feds was watching her house. I took a look at the picture again and traded glances with Theresa.

"We really should call someone in," I said.

"I told you no," Barbara said. "If you can't help me, I'll handle things myself."

"And if I call someone anyway?"

"Then you've destroyed two lives. Angela's and mine."

"So why contact me?"

"I don't trust them to keep their word. That they won't do something to her. But I also don't trust the police, and what would happen to Angela once the authorities learn her status. I looked you up, after your visit. I thought you—"

"Thought what?"

"Might be able to help me. Because of your reputation."

I thought about Helene Paulus. Her description of what she'd learned about me. *See what? That you fell down on the job?*

"I appreciate the vote of confidence. But this is extremely—"

Theresa interrupted. "We need to get their attention. Turn things around."

"What do you mean?" Barbara said.

"Yes," I said. "Do tell."

"They think they've got all the cards now. Your niece and the threat to reveal her secret. They're saying they'll release her, just not when. So we've got to switch that. Get things on our turf."

"How?" I said.

"Trade them something important for Angela."

"Something like what?"

"Something like you, QB," Theresa said.

28

I LOOKED UP AT MARILYN MONROE. I couldn't read anything in those lonely, yearning eyes. I was guessing the feeling was mutual.

"Me?"

"They probably think you know too much anyway," Theresa said. "What better trade for Angela than someone who might screw up whatever it is they're up to?"

"I'm not sure. Is it realistic? Would they buy it?"

"I would betray you in a second," Barbara said quietly. "I would do anything to help Angela. I'm sorry, but it's true."

"Let's be clear on one thing first," I said. "You don't think Abdi Mohamed is a terrorist?"

"Absolutely not."

"You heard about the firebombing at Mount Shiloh?" I told her what Freddy Cohen had confided in me, that the feds had video of Abdi throwing the Molotov cocktail at the front of the church. About the message board threat.

"I can't explain that," Barbara said. "All I'm telling you is what I know from before he disappeared. And none of that is consistent with what they're saying now."

"Even with what his brother did?"

"Even more so. Abdi was devastated by Hassan's actions. I got several e-mails from him, about how upset he was. But he was also furious. He saw it as a complete waste, not to mention a betrayal of America."

I relayed the cryptic comments Henry Fielding had made about Abdi having gang ties. I told her what Mike Parsell, Abdi's soccer teammate, told me about Abdi joshing around with a supposed Agler Road Crip. DaQuan someone.

The counselor nodded. "JaQuan Williams. Talk about a complete waste. But in his case there's no doubt. We had many problems with him before he dropped out."

"Any chance what the Columbus detective is saying is true?"

"No. You have to believe me. Abdi never met a stranger. But he didn't have anything to do with JaQuan outside of school."

"Any idea where JaQuan is?"

"None. I told the police as much, when they came looking for him. Not long after Abdi disappeared."

I leaned back in the booth and drank some coffee. "And you don't know who would want you to perpetuate this lie about Abdi to the authorities?"

She shook her head. Her eyes brimmed with tears again.

"Get with the program, QB," Theresa chastised. "That kid Abdi don't matter right now. Neither does some gangbanger. What matters is Angela."

"You're right. I'm sorry."

"So what are you going to do?" Barbara said.

"We're going to need a plan," I said. "And we're going to need some help."

"Help?" she said nervously.

"Some more muscle. If I'm the target, we need someone who's got my back."

"What about me?" Theresa said indignantly.

"I've got another idea for you."

I looked at my watch. It was past 2:30. We had a little time, but not much. I excused myself, went outside, and fished around in my wallet. I found the card I was looking for and called Otto Mulligan.

"That's some serious shit, Woody," he said when I finished explaining what I had in mind. "And it sounds like it could go wrong in about seven different directions."

"Just like the job you dragged me along on the other day."

"No hard feelings, I hope. How's the eye, by the way?"

"It's been upgraded to medium rare. What do you say?"

"I say I guess I owe you one."

"That's what I was thinking."

I went back inside the diner.

"All right," I said, sliding back into the booth. "I've got an extra set of hands on board. And I think I've got a plan."

"What is it?" Theresa said.

"Here's what we're going to do."

WE SPLIT UP OUTSIDE FITZY'S. THERESA
drove Barbara back to the airport with plans to park her own car
and return to the counselor's house hidden in the backseat of
Barbara's car. I had to assume Barbara would be followed from
her house tonight, and I didn't want her by herself. Short of bal-
listic missiles being fired, I was pretty sure Theresa could handle
her own in that regard.

Mulligan and I were in place by eight o'clock. The warehouse
we'd chosen for the operation sat by itself at the end of a light
industrial park off Refugee Road on the southeast side, not more
than twenty minutes from Barbara's house. The street the building sat on, cleverly named Industrial Park Road, looped around
back onto Refugee, meaning we had a different way out than in
if needed. The warehouse held components used in the manu-
facturing of conveyor belts for recycling facilities. I felt better
about the environment already. Mulligan knew a guy who knew
a guy who was happy to get a paid night off that came with a
bonus in an envelope and a promise the components would be
well guarded even without his vigilant presence. To judge by the

bottle of Jack Daniel's and the box of condoms we found in a drawer in a desk in the small security office, we might have been doing the company a favor.

The setup was basic. I instructed Barbara to text her contact to say she'd caught me following her. That she'd confronted me in a Walmart parking lot. That she'd finally agreed to meet with me where I moonlighted as a warehouse security guard just to get me off her back. That she didn't care what happened to me as long as they returned Angela safely. Me for Angela. She promised she'd stay out of the way and would keep her mouth shut. She'd done it so far, hadn't she?

Closed-circuit TVs in the guard's office broadcast the view from cameras positioned on four sides of the building. We watched as night fell and the pictures changed from boring scenes observed in the shadows of dusk to even more boring scenes caught in the harsh glare of streetlamps, as if we were looking at old-fashioned film negatives. Based on the timeline we'd established, there wasn't much to do besides wait. I read *Dreamland* and wondered idly if Helene Paulus and I would ever discuss the book again. Mulligan played *Words with Friends* while balancing a shotgun on his lap, as you do.

At quarter to ten a stray cat walked past the front of the building. For a moment it seemed to glance straight at the camera.

"'The fog comes on little cat feet,'" Mulligan said.

"Carl Sandburg. I'm impressed."

"Don't be. It's on a coffee mug somebody brought me back from Chicago."

At five minutes after ten the cat trotted back across the asphalt parking lot with something small struggling in its mouth.

"'If cats looked like frogs we'd realize what nasty, cruel little bastards they are,'" Mulligan said.

"Another coffee mug?"

"Terry Pratchett. And it's hard to disagree with him."

Twenty minutes later we saw Barbara's car pull into the parking lot. She turned the engine off but didn't get out. I assumed she was texting Angela's captors to let them know she'd arrived.

"My guess is they're sitting a quarter mile up, waiting for you to come outside," Mulligan said.

"So it's now or never."

"Good luck, Woody."

"See you in a few."

We walked out of the office and parted ways. I turned left and headed to the front of the building. Mulligan went right in the direction of the side entrance, which would put him outside, out of view of anyone up front. His security guard acquaintance had deactivated the alarms for the night to facilitate this kind of movement, though that had taken a couple extra bills in the envelope. I turned the lock at the main doors and stepped out. I eyed Barbara and gave her a little nod for show. She opened her door but didn't get out, as we'd discussed. As Mulligan predicted, a pair of headlights blinked on just down the street, and a moment later a van pulled slowly up, stopping directly behind the counselor's car. I stared at the two people inside. This was not what I'd been expecting.

30

BOTH THE DRIVER AND THE PASSENGER were wearing Guy Fawkes masks. The disguise—black slashes of eyebrows and mouth and Van Dyke beard against white-as-snow skin—had been immortalized in the movie *V for Vendetta* and later as the go-to concealment for everyone from online hackers to the most extreme participants in the Occupy Wall Street movement. There was a reason they'd become so popular, I realized. They were downright creepy in a hide-the-kids-scary-clown kind of way.

The newcomers opened their doors and got out at the same time Barbara stepped out of her car.

"What the hell?" I said. Given the masks, feigning surprise wasn't much of a stretch.

"Where's Angela?" Barbara said. The urgency in her voice made it clear she at least wasn't playacting. "You've got what you want. You've got *him*." A dismissive nod in my direction. "Let me see her."

"What's going on?" I said, taking a step backwards.

The driver took a couple of corresponding steps toward me. He wore black jeans, a black button-down dress shirt and carried a gun in a black holster at his side. He looked like a waiter at an anarchist café.

"What exactly are you up to?" he said through the mask, his language oddly formal.

"I'm not up to anything. What is this?"

"Why are you bothering this lady?"

"I'm not bothering her. I'm trying to help."

Where the hell was Mulligan, I thought.

"Who are you working for?"

"I work for myself."

"Nonsense. You've been asking her about the terrorist, haven't you?"

"Abdi Mohammed? What about him?"

The person beside him, the van passenger, unholstered his own gun and pointed it just above my solar plexus.

"You're not asking the questions here, dipshit," he said, in decidedly informal fashion.

Now would be good, Otto, I thought. This particular moment would be just fine.

"I'm not answering jack. I don't know who the hell you are, but you need to leave this lady alone. And while you're at it, put the gun down."

At that we all glanced at Barbara. She was shaking so hard she was holding the car door with her right hand to steady herself.

"You have him," she said. "Just give me Angela. Please."

"Just as soon as we get a little more information," the driver said. He nodded at the other guy, who raised the gun and took a couple of steps toward me.

Otto, I thought. What the—

The rear passenger door of Barbara's car flew open just then and a scream pierced the warm summer night, like a car alarm that goes off in the street just as you're finally dropping into REM sleep. An object I recognized dimly as Theresa Sullivan hurtled out of the car and leaped onto the back of the driver, her hands clawing at his mask, yelling like a banshee who's caught Mr. Banshee with another ghoul. The man shouted something in surprise and began spinning around as if he were trying to control a firehose, reaching in vain behind him to grab Theresa. His partner turned and watched the scene unfold, his gun hand dipping a centimeter or three. I didn't hesitate. I hurled myself onto him from the side, knocking him hard against the hood of Barbara's car. He grunted in pain and we rolled off the hood and hit the pavement and rolled around a couple more times. When we came to a stop I grabbed his gun hand and smashed it one-two-three times against an extruding nut on the front hubcap until he yelped in pain and dropped the weapon, which spun away under the front of the car. I used my free hand to grab his mask and I had it partway off when his left fist smashed into my medium-rare eye and I yelped myself, and not quietly. I raised my hands and warded off a second blow and then heaved myself toward him, tackling him by the waist. He started scrabbling forward, toward his gun.

"Don't move."

I stopped. I turned my head. The driver stood above me, his gun out of his holster and jammed up against Theresa's jaw. His mask was still on. He had his left arm around her head in a half nelson that was making her grimace with pain and me roil in anger at the expression on her face. She looked terrified but also furious. Theresa didn't like losing control of situations. One of the things I liked about her—and was a little scared by at times.

"Release him," the driver said, the comment directed at me, his voice slightly distorted by the mask. I looked at his gun and at Theresa's expression and reluctantly let go.

"Get the gun," the driver said, and the passenger started to crawl toward his long-lost weapon.

Where the hell—?

"Don't move."

Same words, but a new voice and with a touch more urgency. I snuck a glance to my right. Mulligan was standing behind the driver, the barrel of his shotgun pressed against the back of his head. Speaking of little cat feet. Or nasty bastards.

"Let her go," Mulligan said.

"I will not—"

Mulligan racked a shell into the shotgun chamber. It's a sound, like the first robin of spring or a baby's giggle as Grandma scoops her onto her lap, that never fails to inspire.

The driver let Theresa go. She spun away, rubbing her neck, spitting fury from her eyes.

"Now the gun."

"Perhaps we can talk about this—"

"You've got three seconds before I turn your head into cherry pie," Mulligan said. "You understand what I'm saying? We're not talking closed casket. We're talking coroner's office wet-vac to clean it all up. One. Two—"

The driver dropped the gun.

"Theresa," Mulligan said.

She walked over and picked it up, staring at the driver the entire time.

"Get the other one, Woody," Mulligan said.

I stood up, grabbed the passenger by his belt, pulled him backwards, reached down, and grabbed the gun that had spun under the car. Mulligan forced the driver onto his knees, shotgun still pressed against the back of his head.

Satisfied things were under control, Mulligan said, "Sorry about that. Took me a minute to figure out the best angle."

"And here was me thinking you aced geometry," I said. "Where's the girl?"

The driver stayed silent.

"Wet-vac," Mulligan said.

"*In the van,*" the driver said, clearly frustrated.

"Woody," Mulligan said.

I walked to the van and slid open the rear side door. Angela was sitting in the backseat, gagged with her hands and feet bound. Her eyes went wide when she saw me. I turned and gestured to Barbara. She rushed over. I pulled out my keys and opened the blade on the Swiss Army knife I keep on the key ring for slicing up apples and for emergencies like this. I cut through the plastic zip ties binding the girl. I untied the gag around Angela's mouth and helped her out. She and Barbara embraced as both burst into tears.

"All right," I said, turning around. "Time for some answers."

Otto yanked the driver's mask off. We stared at the face of a man whose features were distorted by a stocking pulled over his head. Clever: a double disguise. Otto went to pull the stocking off when the night came to a sudden conclusion. Up the street we heard a siren. It was hard to tell where it was coming from, but it was definitely close. Maybe Mulligan's security guard pal had forgotten to deactivate one of the silent alarms. Maybe the cop was responding to a traffic accident two miles away and it was a complete coincidence. Either way, things went to hell fast. The driver used the momentary distraction to roll away from Mulligan. When he righted himself he'd produced a gun we'd missed, hidden in an ankle holster. As he and Mulligan faced each other in a stand-off, the other man charged the van. I pulled Barbara and her niece out of the way.

"Let's go, Woody," Mulligan said.

"But—"

"I put people in jail for a living. I ain't going there myself."

"We need to know who these guys are."

"Ain't gonna help if we're in a cell. Or a grave. C'mon."

Reluctantly, I backed off. Theresa and Barbara and Angela piled into the counselor's car, Theresa at the wheel. I jumped into my van with Mulligan in the passenger seat. We drove away fast, leaving Guy Fawkes I and II behind us, taking the turn on the curving loop with a genuine seventies cop show tire squeal. In another minute we were back on Refugee Road with Barbara's niece safe but still no idea who her masked captors were.

31

THERESA AND I SPENT THE NIGHT AT
Barbara's house. The counselor told me it wasn't necessary, that
she would be all right. She said it with the conviction of a woman
staring out the locked second-floor window of a house as it goes up
in flames. I gave Mulligan the keys to my van and told him to obey
the speed limit and to let the dog out when he got to my place.

"I can't believe you're making me drive this thing," he said,
eyeing my Odyssey. "It's got a big butt. It's the kind of thing a
soccer mom would drive if her first car was in the garage. It says
private investigator like a girdle says sexy."

"If you wouldn't mind putting some kibble in Hopalong's
bowl while you're at it, that would be great," I replied. I'd long
ago given up defending my vehicle of choice. It held my collection of eighties music CDs, my Louisville Slugger, and both my
boys and a friend or two just fine. Plus, he was wrong. I'd dated
at least one soccer mom who liked hers plenty, though it was true
she'd gone with a Jeep when it was time to trade up.

We didn't talk much after Mulligan left. We put Theresa in a
guest room in the basement. I took the couch downstairs.

"Thank you," Barbara said as she went upstairs with Angela. "I'm glad it worked out."

I lay awake for almost an hour, going over the events of the night, trying to figure out what was happening. Who the clowns in the scary clown masks were. At last I dozed off, snuggled up with the aforementioned baseball bat. I slept fitfully, dreaming of omelets and cats that looked like frogs and people in Guy Fawkes masks dancing around bonfires like giant marionettes, the strings stretching high, high up into the sky.

I AWOKE TO THE smell of something cooking. I sat up and gingerly rubbed my reinjured eye. I blinked. Sunlight illuminated the edges around the drawn shades in the living room. I found my phone and checked the time. It was just 7 a.m. I saw I already had texts from both Kym and Crystal about Red, White & Boom arrangements. Just three days away now.

Three days, I thought, getting my bearings. There's a certain symmetry to that length of time one has to admire. No extraneous days you're not sure what to do with: there's a beginning, a middle, and an end. Three is a prime number, of course, which is always special. And it's a phrase full of historical and artistic significance. The length of time Jesus spent in the tomb. *Three Days of the Condor*—a book my dad once called his favorite ever. "Three Days," a decent 1990 song by Jane's Addiction that I always claim for the eighties, which didn't really end until the Gulf War anyway. And most pertinent to my situation, the number of days of grace accorded under old English law before someone had to appear in court to answer a summons.

Three days. The amount of time the food left in my refrigerator would last without another trip to the grocery store, tops, assuming I went easy on the eggs and Black Label, and also assuming I had any money to replenish my supplies.

Three days. The amount of time I had until a painful appointment with destiny in the form of accompanying Joe and Mike to Red, White & Boom thanks to the generosity of Anne's new boyfriend.

Three days. The amount of time I likely had to either find Abdi Mohamed or let Freddy Cohen know—and therefore the authorities—that Barbara Mendoza was lying about the boy. I hadn't told her that in so many words. But she and I both knew we had to get to the bottom of this situation and fast. For Angela's sake, if not for Abdi's.

I WALKED INTO THE kitchen. Barbara was standing over the stove tending to a cast-iron skillet filled with sausage and eggs and potatoes and onions and green peppers.

"Are you OK?" she said, the corners of her mouth turned down in concern.

"Little sore. Fistfights aggravate my arthritis."

"You were . . . You were snoring so loudly, I thought—"

"Occupational hazard. I'm fine."

She smiled for the first time since I'd met her. "There's coffee," she said, pointing at a drip machine and a pair of cups beside it. I helped myself and sat down at the kitchen table.

"How is she?"

"Still asleep," she said. "She stayed with me in my bed. She couldn't bear to be alone."

"You're sure they didn't hurt her?"

"Yes. Other than tying her up and blindfolding her, they didn't touch her. They even asked her what she wanted to eat."

"Any idea where they kept her?"

"None. She said she never saw anything or anyone, other than a flash of a face when the van pulled up. It happened so fast. There was a lot of driving around, and then stopping someplace, and then they took her into a building of some kind."

"And no idea who they were?"

She shook her head. "But there's one thing—"

"Oh?"

"My phone died. What time is it?"

I looked up. Theresa stood before us in bare feet, rubbing her eyes. Her brown hair, normally held back with pins or a hairband, flew around her head as if she'd awakened, brushed her teeth, and jammed a finger into an electric socket. Her freckled face was puffy with sleep.

I stood up and handed her my cup of coffee, which I had yet to touch. She took it, nodded her thanks, and stumped over to the kitchen table. She sat down heavily in a chair next to mine. In past years her thrift-store outfits left one with the impression of a grown-up Pippi Longstocking on the way to the shooting range or a graduate seminar. She'd toned it down for last night's adventure, opting for a black skirt over black yoga pants and a black-and-white striped sleeveless top. She looked like someone out of one of Bonnie Deckard's manga comic books. Like someone scary clowns wouldn't want to mess with.

"How're you doing?" I said.

"Better than those two guys." She grinned. I couldn't help myself. I grinned back.

I poured myself a new cup and refreshed Barbara's.

"You were saying?"

Barbara pulled three plates out of a cabinet to her left, one yellow, one red, one green. She opened the oven, reached in, and removed a flat bowl. She set it on top of the stove, lifted a tortilla out of it, and laid the tortilla on the top plate. She spooned a large helping of the skillet concoction on top, doused the results with salsa, sprinkled on cheese, rolled up the tortilla, and handed the plate to me. I handed it to Theresa. Barbara repeated the process for me, and then served herself. She sat down on the other side of the table.

"Angela heard something. In the van, right after they took her."

"What was it?"

"A word or a name, she wasn't sure. 'JJ's.' One of them said it, the passenger, I think, and then the driver told him to shut up. It seemed important."

"'JJ's'? She's certain about that?"

"Yes."

I flashed back to Grizzle in the parking lot, holding up his phone. Mike Bowden, I knew now. *He's saying JJ's.*

147

"Does that mean something to you?" Barbara said, seeing my reaction.

"Maybe." I told her about the reference from the assault on Kaltun Hirsi.

"Which means them two last night are connected to your parking lot guys," Theresa said. "Same ones?"

"Young guy, maybe. The older guy with him that day was moving a lot slower than either of those two." I told them about the call from Patty Bowden, how her brother and nephew were missing. "But what's the connection?" I said. "And if it's not them, why would those guys"—meaning Bowden and his son—"have anything to do with the people who took Angela?"

32

AS WE DISCUSSED THE POSSIBILITIES, MY phone buzzed with a text. I replied and stood up.

"What is it?" Barbara said.

"We've got some visitors—don't worry," I said, seeing the expression on her face. "Someone I asked to stop by. Someone who's going to help us."

"Who?"

"More people we can trust."

I walked through the living room, opened the front door, and looked up and down the street. Satisfied the coast was clear, I signaled for the occupants in the car in the driveway to come inside.

"THEY'LL KNOW SOMETHING IS up," Barbara said, tears back in her eyes. "Seeing strangers like this. No offense, I'm sorry."

"It's OK," Bonnie Deckard said. She was working on her own breakfast burrito and coffee. Her boyfriend sat next to her. Troy hadn't touched his food yet. He was attending to the third visitor, a mastiff sitting by his side, motionless but eyes glued on Troy. She was the biggest dog I'd ever seen. She would have swamped pleasure boats, and not small ones. It was not out of the realm of possibility that Hopalong's entire head could fit into her mouth. Her name was Goldie. She was a rescue that Troy brought home from the kennel where he worked on the northeast side of town helping to foster dogs captured in police raids of dogfighting rings and drug houses. Troy was wearing shorts and a black T-shirt and sporting a pair of muttonchops that wouldn't have looked out of place on HMS *Intrepid*.

"We've got a window here," I said to the counselor. "They're going to lay low after last night. Like Theresa said—we needed to get their attention, and we did it." Theresa gave me a smile of triumph at the recognition. "The ball's in our court now. They have no idea how much we know, or even if we may have figured out who they are. And if they do get any ideas, we've got them outnumbered." I reached out and carefully patted the top of Goldie's head. "Seriously outnumbered."

"But why are they here?" Barbara said, glancing at Bonnie. Bonnie smiled encouragingly. She was wearing black workout stretch pants that stopped midcalf and a black sleeveless tank top over a green Arch City Roller Girls shirt. Her auburn hair lay across a shoulder in a thick braid. Her muscular arms looked like she could juggle two Guy Fawkes mask–wearing clowns with ease and look around for more. She'd added a couple of ear gauges recently, which suited her personality, if not my tastes, though I noticed no one had asked me my opinion.

"Bonnie's here to help us figure something out. Troy's here because I prefer the odds with him around. Him and Goldie."

"Figure what out?"

"These people learned the truth about Angela somehow. I assume, based on what you've told me so far, it's not something you've told anybody?"

"Of course not. I've told no one. *No one.*"

"So that leaves one other possibility. Do you keep files about her case on your computer?"

She reddened. "A few. Some documents. I didn't think—"

I raised my hand. "No one's blaming anyone. But it makes it conceivable you were hacked. That's the only thing I can think of." Bonnie nodded.

"I'm very careful," Barbara protested. "I have to be."

"Everyone is. But it's like the feds say about fighting terrorists. You have to bat a thousand keeping your laptop secure. Hackers only have to crack the code once." I turned to Bonnie. "Let's assume she's been infiltrated. Is that something you could detect?"

"Depending how good they are, probably. And if she was, there's all kinds of debugging software I can use. But given the circumstances, it might just be easier to start completely over."

"What do you mean?"

"Everything. Totally new laptop. Just junk the old one."

Barbara shook her head. "I couldn't. All my files—the information on Angela. School things."

"I figured as much," Bonnie said. "It's OK. I can find a way around that. But if we can isolate those files, it still might make sense to get a new laptop, just to be sure."

The counselor nodded, accepting the reality, though I could tell she wasn't happy about it.

"You know about phishing?" Bonnie said. "People send you fake e-mails with links that hide viruses—"

"Yes, yes, of course," Barbara said impatiently. "The district is very strict about that. We get reminders constantly."

"I think it's still a possibility, since like Andy says, they only have to succeed once and they've gotten quite sophisticated. They phish the e-mail of someone you know, ask to share a Google doc, and it's game over. It's even happened to me. But let's think about other possibilities."

"Such as?" Barbara said.

"Do you go out with your laptop a lot?"

"What do you mean?"

"Libraries, coffee shops, that kind of thing."

"Very rarely. Why?"

"Public wireless can be just as dangerous. Even more so, because the connection isn't really secure."

I thought about the number of times I'd sat in coffee shops in recent years working off free wireless, including at Tim Horton's just the other day. It made my job infinitely easier, especially at times I'm on the far side of town and won't be home for hours.

"There is one place," Barbara said after a moment. "I went there once after school, this spring. A meeting ran late and I had an early evening event at church. Angela was home doing homework, so I felt all right about it. Of course, this was before everything happened."

"Anything suspicious when you were there?" Bonnie said.

The counselor shook her head. "I didn't stay. I was disappointed, because I had a lot to do and I wanted a chance to sit by myself out of the office, away from the school environment. But as soon as I walked in I knew it wouldn't work."

"Why not?" I said.

"It was full of students. It was a popular place. It's in a strip mall near the high school. All the conversation stopped when I entered. I smiled and waved, but I felt too self-conscious. I bought myself a coffee and left."

I recalled something Mike Parsell, Abdi's teammate, had said about a coffee shop all the students hung out at. "OK," I said, disappointed.

"I happened to mention it to Helene the next day. She laughed and said I'd walked into the Ninth Period."

"Ninth Period?"

"That's what they call the place, apparently. Because so many students go there after school to drink coffee while they log back into their lives. They're desperate for a connection after a day without. It's ironic, when I think about it now."

"Why?"

"Because Abdi Mohamed was one of the students I saw there that day. He and Faith Monroe and a couple other kids were sitting at a table, their laptops open, doing homework."

33

I SHOVELED A FORKFUL OF BURRITO INTO my mouth. Making sure Troy wasn't looking, I pinched a wad of egg and sausage and slipped it discreetly under the table. Goldie took it, kindly leaving my fingers intact.

I said, "Did you talk to them? Any students?"

"No. As I said, it was an awkward situation."

"So you must have been hacked some other way—"

"Back to Abdi, then," Bonnie interrupted.

"What about him?" I said.

"Maybe he's the one who got hacked after all."

"But how?"

"I've got some theories. The problem is, teens are extremely vulnerable, despite how tech-savvy they seem. They take everything digital and Internet-related for granted, like it's just there—like air or something, and nothing could possibly go wrong."

"But why would someone hack Abdi?" Barbara said.

"I'm not sure," I said. "But other than the feds, whose job it is to doubt everyone, I haven't run across a single person who thinks what he was posting was in character. Maybe someone hacked his account and put that stuff up in his name."

"But why?" Barbara repeated.

"To get him in trouble?" Bonnie said, spooning up some egg and sausage that had slipped free of the burrito. "Because they hate Muslims or something?"

"But if that's true, why would he disappear?" the counselor said. "Wouldn't it be easier for someone to post those false things and wait for him to be arrested?"

"That's what makes this case so perplexing," I said. "A kid with no animosity toward anyone and no reason to go anywhere does the two things most contrary to his personality. And nobody can explain why."

Bonnie interrupted. "Did you get e-mails from Abdi after that day?"

Barbara thought about it. "Probably. Yes, I'm sure of it. He had a lot of questions about Ohio State and his classes. And later, telling me how upset he was about Hassan."

"That could be it," Bonnie said. "If someone had control of Abdi's computer, it would have been much easier to hack into yours. And it wouldn't have had to be a link. They could have booby-trapped a document. Anything."

Barbara nodded. "He sent me documents, yes."

Bonnie looked at me. "I'll have to take her laptop, check it out to be sure. But we may have our answer."

I suddenly thought of Ronald McQuillen, attacking his keyboard in the darkness of the Garden. The way he'd reached out to me unsolicited after the attack. The document he'd sent me about the '76 Sentries. Calling him a quirky fellow was like observing giraffes had long necks and spots. But was there more to his interest in me than met the eye? Was it possible—

The doorbell rang. Barbara started. "More friends of yours?" she said.

"Not that I'm aware of."

"Otto?" Theresa said.

"I don't think so," I said, pulling out my phone. Additional texts from Kym and Crystal and now Anne, wondering about Red,

White & Boom. But no one else. "He had a full morning. That's why I let him go home last night. Are you expecting anyone?"

"No," Barbara said, color leaving her face.

"Stay here. Call 9-1-1 if anything sounds off."

The comment went to Theresa, Bonnie, and Troy. Barbara was already out of the kitchen and bounding up the stairs.

I walked into the living room, Theresa and Bonnie close behind, phones at the ready. Behind them Troy, standing beside Goldie, fingers brushing her collar. I reached down and retrieved my bat from the couch. I approached the door. "Stand a little ways back in case I need some swinging room," I said without turning around.

"Has that thing ever helped you?" Theresa said.

"Let's try to keep this positive, shall we?"

I unbolted the lock, turned the knob, and pulled the door open quickly.

Helene Paulus stood on the doorstep, shock filling her eyes.

"You!" she said.

34

"THERE'S ANOTHER POSSIBILITY," BONNIE SAID.

"Like what? Me getting sued by the Columbus school board?"

"OK. Maybe two possibilities."

A couple hours had passed. We were sitting at Scarlet & Gray Grounds, the coffee shop favored by Maple Ridge High students. The Ninth Period.

"Something more sophisticated," Bonnie said. "Something I didn't want to mention back there. At the counselor's house."

"What is it?"

"It's scary, is what it is."

Explaining our presence at Barbara's to Helene Paulus after the principal's unexpected arrival without giving up the counselor's secret had nearly rivaled our derring-do outside the warehouse the night before. Helene had been about as pleased with our stony silences and monosyllabic responses as an actor discovering on opening night her role has been axed. Somehow I talked our way out of it, apologizing and prevaricating and suggesting we talk again in a day or five. Eventually, Helene acquiesced in my request to leave, though not without pointedly asking Barbara more than once—all the time glaring at me—if she was really all right. Theresa, Bonnie, and I left soon after, taking Theresa to the airport to retrieve her car before we headed to the coffee shop. Troy and Goldie were still at Barbara's house, taking the first shift of guard duty. I wasn't convinced we had anything to worry about for now, but it made me feel better knowing they were there.

Scarlet & Gray Grounds was tucked between an AT&T store and a bargain basement haircut place in a newish strip mall off Stelzer Road. While Bonnie got her laptop up and running I went to the counter and ordered us coffees from a young barista dressed in jeans, suspenders, and a white T-shirt, sporting a full beard and with his hair knotted into a tight bun on top of his head. He looked like someone from Planet Lumberjack in a Buck Rogers movie. When I sat down beside Bonnie with our drinks she was typing with a fury that would have done Ronald J. McQuillen proud.

"Scary how?" I said.

"What happens is that people set traps in places with public wireless. Coffee shops are ground zero for this kind of thing."

"How's it work?"

"They start by creating a wireless network with a similar name and a fake SSID number and trick you into logging onto that instead. Once you do, they're in your system and you're hosed. It's called an Evil Twin attack."

"Sounds like a blind date I was on once," I said. "But not sure I follow."

"Well, take this place. Their wireless connection is 'SGGroundsNetwork.' I'm not seeing anything out of the ordinary now. But if someone was serious about it, they might create something like 'SGGroundsNetwork1.' Something like that."

"But you're not detecting anything today?"

"Just a bunch of people using their iPhones as hot spots. Which also is kind of risky."

I took in our fellow patrons. The place was filled with twenty-somethings feverishly engaging with the virtual world in one form or another. I thought of a probably apocryphal story I'd read of a man in line at the grocery store trying to catch the eye of the woman ahead of him, only to give up after realizing she was too engrossed in writing a Facebook post on her phone lamenting how hard it was to meet guys. None of the people in the coffee shop looked like hackers to me; except that all of them did, if I was being honest about it.

"OK. Wait here," I said.

I stood up and went back to the counter. I gestured at Lumberjack Man.

"'Sup?"

I handed him my card. "Hoping you can help me. I'm trying to find a guy." Or gal? Who knew? "He's been messing with wireless connections around town."

He examined the card with interest. "Messing how?"

"Trying to hack people."

"Who is it?"

"Not sure." I described Mike and Todd Bowden to him. He shook his head. I thought about JaQuan Williams, then realized I had no idea what the gangbanger looked like. For the heck of it, I described McQuillen.

"Like, older guy?" he said. "Like you?"

"Something like that. Forties maybe. A bit, ah, disheveled. Drinks a lot of Mountain Dew, which I take it you don't serve here?"

He made a face. "Not that stuff. We have some artisanal sodas if you want."

"I'm a grape pop man myself."

He made another face. "It does kind of ring a bell, this guy. Most of the people in here are a lot younger than that. Maybe if I saw a picture. You think I should let my manager know? Like, is there a problem?"

"I don't think so. I'm pretty sure it was a one-time thing. Any idea when he was here?"

"I'm not really sure. Maybe a couple months ago?"

The timing was right for Barbara getting hacked. But the vague nature of the barista's response wasn't sounding like something that would stand up in court anytime soon.

"If you see him again by any chance, or anybody similar, could you give me a call?"

"Sure. No problem."

I returned to the table and reported the conversation to Bonnie.

"You think it could be this guy McQuillen?"

"I don't know. It's the only person with a connection to any of this that seemed to jog his memory."

"But why would he be involved with Abdi?"

"No idea. I think this is pointless. It could be anyone."

Pulling out of the parking lot a few minutes later, I pondered the notion that Abdi was innocent of the dark postings he'd placed on Facebook and tweeted after his brother's death. If someone had used this fake SSID number to take over his computer, as Bonnie explained, it would back up what everyone was saying about him; the surprise they were expressing. The problem was, it was hardly the whole story, given the firebombing at Mount Shiloh Baptist. That one was a lot harder to explain away.

ABUKAR ABDULKADIR INTERRUPTED, SHAKING his head over what I'd just told him.

"Abdi. Dating the minister's daughter? You cannot be serious, Andy Hayes."

"It's the truth."

"And you think that had something to do with his disappearance?"

"I don't know. The family's not talking—the mom and the daughter, anyway. The father knows how bad it looks, but I'm not sure what he's going to do about it."

We were sitting over plates of goat stew and flatbread inside Hoyo's Kitchen off Cleveland Avenue a few hours later. Abdulkadir had called me shortly after I left the coffee shop, explaining that Abshiro Ali, the school friend of Abdi's, had agreed to speak with me. We settled on the Somali restaurant as a meeting place. Before I entered I sat in the parking lot and listened to a long voicemail from Helene Paulus, asking again if there wasn't any way I'd reconsider and tell her what was going on. I thought about it. I decided there wasn't.

"I will tell you this," Abdulkadir said. "That minister is not friendly to Muslims. It's boys from his church who threw rocks at the mosque. He did little to stop it."

"Could that have motivated Abdi to attack Mount Shiloh?"

"I would hope not. That's nothing like who the family says he was. Who he is."

"I think we've established that. You know the community well, though. That must be going through people's minds. Not to mention the minds of the feds."

"It is likely," Abdulkadir said sadly.

"One other thing." I told him about my conversation with Patty Bowden, and how it appeared her brother and nephew were the men who attacked Kaltun Hirsi. He nodded, but not with the enthusiasm I'd expected.

"And now the police will be able to find them?" he said.

"Maybe. Except the only reason I know who they are is because they're missing."

"It will be good to locate them." He took a sip of his Somali tea. "To ensure that justice is done."

"Indeed," I said, waiting for him to continue. But he stared moodily out the window, unresponsive.

A minute later Abdi's friend came through the door. Abdulkadir introduced us. I started explaining what I wanted to know.

"You're wasting your time," the teen interrupted. "I don't know anything."

"I take it you were surprised when he disappeared."

"Yes. It wasn't like him."

"In what way?"

"He's a goofball, you know? Not like his brother." He was thin, dressed in jeans and a Cavaliers shirt.

"Which brother?"

"Hassan, of course. Who else?"

"He has another brother."

He waved dismissively. "Aden isn't part of this. He's too serious. And dutiful. He wouldn't hurt a flea."

Aden and Hassan, making Abdi the third brother. Idly, I recalled Ronald McQuillen's tale of David Derwent and the right-wing theology of "Seth," the brother of Cain and Abel. I shook my head. I was starting to see highly unusual coincidences everywhere.

I explained what I'd learned about Abdi's girlfriend. "Did his family know?"

"No," Ali said, sullenly. "They wouldn't have approved."

"So how did Abdi and Faith manage it?"

"They saw each other in school. Or at his games. That was easy, since Faith's brother played on the team."

"Could Abdi have gotten mad at the family? Mad enough to do something to her father's church?"

"Abdi? No way."

I thought of the ominous posting on a message board after the church fire. *This is only the beginning.* I said, "Ever heard of a guy named JaQuan Williams?"

He frowned. "I know who he is."

"Ever see him and Abdi together?"

"A couple times, in the halls or something. But they didn't hang out. JaQuan was a bad dude. He and Hassan were buddies for a while. Until Hassan, you know . . ."

"Have you seen this guy around?"

"Not since school's been out."

"I heard the police were looking for him."

"Good for them. He's gonna be hard to find."

We chatted for a few minutes longer, and then he excused himself abruptly and left. I was no expert on teenagers, but Abshiro was either the world's greatest liar or was in the same boat as everyone else—clueless about his buddy's disappearance. I told Abdulkadir what I was thinking.

"I do not believe Abdi is a terrorist," Abdulkadir said. "And I do not believe that this relationship is connected to what happened."

"Odd coincidence, though."

"Yes," he said reluctantly.

"And it gives him a motive, for the church fire, anyway."

He conceded it.

"Have you known the family long?"

"Yes. That's why I was happy to help with everything."

"You've been here a while?"

"More than twenty years."

"Before that?"

He bowed his head, focusing on his food. "Kenya. A refugee camp. Very difficult. Harsh conditions. This is home now."

"Is all your family here?"

"Many."

"Any in Minneapolis? Isn't that the biggest population in the country?"

"I have a brother there, yes."

"Do you ever see him?"

A pause. "Once a year, perhaps. On one of my trips, if it's on the route."

"Route?"

"My work. I drive a truck most days, during the week."

"A truck?"

"A shipping truck, yes. It's my business."

"Where do you drive?"

He still wouldn't meet my eyes. "All over the Midwest. Detroit, Chicago, Indianapolis. Kentucky, West Virginia. And of course Ohio."

"What's in your truck?"

"Everything, Andy Hayes," he said, looking up, the slightest hint of annoyance on his face at all the questions. "Furniture, appliances, shipments of clothes. Whatever they need transported."

"Is that something you did before?"

"Before?"

"In Somalia."

"The roads in Somalia are not like here. There would not be room for such big trucks."

"So what did you do? Before the civil war?"

"Many things. Many things. You did what you could to survive in those days. Even before the war, jobs were becoming scarce."

"Would you ever go back?"

"To Somalia?" He took a bite of goat and added a large spoon-ful of rice. He chewed for a minute. "I have been back, a couple of times, to see family. But permanently? I don't think so. It's very dangerous still. There are some very bad people there. Al-Shabaab— you've heard of them?"

I nodded. Given the size of Columbus's Somali community, I'd read enough stories over the years about the efforts, largely successful, to keep youth here from joining the terrorist group back home.

"I appreciate all your help," I said. "But we may be near the end of the case."

"What do you mean?"

"Once the feds find out about Abdi and Faith, it could change everything. Probably make things worse for him. The only good news is, I'm guessing he'll turn up sooner rather than later, now. That the farthest he got was a couple blocks from his girlfriend's house, and he's just living under the radar here. Who knows? Maybe he's hanging with this JaQuan kid."

"I don't think that's possible," Abdulkadir protested.

"We've got to look at the facts. And they aren't good right now."

36

ON MY WAY BACK HOME I STARTED HAVING doubts again about Abdi and Faith Monroe. Their relationship and the hostility he likely faced from her parents gave him motivation, however irrational, to attack the church. Yet I still felt as if I were missing something. As though—there was no other way to put this—the solution was too easy. Boy meets girl. Girl's parents object. Grieving boy-turned-extremist lashes out. Voila.

What wasn't I seeing?

I took Hopalong for a long walk when I got home, feeling guilty at ignoring him so much in recent days. The air was muggy and still. At Schiller Park I passed a few other dog walkers. Over on the tennis courts somebody was having a good match despite the heat of the day. The repetitive thwock of the ball hit back and forth across the net continued for several volleys at a time. I tugged Hopalong in that direction to take a look. A man and a woman were battling it out, nearly evenly matched. A couple of guys watched, intent on the game.

Back home, I was hanging up the leash on its brass hook in the kitchen when my phone rang.

"You said you were coming."

It took me a moment. Patty Bowden. Wanting help finding her missing brother and nephew. A fool's errand forty-eight hours earlier. Now? I thought of the word Angela heard during her captivity. *JJ's.* Suddenly I was interested.

"Right. I'm sorry. Something came up."

"Like what? You promised."

"Give me the directions again. I'll be right there."

I PARKED BESIDE HER double-wide trailer down a country road off U.S. 40 just under an hour later. Her house backed up to a wide soybean field, the bushy dark-green plants approaching knee level with July almost here. In the distance, cottonwoods following a river snaked in a curving line along the edge of the field. "Don't Tread On Me" said a yellow flag with a depiction of a segmented snake that hung from a pole at the front of Bowden's house.

The woman who answered the door looked to be in her mid-fifties and feeling every day of it. She had graying blond hair she kept pulled back in a ponytail like a schoolgirl. She moved slowly— even more slowly than Freddy Cohen—and like him used a cane. "MS," she said flatly, and waved away any further conversation on the topic. She was wearing jeans and a loose-fitting pullover beige blouse. The inside of the home was tidy, but the furniture looked worn and the counters in the kitchen had bare patches here and there where the linoleum had worn through. Still, it would have been three degrees from cozy but for a pair of Yorkshire terriers that crouched at her ankles and yapped incessantly at my presence. They were as comforting as broken smoke alarms you can't silence when Dad's trying to nap in the other room. The dogs made their displeasure clear as I followed Bowden into the living room and sank at her instruction into a red recliner whose springs felt as if they'd seen better decades. The dogs hopped on a couch beside Bowden, taking up glowering stances on either side like tiny macramé gargoyles.

"When you called," I began, "I wasn't sure this was something I had time for. But some things changed recently."

"Things like what?"

Without divulging the details of the warehouse escapade, I mentioned the word "JJ's" and the fact it appeared her brother and nephew, based on the false license plate and her nephew's tattoo, were militiamen or Sovereign Citizens or both. I looked at her for confirmation. The dogs eyed me suspiciously. I wondered whether they'd make even a single meal for Goldie.

"Yeah, that's right," Bowden said after a moment. "They're Sentries, whatever that means. What about it?"

"Nothing, I guess. Unless it has something to do with 'JJ's' and that has something to do with what happened to them."

"Don't know nothing about 'JJ's.' But I do know those two are a couple of nitwits. Too lazy to get a driver's license and too cheap to pay taxes, and all of sudden they're antigovernment protesters. Real convenient."

"You don't agree with that movement?"

"Didn't say that, did I, soldier?"

"Then what?"

"I don't agree with what a cock-up my brother's made of his life, excuse my French. I couldn't care less if aliens were probing his butt or he believed in the Ohio Grassman, long as he cleaned up his own shit. Which he didn't, of course."

37

I GLANCED AROUND THE ROOM. AT THE far end a framed painting of a Civil War battle hung over a fake fireplace, the blues and the grays caught up in a smoky swirl of mortal combat. Paperbacks and hardcovers about the Civil War lined the shelves of a small bookshelf to the right of the couch. I recognized a bunch of novels by John Jakes and Michael and Jeff Shaara, but also the Shelby Foote histories. On the top shelf sat a small walnut frame holding what appeared to be an authentic Civil War musket ball nestled on a bed of red velvet.

"Ohio Grassman?"

"Local legend," she said. "Like Bigfoot, only smellier. And a vegetarian, which doesn't seem likely if it's from Ohio. Anyway, I didn't call you because of what they believe. I need them found."

"Why? No offense, but you don't seem like you're all that close."

"We're not. But we're family, for what that's worth. Plus Mike owes me five thousand dollars, which believe me is the last money I'll ever lend him. I need it back plus the interest he promised. I'll give you five hundred once you find him."

"I'm not sure—"

"OK—seven hundred, but that's it. I've got repairs I need done around here and no man to do them, and I'm two payments late on my truck. I'm not made of money, like you people over in Columbus."

I said a little prayer for my lost groceries and let the comment go. "What if I find him and he doesn't want to come back?"

"You leave that to me. Once I know where he is I'll make sure he listens to reason."

I sat back and considered the offer. Patty Bowden didn't seem like the kind of woman who could afford to shed seven hundred dollars, even from a payback that large. Assuming her brother even had the money, which seemed about as likely as him making a donation to a local mosque anytime soon. But to tell the truth, it wasn't the money I was interested in right at the moment.

"Back to 'JJ's.' Sure it doesn't ring any bells?"

"Like I said, don't mean nothing to me. Mike had been running over to Brenda Renner's a lot recently. I told him to leave the old woman alone. But he wouldn't listen. You could ask her."

"Who's that?"

"Used to be a midwife, back in the day. Home births were real popular with those militia types in the seventies and eighties. Nobody wanted nothing to do with hospitals. Plus no one had insurance, of course."

"Why'd your brother go to see her?"

She gave an exasperated sigh. "Rumor was she ran with a big-deal antigovernment type once upon a time. Delivered babies for his followers. I'm not sure half the shit they say about her is true, excuse my French again. But she's got a little shop people like to hang out in and listen to war stories."

"Who was it?"

"Who was what?"

"This guy she ran with."

"Nobody you'd know. Fellow named David Derwent."

"Derwent—the Third Brother guy?"

She looked at me, surprised. The Yorkies launched themselves onto their feet, bristling like electrified mopheads.

"You've heard of him?"

"A little bit. He's the one who killed the prosecutor. John McQuillen. And then blew himself up two days later."

"That's him, all right."

"Weren't there rumors about him fathering children with his followers? Were those the babies this lady delivered?" I told her the story McQuillen had relayed of a girl—a young woman—who'd died in childbirth along with her baby.

She shrugged. "Who knows? And who knows if any of it's true? Brenda left town at some point, so it probably couldn't have happened anyway. Plus, some people say Derwent killed deer with his bare hands and ate their hearts by moonlight. Hard to know what to believe."

"Where's this shop?"

"Couple miles down the road. It's in an old converted garage. Her son has a little repair place next door. Kind of junky looking, you ask me."

"Maybe I'll check it out. But—"

"But what?"

"The thing is. If I find your brother, and his boy, I'm going to have to tell the police. I don't care about what happened to me. But they attacked that woman. I can't just let that go—and neither can the cops."

She shook her head wearily and shifted herself, trying to get comfortable. The Yorkies shifted with her, scrambling for purchase on her lap. "Fat lot of good it's going to do me, them sitting in jail and no way to get my money back."

"I understand. I just wanted to be upfront with you."

"You ain't going to get paid either, that happens."

"I suppose that's right."

She sighed. Her shoulders sagged and she aged almost before my eyes. It occurred to me she'd probably spent much of her life cleaning up after her ne'er-do-well brother. It would get to you after a while. I should know. I'd seen the same look on my own sister's face, more than once.

She said, "I'll make your share a thousand if you call me first. But that's as high as I can go."

"You really don't—"

"I'm not saying you can't call the police, all right? I'm just saying call me first. Give me a couple hours. I just need to get my money. After that, you can call the CIA or the KGB or whoever the hell you want to get ahold of. I just want two hours first. Is that so much to ask?"

I eyed the Yorkies, who were poised for attack again. I'd seen friendlier-looking Tasmanian devils.

"It's not too much," I said at last.

38

THE LIGHTS WERE ON AT THE SHOP
Bowden had described when I pulled up a few minutes later.
Brenda's Books 'n Things sat at the end of a gravel drive, and
looked—as Bowden had suggested—like it started life as an old
stone-block Sinclair gas station. At some time in the past the station's familiar white-and-red color scheme had been replaced
by a coat of baby-blue paint now starting to fade in places. Blue
seemed to be a theme with the place, from the paint job to the
hand-lettered sign over the door to the painted bluebirds in little
nests that formed the O's in "Books." A sign on the trailer to the
side of the shop advertised the son's repair business. Behind the
store the driveway swooped farther up a small incline to a large
pole barn. My van joined four other vehicles. The compound
looked like something you often see in rural Ohio, a conglom-
eration of small businesses lumped together on a single piece of
property, the sum of whose parts adds up to just enough of a
whole to spell economic survival.

The inside smelled of mildew and candles and coffee. A couple other customers browsed the shelves, which looked heavy on

Beanie Babies, porcelain figurines, and paint-by-number kits, and light on books other than fat paperback copies of Ludlum and Clancy and Patterson thrillers. Midway down the shelves several wooden bins held heaps of wrapped hard candy. Brenda—she acknowledged her name with a smile when I inquired—was sitting at a counter at the back that was crowded with paper and trinkets. She was reading a devotional of some kind. The smile turned to a frown when I presented my card and explained the purpose of my visit and my search for Mike and Todd Bowden.

"I know who Mike is," she said in a voice barely above a whisper. "I haven't seen him in a while."

"How about his boy?"

"He was never here that much."

"Do you have any idea where they might have gone?"

She looked around the shop, as if hoping to find the answer on one of the shelves. She appeared to be in her late sixties or even early seventies. But despite the reading glasses perched on her nose, she had a youthful demeanor in a spacey, once-a-flower-child sort of way, as though she wouldn't look out of place teaching yoga on a beach in California. She wore a simple denim dress with her long, gray hair plaited down her back.

"I really don't," she said vaguely. "I'm sorry I can't help you."

"Patty said you midwifed, back in the day."

"Did she?" she said with a faint smile.

"She also said you knew David Derwent. And that Mike liked to come by and hear the stories."

It took her a few seconds to respond, and when she did her voice was even quieter. "That was all a long time ago. I can't remember half of it myself."

"You were a midwife, though?"

Another long pause while she looked around the shop. "I delivered a lot of babies under strange conditions back then. Sometimes you didn't really know who or what was up, or even their names. It was cash only and the fewer questions, the better. Like I said, it was a long time ago."

"Do you still deliver babies?"

She shook her head with a smile.

"Did you know Derwent?"

"A little. I knew who he was. A good man. He paid me if people didn't have the money for my services."

"People? Like his followers?"

"I don't know anything about that."

"Really?"

"Was there anything else?" she said softly.

"Yes. Mike Bowden mentioned a place called 'JJ's.' Or maybe a person. Does that mean anything to you?"

"I'm sure it doesn't."

A tinkle of a bell as the door to the shop opened. A man walked in wearing a blue work shirt and work pants.

"Ma. You got a second?"

"Trey," Brenda said, her face brightening. "Maybe you can help this gentleman. He's asking about Mike Bowden."

"Hey, how's it going? Trey Renner." He approached and shook my hand. His was the first in a while whose grip wasn't north of finger-numbing. He had a funny, bowl-shaped haircut that made him look vaguely Amish, and a thin, angular face. His smile was easygoing and open.

"Not too bad." I looked between the two of them. "You're her—?"

"Son and chief troublemaker, that's me. What can I do for you?"

I reviewed my run-in with the Bowdens and Patty's request that I try to find them.

"Mike Bowden's a bit of a loose cannon," Renner said. "He liked to come in here and stir things up. I asked him more than once to leave. I am not surprised, what happened to you with them."

"So that doesn't sound out of character?"

"Not really. His son, Todd—he's the real hothead. But Mike is no slouch in that department."

I gave him the same spiel about JJ's. If it meant anything his face didn't show it.

"Don't know. Perhaps a bar? There used to be a JJ's Tavern down by McConnelsville, but I think it's closed now."

I glanced at Brenda. She was back to studying her devotional. I said, "Patty mentioned her brother liked to come over and talk to your mom about David Derwent. About the old days."

Brenda murmured, without looking up, "I told him that was a long time ago. It's like another life."

"That is about it," Renner said, slowly. He dug his hands into the back pockets of his pants. "Bowden had big ideas about government, about all the problems in the country. All that militia talk. He thought it was better back in the day. Back in the seventies and eighties. But it wasn't like what he made it out to be. It was just a bunch of hippies running around the woods. Isn't that right, ma?"

"Something like that."

"But—if I can just ask," I said, directing the question to Brenda. "The babies that you delivered. Did any of them, you know, belong to Derwent?"

"Listen," Renner interrupted. "I'm not trying to be obnoxious or anything. But that's the kind of thing Bowden kept asking. And what I'm trying to say is my mom really doesn't want to talk about it."

"I'm sorry. I'm not trying to make trouble. All I want is to figure out where Bowden went. Bowden and his boy. The only reason I brought that stuff up is because he did, apparently."

"And I am telling you she doesn't want to talk about it." Spoken in his same slow cadence, but now his smile tightened for the first time since he entered the shop.

"There's also a story out there that a girl died in childbirth. Her and her baby. Is that true?"

"I told you—"

I held up my hand to interrupt him. I could tell from the look in his eyes I'd crossed a line.

"It's OK. I get it. I gave your mom my card. If you have any idea where Mike Bowden might have got himself to, either of you, can you let me know?"

"Sure," Renner said. "But I wouldn't hold your breath. Not with those two."

I thanked them and left them at the counter. I browsed for a couple minutes, finally pulling a Kevin O'Brien thriller off the shelf to buy, just to be neighborly. Brenda thanked me but didn't say more. Outside, Renner was waiting for me by my van. I walked up to him and took in the view. The compound overlooked a cornfield across the road that could have swallowed up a dozen high school football stadiums, a hardwood forest beyond that, lush treetops nearly black in the dimming light of dusk.

"Nice out here."

"God's country," Renner said.

"How's business?" I nodded at his repair shop.

"Booming."

"Really?"

"Sure. Everybody's got a coffee pot or a washing machine or a computer on the fritz, and nobody wants to drive into town to get it fixed."

"Good opportunity, then."

"I suppose so. People don't know how to repair their own stuff anymore. Bad for them, good for me."

"Listen, thanks for the help. Sorry to bug your mom."

"It's OK, pal. The thing is." He glanced behind him, back to the shop. "She's had some memory issues lately, doesn't remember things so well. And when she doesn't, she gets upset. That's why I was trying to cut you off. I've got to look out for her."

"Mike Bowden wasn't helping much, I'm guessing."

"Yes," he said, a kind of formal relief in his voice. "That is what I was trying to say."

"Well, give me a call if you happen to hear anything."

"Will do. Be safe."

We shook hands and I pulled out of the parking lot and headed west, back to Columbus. Other than the paperback sitting on the seat beside me, I wondered how much I'd really gotten out of the past few hours, in the end. At this point, the chances of finding the Bowdens and getting Patty Bowden's money back for her were probably as good as finding Abdi Mohamed. Or the Ohio Grassman.

39

I WAS PULLING UP IN FRONT OF MY HOUSE
just short of an hour later when Helene Paulus called again. I decided to answer this time. We spoke as I unlocked the front door, went inside, opened a can of Black Label, and filled a small bowl with pretzels. Hopalong nosed at the back door and I let him out. I turned to the sink and filled a pot with water. I set it on the stove and lit the flame beneath it.

"I just wish somebody would tell me what's going on," Helene was saying. "Why you and those other people were at Barbara's house. I called her again this afternoon."

"What did she say?"

"Same as this morning. That you were just asking her a few questions. Which is absurd, that early in the day. And why was that dog there? The biggest one I've ever seen. Given how upset Barbara was the first time you stopped by, it doesn't make sense."

I opened my pantry door and pulled out a bag of penne. I tucked the phone between my right ear and shoulder and carefully tore open the bag.

"I'm sorry," I said. "Anything more will have to come from her."

"You've got to be kidding. Why all the secrecy?"

"It's just how it has to be, for now. But as long as we're on the subject." I asked her if she knew that Abdi Mohamed and Faith Monroe were dating.

"Who told you that?"

"A little bird I snooped on. So did you?"

"No. And I find it hard to believe."

"Why?"

"Just how things work, I guess. Abdi was pretty Americanized, but his family is still devoutly Muslim. And Faith's father is a minister, obviously."

"Montagues and Capulets?"

"Please. This is real life we're talking about."

"I agree. Just as I believe love is a many-splendored thing. But if it's true, what's interesting is the way it muddies the water when it comes to the firebombing. On the one hand, it gives Abdi a motive since her father was not exactly enamored with the idea of them being together. On the other hand, if Abdi really liked Faith, trying to destroy her father's church is a funny way to show it."

"Have you asked Barbara about this?" Helene said.

"We've discussed it."

"And?"

"Like I said, you probably need to talk to her."

"Let me get this straight. You can ask me questions about Abdi, but you won't tell me anything about what's going on with Barbara?"

"It's a fair point. There may come a time when I can explain more."

She didn't respond right away. I went to the fridge, pulled out a couple of brats from Schuman's meat market, cracked a second can of Black Label, dumped it into a skillet, and added the brats.

"She's grateful, you know," Helene said.

"Who is?"

"Barbara. I mean, that's the impression I got, whatever it is you're up to. I asked her if she wanted to file a complaint. With the police, for harassment."

"That was nice of you."

"The thing is, her reaction took me aback. It was as if I'd said something insulting. She said absolutely not. That you were a good man. That she didn't know what she'd do without you."

"She said that?"

"Her exact words. She just won't tell me what you did."

"And as I said—"

"So I guess thanks are in order. And an apology."

"For what?"

"For thinking the worst of you. Apparently you have one or two redeeming qualities. I just wish I knew what they were."

After I hung up I salted the water in the pot, waited for it to boil, then dumped in the pasta. I pulled a half-empty jar of Carfagna's marinara sauce from the refrigerator and threw the contents into another pan on low. I turned the heat down on the brats, covered them, went into the living room, and flipped on the TV. I surfed until I found a tennis match being played someplace overseas, which seemed the least boring thing of everything else on at the moment. My phone buzzed with a text. Abukar Abdulkadir, wondering about any updates on Mike and Todd Bowden. I replied with a terse Nothing new. I couldn't see the point of mentioning the gentleman's agreement I'd struck with Patty Bowden, that I'd call her first, before the police, once I located the two. If I located them. He didn't respond.

I watched a game and a half, stood up, went into the kitchen, drained the pasta, and turned the brats. I opened a third beer—technically only my second—and took a long pull. After another minute I turned the heat off under the brats, tossed them onto a plate with the pasta, added the marinara sauce, and went back into the living room. As I ate, I thought about my conversation with Abdulkadir in the restaurant earlier in the day. I thought about the anger and frustration local Somalis were feeling with the eyes of the law on them after Hassan Mohamed's treasonous trip to Syria, and now the allegations against Abdi. I thought about Mike Bowden and his son. For just a moment, I considered the possibility that someone from the Somali community had been a step or two ahead of me and the police and Patty Bowden, figured out who they were, and taken matters into his own hands. Maybe they weren't just missing. I took measure of the idea: was it all that far-fetched?

Most Somalis I knew were hardworking entrepreneurs, scrambling to make a buck like everyone else, and eager to put the violence they'd fled far behind them. But what if some rogue player from the authoritarian government that fell during the civil war had quietly acted on his own? I considered Abdulkadir's vague responses when I asked him what he did back home. Remembered that he drove a truck all over the Midwest. To West Virginia sometimes, which depending on how he went could mean passing Brenda's Books 'n Things. Passing the country road where Mike Bowden and his son lived.

At the rate my mind was starting to churn, I would have thought a lot more about the idea that night. I would have cracked a third beer for myself. But my phone vibrated with a text from Mike, and then one from Kym, and then another from Anne, and before I knew it the rest of the evening was spent on a flurry of preparations for Red, White & Boom. At this point the plan was to grab dinner at a food truck, watch the fireworks on the street, and then return to Ben's office to let the crowds thin out. He had a DVD player and a big-screen TV and plenty of movies and snacks and pop and beer for the adults. Of course he did. Why should I have expected anything less?

40

I CALLED HENRY FIELDING ABOUT MIKE and Todd Bowden as soon as I figured the first pot of morning coffee was on in the homicide desk's sixth-floor offices downtown. I gave him their names and a general idea of where they lived. It wasn't exactly a breach of my contract with Patty, I decided, since it wasn't like I expected to see her money anyway.

Next, I called Ronald McQuillen. As unlikely as his involvement in hacking Barbara Mendoza seemed, there were still plenty of unanswered questions in the Garden. He picked up on the tenth ring, and it was clear I'd awakened him. I apologized and, when I was sure I had his attention, reviewed my meeting with Patty Bowden. I told him the little I knew about her missing brother and nephew, and then explained about Brenda Renner and her son, Trey, and Brenda's Books 'n Things.

"There's a video," McQuillen said, clearing his throat.

"Of what?"

"The Ohio Grassman. I've seen a few seconds of it."

"Give me a break."

"It's true. I'm negotiating with somebody who knows somebody who took it. It's pretty convincing."

"So was Piltdown Man. Back to reality, if it's OK with you. Does any of what I told you ring any bells?"

"Yeah, it's interesting stuff," he said. I could tell from the way he'd lowered his voice that he was warming to the information I'd given him, despite the fact I'd awakened him at the crack of 8:30. "I can run some traps on the Bowdens. I've heard of Brenda Renner. I knew she knew Derwent, but God knows how much she really understood what he was up to. One thing, though, about what you said. The way you said she got paid?"

"In cash, yeah. What about it?"

"Well—" he started to say. My phone pinged with an incoming call. Freddy Cohen.

"Sorry. Other line. I need to take this."

"No problem," McQuillen said curtly. "It's not like I was doing anything before you called, other than sleeping."

"I'll call you back," I said, ignoring his sarcasm. "There's one other thing I need to talk to you about."

"I can hardly wait."

"We've got another problem," Cohen said when I'd disconnected with McQuillen and picked up his call. "Thanks to you, as usual."

"What now?"

"Morris just called. She wants to know what's going on at Abdi's counselor's house. Mendes?"

"Mendoza. Barbara Mendoza. Are they sitting on her?"

"I don't think so. Morris swung by for a follow-up interview. Said there were people there who wouldn't identify themselves. And something about a giant dog."

"That's Goldie. But Irish wolfhounds are bigger, for the record. Some of them are like ponies—"

"Fuck the Irish wolfhounds. What's going on?"

I paused. "It's a little complicated."

"Really? With you involved? What a surprise. Anyway—"

"Actually, it's really complicated."

I TOOK A MOMENT to compose myself. How was I supposed to explain the dilemma that Barbara Mendoza faced without betraying her and the deal we'd struck? My three days weren't up. But I realized I hadn't factored the FBI's continued interest in Barbara's connection to Abdi into my planning. Hadn't taken a lot of things into consideration, to be honest about it.

I decided to come clean. Maybe it was concluding that I couldn't sink any lower in Cohen's estimation because of how much he hated my guts anyway, because of his wife and the affair I'd uncovered. Maybe it was feeling like he deserved to know because of the connection to Abdi's disappearance—or at least the impression someone was trying to leave of the teen as a newly radicalized extremist. Maybe it was because I was exhausted from all the blind alleys. In any case, I ended up telling him everything, up to and including the night at the warehouse.

"Good God," Cohen said when I finished. "You've taken the phrase 'off the reservation' to a whole new level."

"It's not a pretty picture. Sorry."

"Not a pretty picture? It's Nightmare on Andy Street, for Chrissake. Anything else you've lied about up to this point?"

"Leaving stuff out is not the same as lying."

"Don't split hairs with me."

"That's rich, coming from you." Cohen's insistence on letter-of-the-law tactics on behalf of clients was legendary around the courthouse.

"How dare you—"

"Save it for closing arguments. I have another concern I want to share with you. As long as we're laying everything on the table."

"Another concern? You mean this gets worse?"

Ignoring the comment, I told him my suspicions about Abukar Abdulkadir.

"You can't be serious," Cohen said. "A Somali guy creeping around rural Ohio? He'd stick out worse than you attending a performance of *La Bohème*."

"Joke's on you. I went last year and no one noticed." Roy and Lucy had dragged me more or less kicking and screaming. To my surprise, I'd enjoyed it, though I hadn't rushed out to buy an Opera Columbus subscription quite yet. "I know it sounds crazy. But he had incentive and opportunity. He's on the road a lot, including over that way. I don't really know what he did before he came to the United States. Do you?"

"No. Does it matter?"

I said, "Life in Mogadishu made the Wild West look like a carnival ride by comparison, from what I gather."

"If you say so. I take it you have no evidence of anything?"

I acknowledged the point.

"Then for God's sake keep it under your hat. The last thing we need right now is to lose our connection to that community thanks to your conspiracy theories. Got it?"

"Sure, I get it. You can't stand me and don't believe anything I'm saying. But that doesn't mean I'm wrong, either. It's hard to discount anything right now. You have to see that."

"Meaning what, exactly?"

"Meaning it's hard not to wonder if a couple of yahoos getting their rocks off harassing Kaltun Hirsi isn't somehow connected to a couple of other guys in dime store masks forcing Barbara Mendoza to push an extremist agenda about Abdi. Unless it was the same two guys."

"Didn't you say you doubted that?"

"It doesn't seem likely, from what I remember of Mike Bowden. But whoever they are, they want to be damned sure Barbara sticks to the terrorist script. Which suggests at the very least they have a vested interest in perpetuating that story. Or worst-case scenario—"

"They had something to do with Abdi's disappearance."

"Hold the presses. We finally agree on something."

"Last time for everything," Cohen said.

"But the thing is, where's it get us?" I continued. "What do fake license plates and drooling over the third brother have to do with lone-wolf extremism?"

"The third what?"

I explained about David Derwent and the twisted theology involving "Seth" as a kind of Aryan super-sibling.

"Sounds pretty fucked up. But nothing I'm surprised by. Those types are seeing nothing but green lights these days. As far as they're concerned, it's open season if you're brown-skinned and have an accent."

I kept quiet. I knew Cohen was sensitive about the subject of militias, as he should be, since many of their beliefs involved anti-Semitism, sometimes lightly disguised, sometimes full in your face. Even in this day and age Cohen was still the target of the occasional slur. Not two months ago, the uncle of a murdered teenage girl had called him a "dirty Jew" in a courtroom hallway after Cohen successfully brokered a plea deal of thirty to life for his client instead of a possible death sentence.

"OK," I said after a moment. "It's all out there. The good, the bad, and a really ugly dog. I'm sorry I haven't been forthcoming. But the question now is, is any of this useful? Does it help our—*your*—case?"

"It's our case, Hayes."

"I'm surprised to hear you say that."

"Don't be. Because once this is over, we'll either walk free together or hang together. I can't condone any of what you've done, but you were right about one thing—the counselor has legitimate concerns when it comes to her daughter."

I stayed quiet again, not trusting myself to say anything that might ruin this split-second of harmony.

"Everything you've told me muddies the water, that's for certain," Cohen went on. "But here's the central problem: the fact that Abdi's on video throwing a Molotov cocktail at Mount Shiloh clears the water right back up, along with that message board threat that followed. I can proffer all this, for sure. See what they say. But I wouldn't cross my fingers."

"And what about Barbara Mendoza?" I said. "For all I know, she'll go underground the second she thinks her niece is in danger. The feds are going to weigh her story of being blackmailed with the fact she lied to government investigators during a terrorism investigation. Hell, they could charge her, too."

"Believe it or not, I get that," Cohen said. "But I'll have to come forward with all this eventually, and sooner rather than later. If nothing else, it lays the groundwork for an appeal. I can hold off for a couple of days. But not much longer."

"You're saying we're running out of time?"

"Oh, no. We're out of time. Only thing we've got now is the possibility you could do your job for once."

"What's that supposed to mean?"

"It means, would you please find that kid before it's too late?"

41

AFTER I HUNG UP I CHECKED IN WITH OTTO Mulligan, who'd tag-teamed with Troy and Goldie for the day shift at the counselor's house. He reported that with the feds gone all was quiet again, and that his hostess was feeding him more than enough to make up for any lost wages on his part. I told him to be wary of guys in suits and sunglasses pretending to deliver Amazon packages.

Despite Cohen's skeptical reaction to my suspicions about Abukar Abdulkadir, I decided it was time to have another talk with the Somali truck driver. He didn't pick up when I called. I knew he lived in the next apartment complex over from Abdi Mohamed's parents. With nothing else to do I drove there, figuring at the very least that if he wasn't around or on the road somewhere I could look up Abdi's sister, Farah, while I was in the neighborhood and see if she'd learned anything new. Abdulkadir didn't answer his door when I knocked. A neighbor who said he recognized me from the news suggested I try a coffee shop and restaurant in a large indoor Somali shopping center around the corner.

The Global Mall sits in the middle of a strip plaza on Morse Road on the north side, a part of town teetering on the brink of resuscitation after years of decline. Shops packed with scarves and dresses and jewelry fill the mall's interior, each business boasting a brighter and more colorful collection than the last. The air smelled of incense and cardamom and sweets. Women in their own scarves and dresses strolled down the aisles examining the clothes, which hung from floor-to-ceiling racks like the world's largest collection of exotic prom dresses. I made a circuit of the shops, looking around for Abdulkadir. I was paid scant attention, despite being the only white person there. Reaching the other side of the mall, I walked up to a small coffee shop where a line of men stood waiting to place orders. Looking around, I spied Abdulkadir sitting at a table with someone I didn't recognize. His eyes went wide when I approached.

"*See tahay,*" I said, having practiced the greeting.

"Andy," he said. "*Asalamalakim.* Peace be with you. What are you doing here?"

"We need to talk."

"Of course, of course. One moment please." He finished his conversation, stood, and directed me to two empty seats by the window overlooking the parking lot. When we were settled, he said, "What is it? Is something wrong?"

I decided just to come out with it. "Something I need to clear up. Your trucking. Did it happen to take you to eastern Ohio recently?"

He looked puzzled. "I was on route 70 last week, on my way to Wheeling. Why do you ask?"

"The men who harassed Kaltun Hirsi. I told you they're missing. I need to be sure you didn't—"

"Didn't what?"

I looked around the room. I was no longer being ignored. I regretted not taking a minute to order a cup of tea. I needed something to fortify me. "That you didn't have anything to do with their disappearance."

I registered the shock on his face as the impact of the question hit home.

"What are you saying?"

"It's just a question."

"You're saying I did something to them?"

"I have to ask. This case is getting stranger by the minute."

"How could I have done something to men whose names I didn't know? You are the one who told me their identities."

"Do you know the expression, leaving no stone unturned?"

"I have heard that. But I must tell you I am hurt." He leaned back in his chair, shaking his head. "I thought we were friends."

I recalled the offense Helene Paulus took at my tracking down Barbara Mendoza despite her declaration the counselor didn't want to speak to me. The pique in her voice at the perceived violation of some kind of rule of etiquette. I pondered what might have happened had I backed off, not visited, and not ended up leaving my card at Barbara's house for her to use later, to call me about Angela's kidnapping.

I said, "Being friends doesn't eliminate the need to ask questions like this. I'm sorry if I offended you. But I still feel—"

"Feel what?"

"I feel like there's something you're not telling me. What you said at the mosque that day. That if Abdi died because of gun violence or something, at least the community would be spared the suspicion of extremism. You can't really think that's right. And then there's the way you reacted the day of the fire, when those FBI cars rolled up. Like it was you that had something to hide, not Abdi."

He didn't speak for a minute or so, out of character for the normally chatty man. At last he raised his eyes to me. "Can I trust you, Andy Hayes?"

"Of course. I hope that's been clear all along."

"That has always been my feeling, my friend." He adjusted his tie, squeezing the knot so that it fit squarely against the bottom of his Adam's apple. "So, what I have not been telling you is that I think I am in trouble."

I got a funny feeling inside, as if I'd just opened a bill—a big one—for a credit card I'd forgotten I had. "What kind of trouble?"

"Trouble involving Abdi Mohamed."

"What about him?"

"I gave him money."

"Money? Why?"

"To . . . to help him on his journey."

I STARED AT HIM, trying to read his face. "You gave him travel money? You're not telling me—"

"No. *No.*" Vigorously shaking his head, like a man on the witness stand providing last-ditch testimony. "Nothing like that. He needed it for books, and other things. For Ohio State. He didn't have enough from his job at the grocery store, and he didn't want to ask his parents. Sammy, the youth coordinator you met at Masjid Omar, told me a little bit about his troubles. I decided on my own to assist him. I was more than happy to. I know how much this meant to him."

"How much are we talking?"

"One thousand dollars."

I couldn't help myself—I reached out, took his cup, and drank some tea. "It's a nice gesture. But I'm not seeing the significance."

"The significance is that I know the alternative, to not having money. To losing opportunity."

"I don't understand."

Now he was staring straight at me. "My nephew is one of those boys."

"Boys?"

"In Minneapolis. One of the ones that disappeared. That went back to Somalia. That joined al-Shabaab. My brother—he still doesn't know what happened. But it is not good. I thought—"

I nodded, his point dawning on me. "You thought by helping Abdi, it was a way to show your support for someone taking the opposite path."

"That's right. Because of my nephew. I thought I was doing the right thing. But then—he disappeared. And posted those things. And if he did take the money, and use it for other purposes—"

"And the feds connect you to your brother and nephew . . ."

He nodded sadly.

"Then this case just got a hell of lot more complicated."

"I am afraid so," Abdulkadir said.

42

I LEFT ABDULKADIR AT GLOBAL MALL, drove home, opened a beer, went into the backyard, and sat down heavily in my Adirondack. I tried to ignore how badly it needed a coat of paint. I reviewed the problems confronting me. These included, in order: the disappearance of Kaltun Hirsi's parking lot tormentors; the whereabouts of Abdi Mohamed; the blackmailing of Barbara Mendoza by a mysterious group connected to Mike and Todd Bowden; the future of Barbara's niece as a U.S. resident hanging in the balance; Abdulkadir's heavy-hearted confession; and me still without a date for prom.

I was distracted from national security concerns by a call from Kym about more Red, White & Boom arrangements, which led to another hour of my life I'll never get back while I worked the phone to juggle Mike's already busy summer schedules, add input from Joe's mom, Crystal, top it off with uncomfortable back-and-forth texts with Anne, and stir vigorously. I nearly cramped my thumbs promising all those team members that I wouldn't screw it up and I'd be there when I said I would. I didn't help my cause when I flatly turned down Anne's offer to give me her boyfriend's number so I could text him directly if it would make things any easier. It wouldn't. That was communication I needed like a hole in the head.

To add to the excitement, I got a bad-news call from Bonnie Deckard.

"It took me a while to find the spyware on Barbara's computer. But there's no question someone has control of her hard drive."

"Can you figure out who?"

"I'm working on it. But honestly, my immediate concern is you."

"Me?"

"It's possible you're infected too. With everything going on with this case."

"I haven't traded any e-mails with her. Nothing like that."

"I want to check your computer out anyway, just in case."

"Why? If I haven't been in touch with her electronically—"

"We're dealing with something big here, Andy. Everybody could be tainted."

I thought about telling her she was being paranoid. But was that fair, given the course this investigation had taken—the twin, possibly entangled threads of Abdi Mohamed's disappearance and the mystery men with an eastern Ohio connection stalking Barbara Mendoza? After I hung up, I rose with a groan of protest, saddled up my Odyssey, and drove to Linden, Bonnie's north-side neighborhood, with my laptop in tow. Goldie greeted me at Bonnie's door as if I were a long-lost master, but that might have had something to do with the dog treat Bonnie slipped into my hand.

Back in my van a few minutes later, I was debating whether to take a return trip to eastern Ohio, check in with Abdi's family, or just start a new life on St. Lucia, when I got a text message that I definitely didn't see coming.

We need to talk

It was Helene Paulus. *See what? That you fell down on the job?*

Topic?
Barbara Mendoza
OK
And her niece

PAULUS LIVED IN WORTHINGTON, THE
north-side suburb founded in 1803, a decade earlier than Columbus and don't you forget it. It was settled by immigrants from
the wilds of Connecticut, and its downtown of tiny shops and
restaurants and cozy streetlamps looked like something out of a
Currier and Ives illustration of old New England with a bunch of
Honda Fits and Toyota Priuses thrown in. I offered to come to her
house, but she suggested a nearby Old Bag of Nails instead. We
settled with pints of Seventh Son IPA in a back booth an hour
later. She sipped hers. I drained half of mine while studying her
studying me.

"So you know," I said.

She nodded. "Barbara told me this afternoon. I checked in
with her again, and I could tell she was upset. Mr. Hayes, I'm
sorry. When I think about what I said to you, the other day, the
morning I saw you at her house—"

"Listen," I said, taking another swallow of beer. "Most of my
friends call me Andy. Most of my enemies go with Woody. Time
to choose."

"Woody?"

"What everyone used to call me."

"Why?"

I looked at her to see if she was teasing. "You really don't know?"

She shook her head. So I explained, tentatively at first, then warming to the subject, how early in high school I'd been slapped with the nickname of the legendary Ohio State coach's first name. Not, as most people believed, because of my football prowess. Because, just as the real Woody Hayes lost his job when he slugged an opposing Clemson player at the end of the '78 Gator Bowl, I'd punched a player on another team in the state semifinals after he'd directed one too many racial slurs against a black teammate of mine.

"I'm doubly impressed. A knight in shining armor from an early age."

"If armor comes in aluminum foil, sure."

"Well, it didn't make your Wikipedia page, so it must be true. Fine. *Andy.* Anyway, Barbara told me what you did. How you saved Angela. You and your partners."

Partners. Theresa and Otto would like that. Like the Mod Squad with smart phones and weaponry.

"It's a bad situation," I said. "And we're going to have to go to the authorities soon. For Barbara's sake, but also for Abdi Mohamed's. It's gotten too crazy."

"But Angela—"

"That can be fixed, I think. It may be painful, and it may take a while. But the alternative is worse at this point. I know the FBI agent working on Abdi's case. She's got a hard heart and a harder ass. But that heart's in the right place. She doesn't give a shit about an innocent girl caught up in an immigration mess not of her own making, despite what the America First crowd says. The only thing she's interested in is protecting U.S. lives, and doing that means resolving Abdi's case, one way or the other."

"But how? No one knows where he is yet, right? And the firebombing—"

"The firebombing may be the flaming straw that ignited the camel's back, if you'll forgive the metaphor. Which is why we have to find him soon. Why *I* have to find him." Even as I said that, though, I recalled what Abdulkadir told me at the coffee shop about the money he'd given the teen. What if Abdi really wasn't here? What if he'd somehow made it overseas? I shook the thought away.

"Do you have any leads?"

I finished my beer and signaled for another. Helene took hers down to just below high tide.

"Honestly, the pickings are slim. I'm sure Faith Monroe's parents would love to put their God-fearing hands around his neck. But I don't think they know where he is. Whoever these guys are who kidnapped Angela might know, since they seem super interested in making sure no one messes with his new-found extremist reputation. But they're not exactly listed in the white pages."

"Is there, I don't know, anything I can do?"

"You can keep an eye on Barbara, for starters. Make sure she's OK. I mean, emotionally." I explained how Otto and Bonnie's boyfriend, Troy, along with Goldie the mastiff, were rotating security shifts. "And double down on your defense of Abdi if the feds come around again. If they continue hearing contradictory stories, it'll keep them guessing a little longer."

"If I may be frank?"

"Be my guest."

"If I seemed suspicious when you first came into school—"

I raised my eyebrows.

"OK. If I was a bitch. But I want to explain. It's because of how unsettling this whole episode has been. First Hassan, then Abdi. You have to understand, we have a lot of immigrants at Maple Ridge. Seventeen languages at last count. We're hypersensitive to these kinds of accusations."

"I can imagine. And for the record, I may not have acted the perfect gentleman myself."

"So we could both do with a turn at obedience school." She raised her pint with a smile and we toasted our newfound détente. "My point is we're walking around on broken glass over this. We had an expert on extremism come in this spring to talk to some government classes. It was like pulling teeth just to get central office permission."

"Who was it?"

"A very quirky guy. But he knew his stuff. Ronald something."

That got my attention. "Ronald McQuillen?"

"That sounds like him."

"Puts the D in disheveled? Drinks Mountain Dew like water if water was going out of business?"

She laughed. "Yes, definitely him. He was wearing a tie, if that counts for anything."

"It might. When was this?"

She thought about it. "April maybe."

"Before Abdi disappeared?"

"That's right."

"But also when his brother was allegedly abroad."

"I suppose, yes. Why?"

"I'm not sure exactly. I appreciate you telling me."

"Is something wrong?"

"I don't think so." I hesitated. "McQuillen contacted me out of the blue about the guys in the parking lot. Wanted to tell me about them, who he thought they really were. It just seems strange he was at your school, with everything else going on. Another coincidence that I can't tell means anything or not."

"A highly unusual one?"

"Well played," I said, and touched my glass to hers.

"If you don't mind me saying, I'm impressed with how calm you are about all this. You've got people's lives in your hands, but we might as well be sitting here discussing, I don't know—"

"The opiate epidemic?"

"Touché. But seriously. How do you manage it? And how'd you get into this kind of thing in the first place? I take it there's not a school."

"I'll spare you a joke about hard knocks. I thought you checked me out already." I repressed the memory of her throwing the reporter's murder in my face.

"Humor me."

So I gave her the abridged version, starting with the point-shaving scandal my senior year in college that led to prison time and consignment to the basement of public opinion in this football-crazed town. I followed with my ill-advised comeback attempt with the Browns, a decade or two of bad-boy behavior that culminated in a head-clearing summer on my uncle's pig farm. I finished up with the end-of-my-rope job for Burke Cunningham strong-arming witnesses to a murder on the east side that finally won me a path to gainful employment.

"Quite a story."

"That's one way to look at it. How about you?"

"What about me?"

"How'd you become a high school principal?"

She looked down at her hands. "Needed a change, I guess. I taught English for twenty years. My kids were in college by then, and I decided to try something else. Make a little more money." She paused. "After the divorce, to be perfectly honest about it."

"I've got a little experience in that arena, if it's any consolation."

"Thanks. I know."

"You do?"

"That stuff actually is on Wikipedia."

"Not my finest hours, I can assure you."

"For a big, bad, private detective, you're very self-deprecating."

"For someone who called me a snoop not so long ago, you're very forgiving."

She leveled her eyes at me. "Everyone makes mistakes. Right?"

"No argument there. So does this mean we're friends now?"

"If I decide we are, maybe."

"Lucky me."

She didn't reply and instead took another sip of her beer. She'd managed to drain nearly two fifths of it. I eased up and left my second pint half full.

"I don't mean to keep you," she said. "I appreciate you coming out like this. And again, I want to thank you for helping Barbara."

"I'm glad we're on the same page finally."

"Me too."

I paid for our drinks, and walked her around to the back of the restaurant to a municipal parking lot that served several of the businesses in Worthington's annoyingly quaint downtown. Night had fallen. It was warm out and the air was muggy with a hint of summer sulfur in it, as though it might storm.

"This is me," she said, stopping beside a red mini-SUV. "Thanks again. I'm really grateful."

"You're welcome."

She put her key in the lock but didn't open the door. Her eyes lingered on my face. Mine lingered back. The sound of crickets filled the evening air. I stepped forward, put my right hand on her left arm, leaned in, and kissed her. She didn't resist, and for a moment I tasted the stirrings of reciprocation. Then she whispered, "Stop."

I stopped.

She looked up at me. Even in the orangey glow of the street lights I could tell she was blushing.

"Why did you do that?"

"My apologies. I didn't mean to—"

"Answer the question."

"I did it because I find you very attractive. I have since I walked into the school that day. And also because you have George Bellows prints hanging on your office wall."

"Oh, for God's sake. You're supposed to be saving the day. Not—"

"Not what?"

"Not, I don't know, saying things like that. About me."

"I'm sorry if I upset you."

"You didn't upset me. It's just—"

I waited. She examined me like a scientist pondering an interesting discovery in a petri dish.

"It's just that I need to go," she said, opening her car door and sliding inside.

"Good night."

"Good night, *Woody*," she said, shutting her door with a very small smile.

I stepped back and made sure she got out of the lot OK. I waved but she didn't return the gesture. Then I got in my van, the one with the big butt, and drove home.

44

AFTER A CUP OF COFFEE AND A GLANCE AT
the paper the next morning, I threw on a shirt and jogging
shorts, laced up my shoes, and lumbered down the street to
Schiller Park, where I dodged real runners, cyclists unaware of
city biking laws, and dog walkers—including the two Kevins
and their pugs—as I circled the park for forty-five minutes, give
or take a knee pain or two.

The evening before had given me a lot to think about, and
that wasn't even counting the way it ended under the roman-
tic glow of a sodium-vapor lamp in the restaurant parking lot.
Reviewing the twists and turns of Abdi and Barbara's situation
over beers with Helene had brought to bear the similarities in
the cases I'd somehow become entangled in. Namely, Ohio's very
own white supremacists and the extremists of Islamic fundamen-
talism. Similarities, but—as with the story of Ronald McQuillen
at Maple Ridge High—any connection?

I was walking the last two blocks up Mohawk to my house
when Abukar Abdulkadir called, panic in his voice.

"I need help. Someone is outside my apartment."

"Someone like who?" I thought of the mask-wearing kidnappers.

"People in big black cars. They are watching my window."

"Stay inside," I said immediately. "If they knock on your door, cooperate but keep your mouth shut."

"But—"

"I'll be right there."

I skipped a shower, dressed, and got into my van. I called Freddy Cohen on the way. I made it to Abdulkadir's parking lot in less than twenty minutes. I walked straight to his door without looking left or right. On cue, I heard a car door open and slam shut and my name called before I put fist to door.

"Hayes," Cindy Morris said, striding toward me with fire in her eyes. Hell hath no fury like a government agent scorned. "What are you doing here?"

"I'm in the market for a north-side chalet. There a law against that?"

"There is now." She turned and waved in the direction of a pride of black Ford Explorers. Several more doors opened and shut. She turned back to me.

"You need to step aside."

"Right of free assembly."

"On public property," she snapped. "As you well know."

"I—"

"Spofforth," Morris said in a voice just shy of drill sergeant with a gut ache. "Assist Mr. Hayes in getting out of my way. If he resists, arrest him."

"On what charge?" I demanded.

"First-degree dumbass," she said, but something in her voice had changed, and I could tell she was seriously angry.

Spofforth approached—we'd met before, on a side street in a subdivision, where he waited like a linebacker ready to upend me—but push never came to shove. The apartment door opened a moment later and Abukar Abdulkadir stood before us, arms by his side.

Morris addressed him by name.

He nodded, misery clouding his eyes.

"I need to ask you to come with me."

"You've got this all wrong," I said.

"Stay out of it," Morris said.

"You're making a big mistake."

"And you're making an even bigger one if you don't get out of my face in the next three seconds."

I did as I was told. Abdulkadir looked at me sadly.

"*Nabadeey*, Andy," he said.

"Sorry?"

"Goodbye."

IT TOOK A CALL from Cohen to the U.S. Attorney's Office and some high-stakes negotiating with Cindy Morris, but eventually I was allowed to retreat from the field of battle with most of my civil liberties intact. I was driving back down Agler Road when I was interrupted by a call from Bonnie.

"It's what I was afraid of," she said. "You've got a serious virus problem."

"I do?"

"You get all that information about phishing I send you, right? The ways to protect yourself?"

"I'm very careful," I protested. "I learned my lesson after a Nigerian prince offered me two million pounds."

"Don't even joke about that. My friend's aunt lost $4,000 in one of those scams. You're sure you haven't communicated with Barbara Mendoza electronically?"

"Positive. Until recently, talking to her in person was hard enough."

"No clicks on suspicious links?"

"None. Promise."

"Opened any files from people you didn't know?"

"Files?"

"Word documents. PDFs. Spreadsheets. Anything like that."

I thought about it. Anything fitting that category came from either Burke Cunningham, or more recently Freddy Cohen, or

Kym and Crystal. I was about to answer in the negative once again when I thought back to the parking lot escapade.

I said, "Ronald McQuillen? The militia hunter I told you about?"

"What about him?"

"He sent me a PDF about an outfit called the 1776 Sentries. But it was just a simple document. A history of the movement."

"When?"

"Couple weeks ago."

"OK. I'm going to check that out."

She called back twenty minutes later, just as I arrived at Cunningham's office, ready to brief him and Cohen on Abdulkadir's arrest.

"You might want to give that guy a call."

"Why?"

"That document had an .exe file attached to it. That's where your virus came from."

"Really?"

"Do you trust him? Because that's a little sophisticated."

"I suppose." Maybe. Possibly? "He's been helping me with the two guys I chased away in the parking lot."

"How'd you find him?"

"I didn't. He found me. He called, after it happened, told me his suspicions."

"How'd he know about you?"

I was getting a bad feeling about this. "The way the rest of the world did, I guess. Saw me on the news."

"You may want to check him out a little further. Something's not right here."

I thought of Helene's story of McQuillen's visit to Maple Ridge High. "Yeah," I said. "I'm starting to get that impression."

I hung up and walked to Cunningham's door and waited for LaTasha to buzz me in. Could things get any stranger? Ronald McQuillen hacking my computer as I recovered from challenging two guys who may have been connected to Abdi

Mohamed's disappearance? Highly unusual coincidence indeed. And not one I needed to deal with right at the moment. Because if we'd been running out of time before, Abdulkadir's arrest had pushed the clock hands about as close to midnight as they could get.

MCQUILLEN ANSWERED HIS DOOR WITH a frown two hours later, blinking at the daylight and clutching a bottle of his ubiquitous Mountain Dew like a dog zealously guarding a rawhide chew toy. Today's T-shirt bore a picture of Darth Vader and the caption "Who's Your Daddy?"

"You know what time it is, right?"

"Time to talk."

"I'm barely awake."

"I don't think that's a disqualifier."

Reluctantly, he stepped back and let me inside. "So what can I do for you?"

Standing in the cramped hallway, I told him what Bonnie had uncovered, the PDF and the infected .exe file.

"Yeah. So?"

"So? You hacked my computer, didn't you?"

"Get lost," he said. "I don't have to tell you anything."

"Maybe not on Planet McQuillen. But we do things differently here in the real world. Which reminds me." I went over what Helene told me about his talks to student government classes.

He took a swig of the soda and tried to blink the sleep out of his bloodshot eyes. His hair and beard jutted out in odd directions, as if no longer subject to gravity. He looked like a folksinger who'd been dragged from his bed by the Ohio Grassman. He turned and walked farther into the house.

"Follow me."

WE WERE SEATED IN the Garden. Lights on various computers and routers and monitors blinked not much more frantically than cockpit controls on takeoff. On the TV the BBC was reporting a thwarted suicide bomber truck attack in Paris. I turned down the offer of my own two-liter Mountain Dew bottle. McQuillen shook his head with a look of surprise when I asked about coffee, as if I'd raised the possibility of traveling to Jupiter's third moon. Instead I sipped tap water from a plastic Columbus ComicCon cup as I unveiled my indictment.

When I finished, he said, "I don't have anything to do with Abdi Mohamed."

"Oh really? So it's just a coincidence his counselor was hacked around the same time you were at the high school?"

"Yes."

"Are you also denying you went after my computer?" I said, making no effort to hide my frustration. I looked around the Garden, wondering how Bonnie would fare *mano a laptop* with McQuillen.

"That's irrelevant at this point. What you're talking about with the Evil Twin attack is much more—"

I sat back and folded my arms.

"Fine. Be a baby. It was research, OK? Pure and simple."

"Research? About what? The bills I owe? My attempts at online dating?"

"Your accounting is pretty shitty, I have to admit. I've got a couple software programs I could recommend. And I'd steer clear of 'Melissa in Dayton' if I were you. But in this case, I'm talking about the guys who rolled you in the parking lot. The Bowdens. That's why I called you to begin with."

"In order to hack me? You couldn't have kissed me first?"

"I didn't know you, beyond what's out there in the news, which isn't always flattering, just FYI. I have no idea if you would have told me what I needed to know. Or if you'd even know what was important."

"So you decided just to invade my privacy instead?"

"I'm fighting a war here, Hayes. I've got to take certain precautions. Hurt feelings don't concern me. And it's not like I messed with your files. I only care about things you came across that could help me understand what these alt-right twits are up to next."

"You're paranoid, is what I think."

"Am I?" He glanced at the framed newspaper clipping about his father's murder.

"With all due respect, yes. But putting that nuttiness aside, why hack Abdi Mohamed? And his counselor? What do they have to do with any of this?"

"I told you, I didn't do that."

"Why should I believe you? You were at his school." Something occurred to me from my conversation with the Lumberjack Man barista at Scarlet & Gray Grounds. I asked him if he'd ever visited the coffee shop.

"Do I look like someone who visits coffee shops?"

"They have soda. Artisanal—you could broaden your horizons."

"They're broad enough, thank you."

"If you insist. Mind if I take your picture?"

"Yes."

"Too bad," I said, whipping out my phone and snapping a couple frames.

"Hayes—"

"I'll keep these off Instagram if you behave. I just want to check something."

"Like what?"

"Like I'll let you know. Back to the school—"

"I did that as a public service," he said, clearly angry now. "I didn't charge—did the principal tell you that part? I speak all the time. Trying to get the message across."

"What message?"

"The one I've been trying to get through your thick skull for two weeks. I don't care about Islamic extremists or whatever. I mean, I care, but it's not what I do. I've got my hands full dealing with these homegrown wackos. It's like I told you before. We're shitting our pants over brown-skinned guys in robes when we've got just as many true-blue Americans sitting around in trailer parks with more guns than an artillery unit in Vietnam and ten bags of fertilizer around back they're trying to figure out what to do with. And believe me, they've got plenty of targets to choose from."

46

I TOOK A DRINK OF MY WATER. "THEN WHO?"
I said.

"Who what?"

"Who hacked Abdi Mohamed and Barbara Mendoza?"

"I have no idea. But Evil Twin is sophisticated," McQuillen said. He brushed his hair out of his eyes. I noticed for the first time what appeared to be crumbs of toast in his beard. "Go over the scenario again."

Reluctantly, I explained what Bonnie theorized, about the hacker gaining access to Barbara Mendoza through an attack on Abdi at Scarlet & Gray Grounds.

"They did their homework, whoever it was," McQuillen said. "Assuming they didn't just stumble onto the counselor's secret, someone had the smarts to check her out. But who would know the two of them were close, other than someone at the school?"

"I have no idea."

"It was a good move, especially if she's as vulnerable as you're saying. Because who's she going to tell? It isolated her even more. Well, at least until you stumbled along."

A calculated effort to leverage a secret. It made sense, as much as I hated to admit it. After all, chasing secrets was at the heart of everything I'd encountered in the past few days. Barbara Mendoza and her undocumented niece. Abdi's relationship with Faith Monroe. Abukar Abdulkadir's efforts to help Abdi pay for books. The midwife and her babies . . .

"*Hayes.*"

"Sorry."

"Did you hear what I just said?"

"No."

"I said I could run up the street to Panera and get you some coffee. If you think you're going to be here a while." From the look on his face, I could tell that playing three-on-three hoops in the hot sun with some 1861 Copperheads would have been more appealing to him.

I shook my head. "I can't stay. I need to find square one and dust it off."

He didn't bother disguising his relief. "I'm sorry about the hacking. Nothing's going to come of it, I promise."

"You'll forgive me if I take a wait-and-see approach."

We were passing through the living room when I remembered our conversation the day before, after my trip to Brenda's Books 'n Things.

"What about it?" he said impatiently.

"You started to say something about the way the midwife got paid, before I had to take the other call."

"Oh yeah. I'm not sure how big a deal it is."

"Try me. I'm not taking anything for granted at this point."

He put his hand on the back of the couch. "It's just that some people may have paid her in cash, but not Derwent."

"What do you mean?"

"He rarely if ever used money—American money. He claimed U.S. currency wasn't legitimate. He'd figured out how to do small-scale minting and made these special coins. Probably from the gold he took down in the Brink's job."

"Coins like what?"

"Here. I'll show you."

We walked back into the Garden. He rooted around in a file drawer. "Ah," he said after a moment. He pulled something out and handed it to me. A gold coin, a little thicker and a little bigger in circumference than a Kennedy half dollar. On one side was imprinted what appeared to be a rainbow over a ship beached on a mountaintop.

"Noah's Ark?"

"Good. At least you didn't flunk out of Vacation Bible School."

I turned the coin over and examined three figures in a freshly plowed field. The man on the left was kneeling, his hand on his heart as if mortally wounded. The man on the right was about to walk out of view, his head in his hands like someone weeping. The man in the middle was lifting his arms up to the sky with his fists clenched. I looked at McQuillen and shook my head.

"It's a lot tougher. That's Abel on the left, just after Cain struck him. Cain's on the right, walking out of the garden. In the middle—"

"The third brother. Seth."

"You got it."

"This was Derwent's currency?"

"He used it as much as possible. It's real gold, so it has value. He was hoping to create an entirely new monetary system, based on him. No ego issues there. Of course, most people just pawned them for cash."

"Wonder if Brenda Renner did."

"Who knows? But I'll tell you this much. If she told you Derwent paid her in cash for delivering babies, she's lying. He wouldn't touch the stuff."

47

I PULLED INTO THE PARKING LOT AT
Scarlet & Gray Grounds half an hour later. The business was
nearly empty, with only a couple twenty-somethings working on
laptops, a guy reading the *Dispatch*, and two Somali ladies having coffee while their kids played in chairs beside them. I spied
Lumberjack Man behind the counter. He was pouring hot water
into a silver, single-cup coffee filter cone perched atop a mug with
the concentration of a man performing eye surgery. I approached
and reminded him of the previous visit.

"The guy I was looking for. Is this him?" I showed him my
phone and the picture of McQuillen.

"Nah," the barista said, reluctantly pausing in his task. I de-
tected a hint of derision in his voice at the sight of McQuillen's
wild appearance. By contrast, the barista's beard was a trim rectangular shape like something you'd see in a tale told with hi-
eroglyphs, with his bun coiled as firm and tight as a lacquered
doorknob.

"You sure?" But even as I asked I realized in my heart I believed McQuillen when he said he hadn't visited the shop.

"I don't remember him. The guy I was telling you about was more"—he paused, considering—"more, I don't know, Amish-ey."

"Amish-ey?"

"You know. The whole beard with the upper lip shaved. Bible-ey."

"Bible-ey."

"Yeah. He definitely stuck out. I mean, we get all kinds in here. But it's a lot of high school kids or ladies like that"—he nodded in the direction of the Somali women. He returned to his pour. "My manager made a joke about looking for a buggy."

"Did he have a laptop? A computer of some kind?"

He removed the cone filter and gazed admiringly at the black brew in the mug. The coffee looked and smelled to me like the Folger's French roast I'd had that morning at home, but I didn't admit as much.

"Pretty sure. Because that's the other thing we noticed. Amish guy with a computer. Sort of steampunkish, if you know what I mean."

"I'll take your word for it. Was he here a lot?"

"I'm not sure. I don't think so. I would have noticed. Couple times, maybe. You think that's the guy? Who was messing with our wireless?"

"I'm not sure. It's possible."

"Hope you find him. You can't miss him. Real Old Testament-ey."

"I'll keep that in mind."

IT MIGHT BE ONE more coincidence, I thought, getting on the highway to head east a few minutes later. After all, Trey Renner, Brenda's affable if protective son, didn't have a beard, despite his—well, Amish-ey—haircut. But Lumberback's description of the potential hacker, combined with the coin that Mc-Quillen showed me and his contention that Brenda wasn't telling the truth about one aspect of her midwife days, was enough to merit a return trip. Even if I was just crossing more people off my list. The important thing was, I still had plenty of time to

pick up the boys before braving inbound traffic for Red, White &
Boom that night.

I was parking in the gravel lot at Brenda's Books 'n Things
less than an hour later when my phone rang.

"Well, don't bother now."

"Who's calling?"

"It's Patty Bowden. And I said don't bother."

"Don't bother what?" I said, looking at the store. The inside
was dark and the sign on the door said it was closed.

"Don't bother looking anymore. For Mike and Todd. I mean,
what's the point?"

"What do you mean? Did you find them?"

"Find them?" She laughed weakly, like someone making light
at a bankruptcy hearing. "I got more important things to worry
about now."

"Like what?"

"Like finding a place to live. Got burned out last night."

"What?"

"You heard me, soldier. Trailer went up in flames. Only reason I'm alive is the dogs. Woke me out of a deep sleep, smoke
pouring through the house."

"Are you OK?"

"I'm alive, but that's about it. Staying with an aunt right now.
Don't suppose you've got any idea who did it."

"Did what?"

"Torched me. Sheriff says it was arson."

"Arson?"

"I mean, just seems odd, Mike and Todd missing, I talk to
you, then this? Starting to wish I never called you."

"Why?"

"Makes me think you're one of them people brings trouble
with you wherever you go."

We talked for a couple more minutes. I told her how sorry
I was. I also told her I wasn't going to give up trying to find
her brother and nephew, and she didn't have to worry about

payment. She called me soldier again and said that was the least I could do. I hung up and got out of the van. I debated bringing along the Louisville Slugger, but decided against it in the end. You could never tell with that thing, what good it might or might not do.

48

I PEERED INSIDE THE SHOP DOOR BUT SAW NO one. I knocked. The glass in the door rattled loosely, but no one came. I took a couple of steps back and examined the front of the store. In the light of day the window displays looked more tired and ticky-tacky than the first time I'd stopped as evening approached. A jigsaw puzzle of the Manhattan skyline included the pre-9/11 twin towers. Dust covered a cellophane-wrapped package of twelve bayberry-scented candles, except where someone had traced a finger along the edge. Something had gnawed at the side of one of the wooden bird feeders hanging from the top of the display. Cobwebs filled corners. The colors on the painting on the lintel above the door—bluebirds in their nest—were fading. I looked more closely at the depiction. In quality it was barely on par with the tole paintings of geese one of my aunts filled her house with when I was a boy. Now that I studied the image there was also something about the birds that seemed off—

I started at a sound. Trey Renner appeared, opening the door from the inside, though the shop was still dark.

"We're closed."

"I can see that. I was hoping to talk to your mom."

"About what?"

"Couple follow-up questions."

"I already told you, it's not good for her to talk about that stuff."

"Maybe you can help me, then."

"How?"

I studied his face. He was clean-shaven like me, with no signs of razor cuts indicating an attempt to hack off a beard. But that had been weeks ago, so what evidence would there be? The bowl-shaped haircut persisted, and seemed oddly out of place on the repairman, like a guy in a kilt wearing a pink nylon fanny pack.

"Excuse the question. But did you use to have a beard?"

Renner looked behind him, and then glanced over my shoulder. "You drove all the way down here to ask me that?"

"Well, that and a couple more questions about David Derwent."

"As I said, that stuff's ancient history. And my mom doesn't want to talk about it. Fact is, I don't want her to talk about it."

"It won't take long, I promise. I'm just wrapping up some loose ends."

It was something to do with the bluebirds' heads, I thought. I wished to hell I'd paid more attention to that stuff as a kid. But of course I hadn't. Because my dad, of all people, was the birder in the family; my mom was too busy with teaching and housework and us kids to care. And since it was him, I'd been automatically dismissive of the things he tried telling me—

"Maybe I can help." Renner stood aside to let me in.

"Thanks." I stepped in, wary. The same musty smell greeted me as before, of books too long on the shelves without someone handling them, of bins of stale candy, of a rug allowed to dry in place after a water leak soaked it.

"So how about it?" I said.

"How about what?"

"The beard."

He sighed. He looked like a man tired of repairing computers whose only issues were the owners hadn't plugged them in.

"I've had a beard on and off. Satisfied?"

"Maybe. Have you ever been to a coffee shop in Columbus called Scarlet & Gray Grounds?"

"Did you say you had questions for my mom?"

"Yes. But what about the coffee shop?"

"Why are you asking me this?"

The heads. That was it. What was I thinking? They weren't bluebirds at all, I realized, even as poorly painted as they were. They were blue *jays,* unmistakable now that I thought about it, with those bright eyes and that distinctive crest. I conjured an image of my father putting out bags of suet for them midwinter, and then sitting for hours in the kitchen watching them through the window.

"Like I said, just tying up some loose ends."

"My mom's back here." He jabbed his right thumb toward the rear of the store. "She can explain everything. Which I guess you deserve to know."

"Everything like what?"

"Like the truth, as long as you've come all this way."

He gestured for me to precede him. I stayed put, my mind working furiously.

Blue jays. Two of them. Side by side. Two jays.

Renner looked back at me. "There a problem?"

Two jays.

Jay Jay.

Jay Jays.

JJ's.

"JJ's," I said, staring at Renner.

"What of it?"

I recalled the urgency in Mike Bowden's voice as he summoned his son. *He's saying JJ's, now.* The snatch of conversation Angela caught after she was taken captive. *The driver told him to shut up.* The link between the two events and the two sets of conspirators the word provided. Since the day I'd walked into Brenda's Books 'n Things it had been right in front of me.

"You're—" I started to say, when I was interrupted by the shop door opening. I turned. A man stood in the aisle, pointing a gun at my head. A man I recognized, but someone I hadn't seen in a couple of weeks. And when I had, he hadn't been pleased to see me.

"You messed up my pretty floors," the custodian at Maple Ridge High said, as Renner stuck his own gun in my back.

49

"THAT'S HOW YOU KNEW SO MUCH ABOUT Abdi Mohamed," I said. "About the Ninth Period, I'm guessing. Him and Faith. And who his counselor was. You had a spy. In plain sight."

The words sounded more coherent in my head. The actual sounds I made were mumbled because of the swelling around my mouth, as if I'd kissed a nest of hornets and they'd kissed right back.

"I prefer the word 'patriot,'" Renner said.

I was sitting in a wooden chair, my butt going numb, hands and feet trussed with plastic zip ties, head ringing from where Renner had knocked me back and forth with a closed fist one or two dozen times. As far as I could tell, half the blows related to information he wanted that I wasn't forthcoming enough about; what I knew about his mom, Brenda; what I knew about Abdi Mohamed; and what I knew about Barbara Mendoza. The rest of the time he just wanted to hit me.

"Tell me this. Was it just a coincidence you found out about the niece?"

"So many questions," Renner said.

"Thing is, Barbara was so secretive about Angela. No one knew. But you put the pieces together somehow." The comment directed at the custodian. He looked at Renner. Renner nodded. The custodian slapped me hard enough to make Renner's blows up to that point seem like puffs of baby's breath in comparison.

When I raised my head again, eyes clearing, Renner said, "Dwayne saw her crying in her office from time to time. When she didn't think anyone was around. It gave him pause. Satisfied?"

A funny formality had crept into Renner's voice. I couldn't place it at first, and then recalled similar phrasing from the night we'd rescued Angela. From a man wearing a Guy Fawkes mask. So I'd met them both before. And had an errant siren not interrupted us that night, everything might have been different.

"Why were you looking for the boy?" Renner said.

"I already told you. His family hired an attorney. In anticipation of charges being brought." *Anticipation* took an effort of ten seconds and what felt like double the syllables. "The FBI was all over them because of what happened with the brother. Hassan. The attorney hired me to find Abdi. That's all there is to it. It was just a job."

"But you were in the parking lot that day. When that *immigrant* assaulted the Bowdens."

I laughed, despite how much it hurt. "Assaulted *them?* She was a mom with kids loading groceries into a car. All I did was what any real man would do." I held Renner's gaze as I spoke. "I tried to help her. I got hired after that because Abdi's family believed I could help them." Mistakenly believed, I thought with bitterness, realizing how badly I'd failed.

"Help a terrorist?" Dwayne said. He had a fleshy face, in contrast to the trim Renner, with a short, gray mustache that looked like something stripped from a squirrel's nest and glued on with Elmer's.

"Somalis aren't terrorists," I said.

"Except for Hassan Mohamed," Renner said evenly.

"There's always going to be few fanatics in the world," I said, looking into his eyes. "Dipshit crazies who don't know any better—

Renner's fist connected with my right temple before I could finish. This time I blacked out for a couple of moments. When I raised my head and my eyes cleared, I saw the custodian holding a knife.

"Please?" he said to Renner. "Asshole's basically asking for it."

Renner made a face at the obscenity. But he didn't reply. My insides went cold as I realized he was thinking hard about the suggestion.

"*We will build a fire of pure white flame that reaches to heaven,*" he whispered. He shook his head. "It's better if he goes out like the rest of them. No questions about time of death."

"Time of death?" Dwayne said. "Like you can tell with bits and pieces. Because that's all that's going to be left."

"Leave it, please." Renner pulled his phone from his pocket and glanced at the screen. "It's getting late. We need to mail the package."

"Mike and Todd Bowden," I said.

"What about them?" Renner said.

"Where are they? Or should I ask, where are their bodies? Since their sister hired me to find them and someone tried to kill her. I'm guessing you shut them up after I entered the picture?"

Renner traded glances with the custodian.

"Or because they put whatever you're up to in jeopardy? Is that it? Did you try killing Patty Bowden for the same reason?"

Renner leaned close and stared at me. His eyes blazed with the clarity of true belief. It occurred to me in that moment that he was a doppelganger for Ronald J. McQuillen, minus the newly shorn beard. Driven by an inner burning. *We will build a fire of pure white flame that reaches to heaven.* Where had I heard that before?

"It is time for you to stop talking," he said.

True belief. The chosen one. The third brother.

I thought back to the day I met McQuillen and took in all his oddities in the Garden. *Fire of pure white flame.* He'd used the same phrase. Attributed it to someone.

To David Derwent, the Son of Seth.

He was their king.

I said, "A girl died out here, a long time ago. In childbirth. Her and her baby. That was the rumor. Your mom took off afterward."

"Please be silent."

"But your mom came back, later. And that baby didn't die, did it? Did he?"

Renner didn't speak. Dwayne lifted the knife and moved closer. I stared into Renner's eyes.

"Did you?"

I waited for the fatal blow. The slide of the knife up under my rib cage. But instead Renner and I held each other's gazes for several long seconds.

"Of course," I said, struggling to enunciate. "That's why Brenda left town for a while. To wait for things to cool down. There'd be too many questions, her showing up with a new baby and the mom nowhere in sight. That poor girl—do you even know her name? Who she was? Where she's buried? Your *real* mother?"

Renner leaned back. "That is enough."

"Derwent made himself out to be this mythical being. 'Seth,' the third son of Adam and Eve. The chosen one. The third brother. But the fact of the matter was, he was an only child. So the story didn't quite fit."

Renner shook his head.

"His first wife couldn't have more children. So he started casting around. Found a follower more than willing to do his bidding. To carry his seed. Which turned out to be you."

"You gonna let him flap his jaws like that?" the custodian said. He waved the knife back and forth. Flick flick. Ice filled my gut. But Renner held up a hand to stop him.

"What was the plan?" I said. "Brenda would stay away for a while, lay low, then show up later with you as her own kid? Reunite with Derwent? Except it didn't work out because he blew himself up after killing John McQuillen. So she was left alone to raise you."

Renner closed his eyes, as if his thoughts were far away.

"A single mom," I continued. "But with a big consolation prize. Because *you're* the chosen one, aren't you? Or so you'd like to think. Your father was David Derwent. But he wasn't the real third brother, was he? You are. Trey—the third one, right?"

Renner opened his eyes. He looked at me and didn't say anything. He turned and nodded at Dwayne. The custodian approached me, and I started to rock in the chair, to fend off the attack even if only for a few seconds. But that lasted only a moment or two. I felt something soft and wet clamped over my mouth and nose and choked at a sickly sweet smell. The dim light of the room dissolved into black, taking all my pain from Renner's blows with it.

50

MY MIND SWAM BACK UP FROM THE depths of unconsciousness, slowly drifting upward toward the ability to conjugate verbs and form full sentences, like a hunk of waterlogged ocean garbage that's spent the day rising and sinking and now, perhaps for the last time, rises once again. Thoughts clicked into place like beads on an abacus. Kaltun Hirsi, tormented in the grocery store parking lot. Freddy Cohen, reluctantly offering me a job. The pain experienced by the Mohamed family. Abukar Abdulkadir, so earnest, and naive, in his desire to help. Ronald McQuillen, glugging Mountain Dew in the Garden while he rooted out enemies of the state, and of his own family. *We will build a fire of pure white flame that reaches to heaven.* Angela Mendoza, trembling as she climbed out of the van and into her aunt's arms. Brenda Renner, the fragile midwife with a deadly secret. Trey Renner: *Time to deliver the package.*

More thoughts: Anne, miffed at my reproach over *Ready Player One*. Miffed, but also disguising regrets? Helene Paulus, so frank and professional, and also so beautiful as I kissed her by her car in the parking lot. Joe, and Mike, and—

I opened my eyes. I was prone on a cool metal floor. It was dark, but not pitch black. An engine was running. My feet were still bound and my hands were still tied behind me, though I realized with some effort I could flap them back and forth and wave and stretch my fingers, for all the good that did me. I'd been gagged, and not politely. My head felt like someone had used it to pound titanium pistons into place. I could move a little, wiggle back and forth, but in the same way a trussed pig wiggles on a hook on the downward conveyor slide toward bacon and baby back ribs and breakfast sausage. A pig, dying alone, the way we all die.

No. Not alone. There was someone else. Someone lying beside me.

"Mmmph," I said.

Nothing. Then a deep sigh.

"*Mmmph.*" The gag cutting into the sides of my mouth.

"Shhh."

"*Mmmph.*"

"*Shut up. They'll hear us.*" A young, male voice, tense with fear. Abdi?

"Mmmph."

"*Shift your head down. By my hands.*"

"Mmmph?"

"*Just do it, motherfucker.*"

Motherfucker. So maybe not Abdi. But who?

Carefully, quietly, I squirmed and inched my body down the floor.

"*Closer. Next to my hands.*"

Squirm, inch, slide. Squirm, inch, slide.

"*Freeze.*"

The sound of voices. I froze. Voices close by, but not in the same space. On the other side of a thin wall of some kind. I recognized the voice of Renner, speaking in formal, uncontracted phrases, and then of the custodian. Dwayne.

I lay there for nearly a minute while we waited, my heart pounding as if I'd climbed a long flight of steps after surviving a car accident. No one came. Nothing happened.

"*OK.*"

I craned my neck, looking around. Realized I was in a vehicle of some kind. A truck.

"*Come on.*"

Squirm, inch, slide. Squirm, inch, slide.

Beside me, tucked below gleaming metal counters, big bags. I made out a word. *Fertilizer.* On top of the bags, wires, and small packets of some kind.

A fire of pure white flame.

Squirm, inch, slide.

My head came level with the speaker's hands.

"*Closer.*"

I shifted until I felt fingers at the back of my head. Fingers that pulled and dug and twisted and—

"Ahh . . ."

"Would you shut the fuck up?"

"Sorry." The word indistinct, with the gag loose but still in my mouth. "Can you—?"

"I can't do nothing. Can't take it off. They'll see. Now slide back up."

Squirm, inch, slide. Squirm, inch, slide. The other direction, now. After a tense minute I was even with him again, back to back.

"*Who are you?*"

A pause. "*JaQuan.*"

It took me a second, synapses firing sluggishly through the storm of my headache.

"JaQuan Williams?"

"Yeah. I know you?"

"No." JaQuan Williams. One of the Agler Road Crips. The gang Hassan Mohamed ran with before he radicalized. A guy Abdi laughed at good-naturedly, friends with everyone.

"Are we gonna die?"

"No." I'd rarely been less sure of anything. "Where are we?"

"Truck."

"Truck?"

"Food truck, far as I can tell."

"How long have you been here?"

"Couple hours. Maybe more."

"Where were you before this?"

"Not sure. A room. It was all black. I got moved today sometime. I'm . . ."

I waited.

"I'm scared."

"Me too. How long were you in the room?" I thought of the storage area behind Brenda's storefront where they'd kept me. Of the pole barn up on the hill.

"Couple weeks, maybe. I don't know. It was always dark."

"How'd you get there?"

"Got zapped."

"Zapped?"

"Motherfucker hit me with a Taser. I went down, next thing I know I'm in the dark in this room, all tied up."

"Who tased you?"

"Dwayne."

"Why'd he tase you?"

"Fuck if I know. I was just trying to collect."

"Collect what?"

"Money. For starting the fire."

"What fire?"

"At the church."

"What church?"

"Mount Shiloh."

Idly, I realized how comforting I found the rumbling engine of the food truck. Memories popped up of overnight trips with my sister in the backseat when seatbelts still didn't matter. In another context, I might have dozed off. A context that didn't include several bags of fertilizer beside me topped with wires and packets whose content I didn't want to think about.

"You started that fire?"

"Yeah."

"Why?"

"Dwayne promised me a couple hundred bucks. Gave me the bottle and the gasoline and some clothes to wear and a scarf—a bandana thing."

"Why would you do that?"

"Needed the money. Plus that church, they got me arrested. Threw me out just for breaking in and playing basketball one time. Why not?"

More advantages to having Dwayne on the inside. He knew JaQuan. Would have helped with the approach, about the job.

"We need to yell. Scream. Get help."

"I tried that. Kicked at the side. Dwayne came back with a knife. Said he'd cut me if I did it again."

"Is it just him and the other guy?"

"Far as I know. And the kid."

"What kid?"

"Somali kid, up front."

"What's he doing up there?"

He paused, and when he spoke again his voice cracked. "I think he's going to blow us up."

51

FOOD TRUCK AS WEAPON OF MASS DESTRUCTION. *Jesus.* No—what was it Roy always said? "Don't say Jesus when you mean shit." Fine. *Shit.* David Derwent. Seth: The third brother. Trey—the third. It made perfect sense, the more I thought about it. Perfect, painful sense. Downtown was flooded with food trucks right now. Portable restaurants offering everything from barbecue to burritos. Even fried kale balls. The new craze. The new normal. They were everywhere. Especially tonight. Because four hundred thousand fireworks-loving visitors were a lot of mouths to feed.

Four hundred thousand—including Joe and Mike, and Anne and Amelia, assuming they'd somehow made it downtown anyway, after I never showed to pick everyone up—

We will build a fire of pure white flame that reaches to heaven.

Jesus shit Jesus.

I thought back to what McQuillen said, was it just a few hours ago? *True-blue Americans sitting around in trailer parks with more guns than an artillery unit in Vietnam and ten bags of fertilizer around back they're trying to figure out what to do with. And believe me, they've got plenty of targets to choose from.*

Red, White & Boom was plenty big. The biggest target Columbus had, other than an Ohio State football game, but that came with the inconvenience—to terrorists, that is—of most potential victims protected inside the stadium. But not the fireworks celebration. What did the experts call people in that situation? Soft targets? I'd never considered just how dehumanizing that expression was until now. Until I realized my sons were in that category.

Bits and pieces. Because that's all that's going to be left.

Lucky me. Renner, in his fanaticism, spared me—and JaQuan—quiet deaths in the countryside in favor of evaporating in a ball of flame at the moment of his greatest triumph. The unfortunate beneficiaries of an ego gone mad.

His triumph. Yet it was Abdi Mohamed sitting in the front of the truck. What was his role in this? They didn't need him to detonate explosives. Any true believer with a cell phone could do that.

My mind raced, trying to figure everything out. A truck. Terror. Blame. Hassan Mohamed, an exception to the rule, choosing terror over integration, but enough to kindle flames of prejudice in a nervous world. And now his brother missing, posting inflammatory threats . . .

I recalled the attack along the waterfront in Nice, France, a few years back, the tractor-trailer plowing into Bastille Day crowds, an assault that killed scores. Similar attacks in Berlin, Barcelona, and London. And now here, in the heart of the heartland. How would it look if Abdi—the brother of a confirmed extremist, someone who'd died in the name of jihad—was seen in the front seat of a food truck as it careened into the crowd, just before igniting into a fireball? Plenty of downtown security cameras would catch that perspective—

Light illuminated the interior. I turned my head and saw Trey Renner step inside, followed by Dwayne the custodian.

"Almost time." Renner said. His voice grave, like a minister beginning a sermon.

"Mmmph." Careful not to give away my ability to speak.

JaQuan pressed himself against the side of the van, hiding his own loosened gag.

"I did not quite catch that, Mr. Hayes."

"*Mmmph.*"

"I tell you what. I'm going to loosen that for a second. If you say anything louder than a whisper, Dwayne is going to cut your throat and then rearrange your intestines. Do you understand?"

I nodded, heart racing again. If they realized what happened with the gag . . .

"*Dwayne.*"

"What."

"I told you to tie these things tightly. His is practically falling off."

"I tied them plenty tight."

"Not tight enough."

Renner fiddled with the back of my gag but said nothing further. Sweat pooled in the small of my back as I waited for the thrust of Dwayne's knife. But it never came. Renner pulled the fully loosened gag down onto my chin. I made a big production of gasping in relief.

"*Quiet,*" Renner warned.

"What is this?" I said. "What are you doing?"

"Making history."

"History?"

"The end times are nigh. Ours are the snow-white wings of salvation. The battle that will decide everything is before us. Just like my father predicted."

"What are you talking about?"

"The final cleansing. The race war. Throwing the garbage out once and for all." He kicked JaQuan, who gave a little moan. Play-acting, or real fear?

"War? I don't see any war."

"You will. Once we light the fuse. Once they begin scraping what is left of a few hundred people off the pavement, people killed by a Somali refugee they welcomed here. Someone who turned on them. Yes, you will see a war. Well, you will not see it, you personally. But it will happen. It is my gift to you both to be there at the moment of victory."

"They won't believe it. The boy. Abdi—that's not his way."

"Do not kid yourself. His skin is brown and he prays to an alien god. They'll believe it. Plus, his brother was a real devil. And he posted all those threats."

"You posted. Including the one after the firebombing, if I'm not mistaken?"

"Does it really matter, in the end?"

"Of course it matters. Your whole plan is based on a lie. A lie that involved kidnapping and blackmail and Internet fraud. What kind of holy war is that?"

"Just because people need a little convincing to get them motivated does not make the cause any less valid, Mr. Hayes."

"Bullshit. You're only justifying what you know is wrong—"

"*Dwayne.*"

"Yeah."

"I have changed my mind. Go ahead and take care of these two. We've kept them alive long enough. This black garbage"—another kick at JaQuan—"knows now the hell he has built for himself. And this one"—pointing at me—"I'm tired of his interference." He moved back toward the front of the truck.

"Happy to," Dwayne said. "What are you going to do?"

"I am taking one more look around. To be sure everything is ready. I'll be back in a minute."

"Hey—" I protested.

"History," Renner said, stepping back up front and shutting the interior door. I heard another door open and close. And then it was just us and Dwayne the custodian and a knife that gleamed in the dark like a carnivore's eyes reflecting firelight.

52

DWAYNE KNELT BESIDE ME. "THIS IS WHAT happens when people get in the way."

"You don't want to do this."

"You're wrong about that."

"You're talking about innocent people out there. Hundreds of them. Women and children, a lot of them. Is that what you signed on for?"

"Every war has its casualties."

"You can't believe that."

"Don't tell me what to believe."

"You won't get away with it. They'll come after you. Then they'll destroy everything you've worked for."

"In the middle of a war? I don't think so."

"At least—"

"At least what?"

Good question. I thought about Joe and Mike. And Angela Mendoza. And Theresa Sullivan and Otto Mulligan. And Helene, staring up at me—

"At least kill the kid first."

Dwayne sniggered. "What?"

"You heard me. Kill him first. Please, for God's sake."

"Why?"

"Because he's a coward. Nothing but a baby." I raised my voice a little. "I've been lying here for hours while he whined and moaned and carried on. You do me first, I'll have to listen to him pissing his pants and crying for his mama because he knows he's next. I don't want that to be the last thing I hear. Listening to a big fat coward while I die. A pussy. A girl. This way—"

"Hey, motherfucker," JaQuan said, raising his head. "Shut your fucking mouth. I ain't no—"

Dwayne turned at the sound of the teen's voice, caught off guard. I rolled hard to my right, knocking myself into the custodian and catching him off-balance. It was my only chance. He fell over with a grunt. I heard the *chink* of the knife handle hitting the metal floor. I braced my feet, arched my back, and dropped my full weight onto him. He gasped like a kid hitting the asphalt after falling off the monkey bars. I gasped too, at the pain shooting up my arms at the impact. I ignored it as best I could, arched and dropped again, harder this time. I heard what might have been a rib crack. I dropped a third time and he went still for a moment. I shifted myself upward and scrabbled for his throat with my bound hands, found his windpipe, and started to squeeze. He came to life, and after a moment began to flail with the knife. I squeezed harder, grinding my fingers into his fleshy neck. He choked and gasped and grabbed my hands and tried to loosen them. I arched my back again and came down on him a fourth time, never loosening my grip, and now he sighed like a man falling into bed after a very long day. I squeezed and Dwayne jabbed and I felt the knife slash at my forearms and for a second my resolve faded at the new pain. But just as quickly his strokes began to diminish, like the weakening motions of a swimmer deep at sea with no land in sight. Ten seconds passed. Twenty. At thirty I felt his body shudder, then relax; the swimmer giving in and sinking below the waves.

I held my breath. The only sounds were the thrumming of the truck engine and in the distance the sound of music and an amplified voice. I rolled off the custodian's body.

I swallowed. "Knife."

"What?" JaQuan said.

"We've got to get the knife."

"Fuck you, motherfucker. Calling me a coward. I ought—"

"Nice job. You picked up on it perfectly. Started talking at exactly the right moment. Just the distraction I needed."

Silence.

Then: "OK, man."

I slid back and forth across the floor, pushing Dwayne out of the way. My forehead grazed the rough plastic weave of a fertilizer bag. *Targets to choose from.* Where the hell was the knife? If it slid under the truck's prep area or stove during the struggle, we were out of luck. We were bits and pieces. And we only had a few minutes, even seconds, before Renner was back. And I was guessing he'd have no trouble finding the knife, or a rough replacement. What would it matter now, how we were dispatched?

"Got it," JaQuan said.

"Jesus. *Shit.* OK, good work. Now hang on."

Squirm, wiggle, slide. Keeping it up until I was back to back again with the boy. I moved my fingers around, found the blade, felt his strong grip on the handle. I maneuvered the plastic tie binding my hands against the blade and started rubbing.

"Hurry up. My hand's cramping."

"I'm trying."

The tie snapped and my hands came free.

I tried not to think about how sharp the knife must have been to cut through a plastic binding so easily.

I grabbed the handle, sat up, and sliced through the ties around my feet. I breathed a little hard as the blood rushed back through my appendages. I turned, crouched, and cut through JaQuan's ties. When I was done he sat up too. He looked sixteen or seventeen going on twelve. A baby face that didn't fit the harsh language spewing from his mouth.

"Let's go," I said.

"Go where?"

"We've got to get Abdi out of here. And warn somebody. We're sitting in a bomb."

JaQuan rubbed his wrists and ankles. "Fuck that shit, man. Not my fight." He stood up slowly, waited to regain his balance, looked around, bent over, grabbed the knife out of my hand, walked to the rear of the truck, opened the door, and disappeared.

53

I LET HIM GO. WHAT WAS THE POINT OF following? He'd served his purpose, helping us escape our captivity, even if he only did it for the most selfish reason possible. Could I really blame him, after what he'd been through? I realized now JaQuan must have been kept alive in case they needed him again, to play the role of Abdi in another attack leading up to tonight. What must that have been like, an understudy always on the brink of death?

I stood up myself, a little shakily. I staggered forward, pulled open the front panel door, and looked around. A person who could only be Abdi Mohamed was sitting in the driver's seat. He was staring straight ahead. His hands were bound to the steering wheel with strips of white cloth, like bindings torn from a shroud.

"Abdi."

Nothing.

"*Abdi.*"

Still nothing. Like trying to chat up a thrift shop mannequin.

I stepped closer, took him by the chin, and lifted his face. His eyes were glassy and his mouth hung open slightly. He'd been drugged; that was obvious enough. Renner must have put him in a doped-up zone perfect for such a mission. Awake but not sentient. A detectable pulse, but not a purpose to it. Who knew how long the boy had been in such a state? How long had he been missing—six weeks? Plenty of time to create a zombie. I looked out the window, orienting myself. We were downtown, east on Broad, just past the cathedral, facing the crowds gathered near Broad and High a few hundred yards away. Far enough to avoid the attention of cops, but close enough for a straight shot down the street. With the steering wheel tied in position, the truck would careen directly for its mark—the throng of thousands. Toward Joe and Mike. I patted my pockets in vain for my phone. I looked at my watch. Three minutes to ten. Almost time for the fireworks to go off. I fumbled with the bindings around Abdi's hands, regretfully recalling Dwayne's knife, now in JaQuin's hands. This was taking too long. I had to get Abdi out of here and get help somehow.

The passenger door opened. "What the hell?"

I turned but was too late. Renner. Hands like bear mitts hooked my shoulders and dragged me away from the boy. He was stronger than he looked, but fanatics usually are. I grabbed the steering wheel, and then the seat, and then several straws of my imagination, but the strength of the man pulling me was too great. He had the fire of heavenly ideology in his loins; I had the headache and bruises from hell. I was extracted from the front of the truck like a late October apple plucked from a low-hanging branch. I slid out and landed in a tumble on the ground. I looked up to see Renner scrambling back into the truck.

"Those are innocent people!" I shouted.

"The war is beginning," Renner said.

I stood up, hearing the rising voice of the crowd several blocks down. A chorus of anticipation. And another sound now, of the truck being slammed into gear. It started to move. Renner leaped out, his eyes gleaming, cell phone in his hand. In the dark, I could see the green disk under his thumb, waiting to place the call of mass destruction. To summon the fire of pure white flame.

54

WHAT WAS THAT NONSENSE OTTO MULLIGAN spouted? The day I met him at Jury of Your Pours? The insignificant play he recalled from the Michigan State game, the one that preserved a first down in the fourth quarter with us up by twenty and nothing on the line. *Who remembers that shit?* Two of us, I guess.

I rolled left, juked, scrambled, and plowed into Renner. Caught in his dreamlike rapture of end times and war, he didn't react quickly enough and went down hard, losing the cell phone as it clattered onto the pavement. I held my breath, waiting for an explosion that didn't come. I gave the phone a nudge with my foot, spinning it out of Renner's reach, and ran.

Ran—not the way I run around Schiller Park, which is to speedy running as ketchup is to five-alarm hot sauce, but like a man possessed. Like a man about to lose everything.

I caught up as the truck passed the Athletic Club by Fourth. Glanced briefly at the name emblazoned on the side of the blue truck: *David's Desserts.* I leaped onto the passenger side running board, swung the door open, was nearly flung off as the truck juddered over a manhole cover, regained my balance, and hurled myself inside. We were moving straight ahead. Renner had calculated it well. In front of me I saw wooden traffic barricades and police officers staring at us, realizing something was wrong. Behind them hundreds of people—thousands—with no idea at all that things were amiss.

We passed Chase Bank, then the Rhodes Tower, with its statue of the late namesake governor James Rhodes, briefcase in hand, as he strode toward another workday, and started to gain on Jack & Benny's all-night diner, filled with patrons.

A hundred feet to Broad and High.

Fifty feet.

Police officers screaming at me, guns in hands.

The crowd screaming too, but oblivious to the approaching danger. People's eyes heavenward. *"Five! Four! Three! . . ."*

I mashed myself against Abdi and cranked the steering wheel as hard as I could. I willed myself to become part of the truck as it veered left, left, left, so reluctantly, with such motorized intransigence, a heavy-laden boat being asked to divert from its expected mooring at the end of a long voyage. Tires screeched in protest and the cops' yelling intensified and Abdi suddenly moaned and the truck ran up onto the corner by the old Huntington Bank building and rumbled back down onto High, bump, bump, bump.

Boom! Boom! Boom!

Night became day as fireworks filled the sky and cut sharp shadows across downtown. Above me, exploding over the Scioto River, brilliant pinwheels of red, white, and blue lights.

The show had begun.

I hit the gas and drove all the way down the middle of the street, past the Huntington Center and the Riffe Center and a guy and a girl arguing about something at a bus stop and brought the truck to a halt at the far southwest corner of the Statehouse grounds. I threw it in park and opened the driver's door and clambered out over Abdi. I stood there, breathing hard, listening to the explosions overheard. I turned and saw men and women in uniforms sprinting toward me.

"Hands up! Don't move!"

"Get away from the truck!"

"Get down on the ground!"

"The phone!"

The phone?

I looked to my right and saw JaQuan Williams sprinting down the sidewalk, chasing Trey Renner, who was limping toward us with the phone in his right hand, raised high.

"Go back!" I yelled at JaQuan.

He stopped, confused.

"Run!"

I turned and tore the bindings loose from Abdi's hands and hauled him out of the truck and threw him over my shoulder and thought just for an instant how light he was, a man in the body of a boy, like holding Joe that morning in my backyard as we sat in my Adirondack chair.

"Run!" I yelled at JaQuan. He ran. And so did I, not away from but toward the police.

"It's a bomb it's a bomb it's a bomb get back get back get back!"

They got back.

Roy and Lucy said later they could hear the explosion at their house, nearly five miles up the road.

55

"YOU'RE ONE LUCKY SONOFABITCH, YOU know that?"

"It's funny, but I'm not feeling all that lucky."

"They would have totally been within their rights to shoot you."

"I appreciate their forbearance."

"Forbearance, my ass," Henry Fielding said. The homicide detective whose beeper went off any time my name came over the radio was sitting inside a fire department squad truck as a paramedic poked and jabbed me with an iodine swab and other instruments of torture. It was not the first time Fielding and I had bonded over my medical treatment. I was guessing it wouldn't be the last.

"Then what?"

"One of the sergeants recognized you at the last second. From the news." He rolled his eyes. "Heard 'bomb' and saw you running *away* from the truck with that kid in your arms and put two and two together."

"And decided not to shoot me."

"Hell with you. Decided to look out for his own people and get them to safety."

"Same difference?"

Fielding shook his head. "Lucky sonofabitch," he repeated.

Lucky, indeed.

Startled by JaQuan's yelling, Trey Renner tripped and stumbled at the last second, dropping the phone. Because he had a messianic complex and was prone to gibbering about history and war and pure white flames, and also because he was crazy, he managed to get up, find the phone, and dial the number that set off the bomb anyway. *David's Desserts.* Cute, if not for the truck's deadly intent. But by that time we—both JaQuan and me and Abdi and the cops and the couple arguing at the bus stop—were several hundred feet away. The blast wave sent all of us sprawling, but miraculously, there was only one fatality that night.

Well, two, if you counted Dwayne the custodian.

Not that there weren't casualties. Dozens were injured in the ensuing panic as police tried to disperse a crowd bigger than the population of most Rust Belt cities in the midst of a fireworks display many of them had been patiently waiting for since early that morning. Nearly two hours passed before Fielding showed up and I persuaded him to let me use his phone to call Anne.

"Oh my God," she yelled in my ear. "Where have you been? Do you know what's going on? They say there was a bomb—"

"The boys—are they all right?"

"Of course they're all right! They were with me! I'm the one who had to pick them up after you just disappeared!"

"I didn't just—"

"Oh, Andy. How could you?"

It was a good question. One I couldn't answer right then. So I thanked her, hung up, and hurriedly called Kym and Crystal, letting them know what was happening. I had a long list of other people to call, starting with Otto Mulligan and working my way down to Theresa Sullivan and my sister and parents and a second cousin in Boulder I hadn't seen for a while, but Fielding snatched the phone away.

"Let's get back to food trucks," he said.

"Fried kale balls. Not a positive trend."

"What?"

"Never mind. Can I go home yet?"

"In your dreams."

56

ABDI MOHAMED WAS SITTING ON THE COUCH
between his parents in the family apartment, looking at pictures
of himself in the newspaper. His remaining brother, Aden, and
his sister, Farah, were seated near him. Two days had passed. I sat
on a chair across from him, balancing a cup of Somali tea on my
thigh. Abukar Abdulkadir sat beside me, drinking his own tea.
He looked tired and haggard, but his smile was genuine. Freddy
Cohen stood behind us, bracing his back against the wall.

"So how are you feeling?" I asked Abdi.

He took a moment to respond. He was even thinner than
the photo Cohen had showed me a couple of weeks ago. Renner
hadn't starved the boy—far from it, from what investigators could
tell so far. But Abdi had also been held in near darkness for weeks,
with no clue as to what was happening and unbeknownst to him
suffering the daily effects of ingesting depressants mixed into his
food. His glazed eyes the night of the foiled attack were no accident. But already doctors were saying he could probably continue
with his plan to attend college in the fall. And his smile was as
ready as that photo had shown, and his eyes bright and liquid.

"Pretty good," he said. "I might be able to go see the Crew tomorrow. Right?" He looked at Farah, who returned a noncommittal smile.

"DC United," I said. "That could be a tough game."

"Yeah. But I think they can beat them, if they actually try." He grinned. He could have been any teenage boy excited about his team.

"Speaking of which." I reached into the bag I brought with me. I pulled out the Juventus jersey I'd purchased online and had had delivered with rush service.

"Oh, man," Abdi said, his smile getting even bigger as I handed the shirt to him. "Are you kidding?"

"I've got the impression that Mr. Andy Hayes doesn't kid around," Abdulkadir interrupted. Everyone laughed at that. Everyone but Cohen. For once I didn't blame him. It had been a long forty-eight hours for him, haggling with the feds. But it was one of the reasons Abdulkadir was sitting beside us and not next to a seatless shitter in a cell in the Franklin County Jail. Brenda Renner wasn't so lucky, and was sitting in a different unit in the same jail on suicide watch. Meanwhile, much to my amusement, Ronald McQuillen had apparently seen both a barber and a haberdasher and had become as ubiquitous on the Big Three cable news channels in the past few days as commercials for reverse mortgages and weight-loss formula. I'd even gotten a thank-you text from Lumberjack Man at Scarlet & Gray Grounds. The shop's notoriety as the place Renner launched the Evil Twin attack that gave him access to Abdi's virtual life hadn't hurt, apparently. Business—most of it media, but they were paying customers too—was booming.

"It's good to see you're OK," I said to Abdi, as he held the shirt up for a round of cell-phone pictures. There was a burst of conversation in Somali, and Farah translated their parents' appreciation for what I did. I told them it was nothing, which drew a small cough from Cohen. A minute later he cleared his throat and said, "You need to excuse me. I've got another appointment."

Over his protests, I walked the lawyer out to his car, on the pretense that I'd forgotten something in my van.

"What's the big rush?" I said, once outside. "The family's genuinely grateful. To me but just as importantly, to you. Would it kill you to let them show their appreciation?"

"Don't kid yourself. You're the one who put your neck on the line. I'm just the schmo taking their money."

"If that's how you see it."

"What do you care how I see it?"

"Listen—"

"Don't. There's just no point." He opened the door to the car. "Now, if you'll excuse me." He started to get in but froze as a spasm gripped his back.

"You OK? Need me to drive you someplace?"

"No."

"Back home?"

"*No.*"

"Sure?"

"Yes. I'm fine, goddamn it. Now get out of my way."

"OK, OK. Where's the fire?"

He turned and stared at me with rage in his eyes. "The fire, asshole, is the James Cancer Center at Ohio State, all right?"

"The James? Are you—"

"I'm fine, no thanks to you. It's Ruth. She has breast cancer. I've been going to her appointments with her." He paused. "She's moved back in. Satisfied?"

"I'm sorry to hear that, Fred. But I'm glad you're back together."

"I bet you are. Now would you please just leave me the fuck alone?"

I did as I was asked. I stepped back and watched him pull out. I waved and got a stony look in return. But at least he didn't give me the finger. It struck me as just short of a miracle that they were back together after I'd pulled the scab off their troubled marriage by discovering Ruth's affair. Fred hardly struck me as the nurturing type, but perhaps Ruth's cancer was the wake-up call he needed to set things right. I hoped it turned out well for both of them. When Cohen's car made the turn out of the complex, I walked back to Abdi's apartment. In fact, I probably had a few things to do myself. But right now I was in the mood for another cup of Somali tea.

57

GANG MEMBER RECRUITED TO IMPERSONATE KIDNAP VICTIM

I lifted my blueberry muffin, split it in two, dipped half into my coffee, took a bite, and checked out the latest headline popping up on my phone. I was at Stauf's on Third around the corner from my house the next day, late in the morning. The story of how JaQuan Williams firebombed Mount Shiloh Baptist disguised as Abdi Mohamed was just now breaking. About time. JaQuan was in a lot of trouble, though not nearly as much had he not grown a last-second conscience and tried to chase down Trey Renner.

I looked up as the door to the coffee shop opened. Helene Paulus stepped inside. She was wearing a yellow summer dress and an air of concern. I stood and waved her over to my table.

"Please don't get up. I mean, after everything . . ."

"It's good for the circulation. Plus I can check the status of the pastry tray like this."

She declined my offer to buy her a coffee. I sat down and waited while she went to the counter. She returned with something icy and creamy.

"So," she said, eyeing me like a museum piece she'd come grudgingly to admire. "Are you all right?"

"Doing better than Trey Renner, I suppose."

"He's the—?"

"The one that started all this. And nearly finished it."

"And would have, except for you. Right?" she said, sharply.

"Something like that."

"Yes, Virginia, private detectives really do save the day sometimes?"

"Investigators. Whatever."

"One thing I still don't understand."

"One thing? There's two dozen I'm trying to figure out."

"The men in the parking lot. What did they have to do with any of it?"

"Ah, yes. Well, it goes back to that old line: You can't get good help anymore."

"Oh?"

"Ronald McQuillen was right. They weren't directly involved in the kidnapping plot, but they were members of the '76 Sentries group. They just didn't have the sense to stay out of trouble. They were supposed to be picking up extra cash for Renner by shaking down casino winners. They'd been scoping the place out that afternoon. Afterward, they bought some beer at Kroger, had a couple, saw Kaltun Hirsi, and thought they'd have some fun. And they would have, if I hadn't stumbled along and tried to be a hero."

"Tried?"

"Anyway, it was pure chance that Abdi's family caught wind of my derring-do and asked Freddy Cohen to hire me to look for him. Once that happened, the two of them more or less signed their own death warrant. Renner couldn't brook that kind of undisciplined behavior. Not with the operation he had planned."

"Which also explains the sister? What was her name?"

"Patty Bowden. She's lucky to be alive. I guess Yorkies are good for something after all." I took another sip of coffee. "How's Barbara doing?"

"A wreck. But thanks to you, one that's still afloat instead of lying at the bottom of the ocean. Your turn to forgive my metaphor, I guess."

"I'm just glad she's OK."

Burke Cunningham was now representing Barbara Mendoza and Angela along with the city's top immigration law attorney. The lawyers had suggested to the U.S. Attorney's Office that the value of the counselor's testimony as the feds probed the conspiracy to use Abdi as a human explosive device to start a race war outweighed Angela's immigration status. Despite the angry rhetoric flowing from Washington these days, the wheels were turning in the girl's favor.

"One other thing I wanted to ask you. About that attorney—Cohen?"

"Yes?"

"At the news conference the two of you had with the family. I would have thought he'd have been more, well, thankful to you, or something."

"I think he is."

"Really? Because to be honest, he looked like he'd been forced to attend marriage counseling at gunpoint. Frankly, you both did."

"That's not a bad analogy."

"So what was the deal, if I may ask?"

I explained the assignment I'd taken on that led to the revelation of Ruth's affair. How angry Freddy was at me over the whole thing—not without reason, I suppose.

"That explains it, then."

"Almost."

"What do you mean?"

I told her the rest of the story. How things got more complicated because Ruth had some underlying depression that helped precipitate the affair. How, when everything broke open thanks to me, Ruth came home and swallowed a bottle of pills. How the good news was that the Cohens' daughter got back from school a little early that day and found her in time. But also how Freddy slipped on a patch of ice as he ran into the hospital where Ruth had been rushed and threw his back out.

"So he blames me for that, too," I concluded.

"That's sounds irrational."

"He knows that. But as he likes to say, he can't help himself and no one's paying him to think differently."

"Did they divorce?"

"They're back together." I explained about her cancer.

"So a happy ending, of sorts?"

"Hopefully. For Ruth's sake. And maybe for theirs."

She thought about that. She took a drink of her iced foam. "Anyway, I just wanted to thank you for what you did. For Abdi and for Barbara. I'm—well, I'm sorry we got off on the wrong foot."

"It's my foot in my mouth that's usually the problem. Big plans today?"

"Not really. Some loose ends at school. I'll actually be back here tonight. *Romeo and Juliet* is opening at the park. Gabe's girl-friend is Juliet. You're welcome to join us."

I thought of Abdi Mohamed and Faith Monroe. Wondered if they'd seen each other yet.

"Only if I can bring the flasks of wine." She smiled and made to get up. I said, "Don't worry about rushing off. You'd only be keeping me if I had someplace to go."

"Don't you have lost puppies to find, or something?"

"Trying to cut back. The real money's in international terror-ism, anyway."

She gave that the demure smile it deserved. "In that case, I'm a little hungry. May I buy you lunch?"

"Lunch? Does this mean you've accepted my friend request?"

"I suppose it does."

"Don't sound so disappointed."

"I'm not. I don't friend just anyone, believe me."

"I'm getting that impression."

We walked out of the coffee shop and went down the street. We lingered a moment in front of the Book Loft, gazing at the display windows.

I said, "The Brown Bag has sandwiches. It's just around the corner from me. We could take them to the park for a picnic."

"That sounds nice."

"Or we could bring them back to my house. You could meet my roommate."

"Oh really? And then you could show me some of your sketches?"

"No George Bellows prints, I'm afraid."

"What then?"

"I'm partial to Thurber cartoons. I have a couple framed ones you might like."

"Now I can't tell if you're joking."

"Only one way to find out."

Twenty minutes later we arrived at my door with paper take-out bags in hand. I let Helene inside. Hopalong lumbered up and greeted her with interest. She knelt and petted him and said things like "What a good dog" that he hasn't heard in a while. I closed the door and turned the deadbolt and she stood up and our paper bags hit the floor with two soft smacks, *plop plop.* I put my hands on Helene's waist and pressed her against the closet door just inside the entryway and as she looked up at me I kissed her neck, and then her cheeks, and then her lips. This time I tasted more than the stirrings of reciprocity.

"You certainly don't waste any time," she said, after a long minute or three.

I pulled back. "Did you want me to?"

She put her arms around her neck and kissed me back. "I guess not."

"Good to hear," I said, loosening the top button on her dress.

"You realize I'm an older woman, right? By more than a couple years."

"It hadn't occurred to me," I said, tackling the second button and kissing her again.

"Really?" she said, digging her hand under my shirt. "Doesn't your ilk chase pretty young things half your age around desks in dark offices?"

"Only in months that end with 'r.' And besides, I'm no spring chicken myself."

"I guess we'll see about that," she said, taking my hands and raising them to the next button in line.

Epilogue

We were spared the sun, so deep in the woods like that. But there was no relief from the July heat and humidity, not to mention the stinging insects. It occurred to me for the first time that my experience growing up in the country—the flat farm fields surrounding Homer, Ohio—was far different than coming of age here, in what felt like a primeval forest about an hour east-southeast of Columbus as the crow flies and light years by any other measure.

"Hang on."

We looked up at the sound of the man's voice. I was standing on the other side of a band of yellow crime-scene tape wound from tree to tree to tree, the barricade marking off a poison ivy–infested patch of ground a hundred yards into the woods from where the remains of a rough cabin, half-house, half-shed, sagged slowly into oblivion as grasses and saplings and vines claimed it for their own. Beside me stood a portly state Bureau of Criminal Investigation agent, face as red as stewed tomatoes and sweat dripping from, as far as I could tell, every pore in his body. Beside him stood Henry Fielding.

The man who'd spoken was standing ten feet away beside a rectangular patch of turned-over soil, a brush in his left hand, a small, narrow-bladed spade in his right.

"Whaddya got?" the BCI agent said. His name was Gil Pollard. He'd worked a case once, more than three decades earlier, with John McQuillen.

"Something. Better check it out."

Breathing hard, the agent raised the tape and trudged forward. At the excavation site he slowly eased himself onto his hands and knees to take a closer look.

"Henry," he said, after a moment. A pause, and then: "You too."

I looked at Fielding. He nodded. We ducked under the tape and approached.

The man with the tools in his hands acknowledged us with a nod. He was a forensic anthropologist from Shawnee State University, down the road in Portsmouth. Trim, bespectacled, tidy beard the opposite of Ronald J. McQuillen's bird's nest. He consulted with BCI and other law enforcement agencies from time to time. As we watched, he crouched down and used the tip of the spade to point at an object in the dirt. It was yellowish white, more than a few inches long, with a rounded knob at one end.

"Tibia," the forensic anthropologist said.

"Animal?" Pollard said.

"No."

"Man or woman?"

"Can't tell for sure. Little small for a man."

Crime scene investigators had been there most of the morning. They'd been directed to the shack—what was left of it—by Brenda Renner, whose memory of events in those woods on a rainy night thirty-odd years ago had improved remarkably as she stared at the possibility of federal terrorism charges.

"Think it's her?" Pollard said.

"Hard to say. Lot of work to do. But chances are good."

Her. The girl—the young woman—taken by David Derwent to carry his seed. To extend the family tree of Seth. The Third Brother. Trey Renner's real mother. Died in childbirth. But not her child. No one was quite sure whether to believe Brenda Renner when she swore that she really didn't know the woman's name. Or anything else about her. Or if Brenda really was looking out for the infant's welfare by disappearing with him to California for a few years, or was just trying to evade the law. But as we stood there in the woods in the heat and humidity, it seemed likely that whoever the dead woman was, wherever she came from, whatever she believed at the time—or thought she did—we were a little bit closer to seeing that she got home again, to where she belonged.

Acknowledgments

I'm grateful to Mahdi Taakilo, editor of *Somali Link Newspaper*, for our conversations about the Somali community's experiences in Columbus and elsewhere. I'm also appreciative of the many Somalis I've met over the years and interviewed for various stories for their openness and candor. The love and respect they have for their adopted home is obvious. Special thanks to Mitch Stacy for help with football lingo, Butch Wilson for the concept of an "Evil Twin" attack, and Robert Bennett for tracking down what Cicero really wrote. With gratitude as always to everyone at Ohio University Press for their continued support, guidance, and awesome cover designs. Finally, with much love to Pam, my no. 1 fan—and I hers—on our journey through life and work.